DiVitto Kelly

World Castle Publishing, LLC

Pensacola, Florida

Copyright © 2026 DiVitto Kelly

Hardback ISBN: 9798279317295

Paperback ISBN: 9798891265028

eBook ISBN: 9798891265035

First Edition World Castle Publishing, LLC, January 12, 2026

http://www.worldcastlepublishing.com

Cover: Design by CC

Editor: Karen Fuller

CHAPTER 1

Late evening, Andrei Popa approached the vacant church situated off a rural road, now boarded up, courtesy of the Romanian government. Clutching a crossbow in one hand, he strode up the familiar stone steps. He extended his arm to open the solid black mahogany door when it creaked open. Despite his advanced age of 75, Popa, a devout Christian and former Orthodox priest at the church, was eager to settle the score.

Clad in a walnut brown sweater, blue jeans, and a cherished pair of square-toed, antique black Frye Conway Harness boots, Popa entered the church, his footsteps echoing inside the stone building still standing after two centuries. He panned the flashlight left to right. He glanced at the holy water font; bone dry. A chill ran through his body. The building smelled musty, like an old refrigerator with cobwebs at home in every crevice. He stepped forward, each step vigilant. He glanced at the pews, now all full of dust. Seeing the ancient church blighted like this made his heart ache. The priest had given decades of his life to the church, shuttered now, a victim of communist rule.

Fearless and strong as his first name, Popa was there to finish up business, to protect the citizens of Dumbraveni, a Romanian town in the north of Sibiu County, in the center of Transylvania. His wife of fifty-five years, Sabina, and their daughter, Myrna, now a United States citizen living in

Queens, New York, with her husband, Sol. Their daughter was completely unaware of what he did besides teaching the word of God. So many urgent late-night meetings. But why? His wife had heard the rumors amongst her friends, but there was never any clear proof. Or maybe she didn't want to know.

But there was an upheaval in the town of Dumbraveni. If it wasn't the iron rule of dictator Ceaușescu, people had to worry about, it was the new breed of vampires, more aggressive than ever before. Perhaps they had watched too many Godfather movies. They were instituting a mob mentality on the townfolk. And it was made plain and simple to the residents. Pay up or die.

Popa was training younger vampire hunters to take his place. But with so many young men forcibly recruited into the military profession, both there and abroad, young fighters were few and far between. He had battled vampires for years… and won. Now, he had one more to kill.

CHAPTER 2

"Here alone, Andrei?" said a deep voice, resonating in the empty building. "How very brave of you. Nice boots, by the way."

"I live up to my name," replied Popa with venom.

"You certainly have," said the voice, both cool and arrogant.

"I am here for one reason...," said Popa. "My reasons are right and just. You've killed innocent people, many that were friends in my town."

"Your town?" said the voice with a scoff. "Why, I've been a part of *your* town, as you put it, for well over one hundred and fifty years. I'd like to think that qualifies me for something. After all, I do keep the population healthy, like a shark, weeding out the weak."

"You justify preying on the innocent?" said Popa in disgust. "Show yourself."

A shadowy figure emerged from behind him. Popa's acute hearing picked up the noise, but his reflexes had slowed with age.

"Here, I am," said the voice, calmly.

Popa turned, ready to shoot, when a gunshot rang out. Popa dropped to his knees, bleeding on the once pristine hardwood floor. The vampire calmly strode over to the wounded man, trying to reach out for his weapon of choice. The man used his foot to kick away the crossbow.

"What a shame. All that blood going to waste," said the vampire, who had preyed on a local citizen mere hours ago. He gleaned at the German Luger, a turn of the century weapon he had commandeered off a German soldier during World War I. "I've become intrigued by firearms," mused the vampire. "Much easier to kill, and not as messy."

Popa lay there on his back, incapacitated, the bullet striking him square in the chest. He coughed up blood, trying to speak as the vampire stood closer.

"There are others," said Popa, his struggling voice coming out as a harsh whisper.

The vampire raised the weapon and pointed it at the former priest. "So be it."

He fired again, striking Popa in the forehead, killing him instantly.

The vampire tucked the gun in his coat pocket and left, taking one last glance at the dead man.

"Like I said, my town."

CHAPTER 3

Ten years later…

It was early March 1979. Sol Hirsch, age 66, retired deli owner, formerly of Queens, New York, was bored as snot. His wife, Myrna, three years younger and holding up quite well, was reading a Stephen King novel, savoring each page as she turned them slowly.

Myrna had convinced her husband of nearly four decades that relocating to Miami Beach last spring not only made sense but was non-negotiable. The two began to bicker as they lounged poolside at their beach condo. Tomorrow, both would be traveling to Eastern Europe to visit Myrna's mother in Romania, the ten-year anniversary of her father's passing.

Myrna put the book down on the frosted glass table. "All our friends are here," she argued, basking in the South Florida sun in a flowery yellow one-piece bathing suit and sporting tortoise shell-framed sunglasses. In her former life, Myrna was an elementary school teacher in Flushing. Savoring retirement but itching to keep active, she volunteered at the nearby public library just off Collins Avenue.

Myrna continued. "We'd be all alone in New York, freezing our collective butts off. And I was tired of hearing you kvetch, as they say in Yiddish, about the cold weather year after year."

"Me kvetching?" said an exasperated Sol, sitting next to his wife in matching blue and white striped chaise lounge chairs. "You're the queen of kvetching, old yeller."

Myrna, who stood five-foot-three with crow black hair with visible strands of gray, had no problem going toe-to-toe, verbally sparring with her occasionally boorish husband, who stood just three and a half inches taller. Myrna, Romanian tough to the core, never took any shit from anyone.

"Let's face it, you and I both couldn't stand the cold," she continued. "It made both of us sick in the wintertime, being cooped up in our apartment for months on end."

Sol nibbled on pretzels and browsed the sports section of the Miami Herald, ruffling the pages loudly in annoyance. "Bang — zoom," he countered, under his breath. He folded the newspaper and dropped it onto the table.

He glanced over at the table. "Salem's Lot?" he asked. "What's that about?"

"Vampires in Maine," she answered.

"Vampires don't like cold weather, do they?" said Sol. "Miami Beach, I could see."

"It's fiction," replied Myrna.

Myrna took a sip of her new favorite drink, vino y soda con hielo, a refreshing mixture of red wine and seltzer on ice that was introduced to her by a retired Argentine couple, Hector and Susana. "Is living here really so bad?"

"Hey, a cup of my chicken soup cured everything," railed Sol, who used to brag that only God made a better chicken soup than him.

He finished off his beer, then reached inside the plastic red cooler and took out another bottle of ice-cold Rheingold, popping the top off and taking a quick gulp. Sol hastily placed the bottle on the table. It started to overflow all over his newspaper. "Ah, crap."

"Buffoon," uttered Myrna, eyeing the spilled suds. She quickly snagged her book and placed it by her side, then handed Sol a couple of napkins. He thanked his wife.

"You know, Florida don't even have a baseball team. How can a place that holds spring training for practically every major league ballclub on planet Earth not have a baseball team?"

"And if they did, what would you call them?" asked Myrna.

"Well, the Miami Dolphins is already taken," said Sol, thinking. "How about the Miami Mackerels?"

"Sounds fishy," jabbed Myrna. Sol smirked.

Sol continued. "Seriously, honey, in New York, I had baseball," he exclaimed, stretching out both arms, palms pointed up. Spring training games won't cut it for me! Besides, the Mets play in St. Petersburg – what's that, six hours away from here?" The die-hard New York Mets fan was working himself into another patented Sol Hirsch lather.

"Oh, the hardship, no baseball," teased Myrna, sarcastically, noting the Yankees played their spring training games in nearby Fort Lauderdale, about thirty minutes north of where they lived. Sol pouted.

"I was born and raised in New York," said Sol, adding he thought he'd never leave… until death do us part. "It's kinda hard to get that out of your system."

Myrna reached over and caressed his hand. "I understand, dear," she said, turning towards her husband. "I miss it too, on occasion, but sitting by the poolside like this with you, enjoying the warm weather. You can watch the games on television – they *do* have television down here in Miami Beach, right?" Sol grumbled. "Not to mention your addiction to Cuban food."

"I do like my Cuban food," grinned Sol.

Myrna continued, "And while everyone's fighting blizzards, crime, corruption, and garbage strikes, we'll be here strolling along the beach, the Atlantic Ocean caressing our feet."

"You know, you should be a writer," smiled Sol.

Myrna took another sip of her drink while embracing her husband's hand, rough and calloused from decades of lugging around oak pickle barrels and other deli necessities.

Sol raised his bushy eyebrows, both sprouting above his black Ray-Ban knockoffs, like shabby, unkempt hedges. "Yeah, yeah," her stubborn husband admitted before breaking into a big grin. "The Plisskens complained about the cold weather worse than me, if that was possible!"

Myrna snickered but couldn't help adding a little zinger at her hubby's expense. "Besides, as a Mets fan, you barely have baseball; they're God-awful every year."

She not so secretly rooted for the Bronx Bombers, who had won back-to-back World Series against the Los Angeles Dodgers in 1977 and 1978. She even owned a baseball cap autographed by fiery Lou Piniella, one of her favorite players.

"I *knew* it!" bellowed Sol. "You really root for those bums in the Bronx – Steinbrenner, what a colossal putz!"

"So, what if I do?" Myrna replied. "I'll root for whoever I want to root for. And besides, why should I follow in your bad taste in sports teams? I mean, the Mets? Por favor."

"Feh!" snarled the ex-deli owner.

Myrna took another sip of her drink. "Stop complaining;

it's just baseball."

"You know that is *so* wrong," countered Sol, as he slapped his hand down on the table. "If you live in Queens, you root for the Mets and Jets; you live in the Bronx, it's the Giants and Yankees – that's sports life in the Big Apple."

Myrna gazed upon her husband with a disgusted face. "Buffoon."

"You wait; this is gonna be our year!" Sol exclaimed, never one to give up on his beloved Mets. "You'll see; 1979 will truly be fine!" Sol thrust his chubby right index finger high in the sky.

"Oh sure," said Myrna with a smirk. "Like they narrowly missed winning their division last year by what, two dozen games? And the year before it was by how many?"

"Uh, 37," sighed Sol, "But who's counting?"

"Ouch," said Myrna. "Face it, hubby, the Mets stink worse than the Hudson River. By the way, who's their manager?"

"Joe Torre," replied Sol with limited enthusiasm. "For the last couple of years."

"Ugh," uttered Myrna. "Like he's gonna bring a World Series title to New York."

Sol slumped back down in his lounge chair and exhaled, a beaten fan. "At least my beer is cold."

"See? Now you're getting it," smiled Mryna. "Cheers." They chimed glasses.

Either way, Sol knew Florida and his tired, achy body were a perfect match for each other. He'd spent all his life working in a deli, starting in middle school, working part-time for his late father, Isaac, in Jamaica, Queens, after school. But after half a century of smelling like pastrami and garlic pickles, it was time to retire and enjoy the omnipresent warmth and sunshine of Miami Beach, Florida. Floating around in the large rectangular pool like a manatee was alright by the stocky senior citizen.

CHAPTER 4

"Let's do Rascal House tonight, dearie," proposed Myrna as she tidied up in the kitchen.

"Sounds good to me," said Sol as he sank into his royal blue La-Z-Boy recliner nestled in the corner of the living room. Their neat and tidy two-bedroom, two bath eighth-floor condominium overlooked the Atlantic Ocean, a far cry from the musty apartment they lived in that faced a soot-covered apartment building.

Sol giggled as he read Garfield, his new favorite comic strip about a chubby orange tabby with a penchant for lasagna. He stood up, petted his own orange tabby, dubbed Rusty, after Mets red-head, Rusty Staub. He walked over and opened the sliding glass door, where he was greeted by a stiff ocean breeze. He stood on the balcony staring out to sea for a few minutes, then returned inside.

"I'm feeling like a thick slab of lasagna tonight."

"As long as you have it with a salad - oil and vinegar, no thousand Island dressing, and minus the endless rolls," chimed Myrna, concerned about her husband's non-healthy eating habits. She had been hoping the ocean would inspire her husband to eat seafood, particularly fish. Sol hated fish, especially gefilte fish. You couldn't pay him to eat that stuff.

Sol shrugged as he glanced at this solidly roundish frame. "Hey, I'm big boned."

"Seriously, Honey. Now that we're retired, I don't

want you croaking any time soon. Remember, your father was your age when he passed."

Sol nodded his head. "Yeah, spending your whole life cooped up in a deli isn't exactly a recipe for healthy eating. But you know I'm trying."

Myrna smiled. "Just remind yourself that vegetables are your friend."

"Hey, I eat vegetables all the time," smiled Sol.

Myrna reached for the telephone and called her friend, Barbara, then covered up the receiver with her hand. "Pickles don't count." She then went back to her call.

"Hey Barbara. You and Donnie want to join us for dinner at Rascal House, 7PM?" Her friend called out to her husband, who gave her the thumbs-up sign.

"Sure," she replied. "Meet you in the parking lot in twenty minutes; we'll drive."

Both couples were bi-weekly regulars at Wolfie Cohen's Rascal House, the premier Jewish delicatessen in Sunny Isles Beach off of Collins Avenue, a mainstay for retired tri-staters (New York, New Jersey, and Connecticut) since 1954. They served up succulent deli sandwiches stacked to the nines and a killer matzo ball soup that featured a baseball sized matzo strategically placed in the center, all of which met Sol's full approval. Sometimes, Sol couldn't help himself, filling up on the free fresh-baked rolls and dipping his hand into the stainless-steel buckets of half-sour pickles and cold sauerkraut. Both Sol and the owner, Wolfie Cohen, a four-term city councilman and successful restaurateur, knew how to construct a premier deli sandwich by planting a heaping full of fresh-cut meat on homemade bread. Cut it in half and amaze your customers.

Sol became friends with the owner, who gave the former deli man a 'behind the counter' tour of the restaurant. Sol was quite impressed, and the chicken soup wasn't half bad either. Brothers in aprons.

***

Donnie and Barbara Falcone were longtime friends of Sol and Myrna. Three of the four grew up in Queens, New York, in the neighborhood of Flushing. While Myrna's parents stayed put in Romania, she had plenty of extended family that made College Point feel like home, a working-class neighborhood where residents leaned towards the Bronx Bombers.

Donnie, tall, medium build with black hair (not all his own) and wire-rimmed glasses, was a retired chiropractor. In his younger days, he was a mediocre stand-up comic making the rounds along the Borscht belt, a resort community filled with summer camps, clubs, and hotels in the Catskill Mountains of upstate New York. His wife Barbara, a retired dental hygienist, convinced him to finish his college degree and put it to good use, noting he could still reach a person's funny bone and make a steady career of it.

***

The four arrived at the restaurant, greeted by the familiar gruff hostess named Delores. With her ever-changing beehive hair colors, the middle-aged woman, a former beauty queen from Bayonne, New Jersey, was a dead ringer for Mrs. Slocumbe from the British TV comedy show, "Are You Being Served?"

She directed them to a booth sandwiched between two elderly couples with a view of coconut palm trees and Collins Avenue, also known as A1A. They sat down as Delores handed them their menus.

"Thanks, Delores," said Sol.

"Water for everyone?" The four nodded, yes. "Be back in a sec to take your orders." She stepped over to another table to present their check, then marched back to the kitchen.

She and the retired deli owner had butted heads a few times prior, with Sol complaining about table location, both people exuding the obstinate gene. In the end, a sizeable tip solved future issues.

Delores reappeared with four waters and placed straws by each glass. With her server notepad in hand, she took Myrna and Barbara's order first, then Donnie's. Sol shifted in the red vinyl-covered seat, making a squeaky sound, then looked up.

"Delores, how's the lasagna tonight? I'm feeling Italian," said Sol.

"A little too dry for my liking," she replied, sometimes honest to a fault. "The spaghetti and meatballs, on the other hand, delectable."

"You sold me, Delores. And throw in a couple extra meatballs if you don't mind."

"Got it. Any sides?" asked the waitress.

"And a house salad, please," he said. "Vinaigrette dressing." Myrna smiled.

"Got it, be back soon," said Delores before picking up the check and cash tip from the table behind them.

"Everyone excited for our trip tomorrow?" asked Donnie.

"I'm a little nervous about the long flight, but it'll be good to see my mother again," said Myrna.

"You said your mother was ill?" asked Barbara.

"She's fine," said Myrna, taking a sip of water. "She just likes throwing a heaping bowl of motherly guilt to get me to visit. I was able to visit her for a few days about five years ago when she actually had an illness: kidney stones." She paused. "I can't believe it's been ten years since my father's death; I wanted to be there for her. She's a tough cookie."

"Runs in the family," said Sol, nudging his wife.

***

After dinner, Sol and his wife returned home to their condominium, saying goodnight to their friends. Despite being only eight floors up, the elevator, with its faulty air conditioning, took an eternity to reach its destination.

"I swear we'd be at the top of the Empire State Building quicker than this heap."

They entered their condo, the air conditioning set at a reasonable 74 degrees. Sweating from the elevator ride, Sol quickly made a beeline to the kitchen and opened the refrigerator, sticking his head inside before snagging a beer. He reached for the shark-shaped bottle opener attached to the refrigerator with a magnet and popped the top off, then took a healthy swig. Myrna went straight for the bedroom to finish packing for the trip. Sol knew not to interfere as Myrna had a detailed method of folding clothes, making everything neat and tidy. He would've created a big-time wrinkle fest, cramming everything into their two matching pea soup green Samsonite suitcases.

Although Myrna tried to educate her husband that the weather in Romania would be comparable to that of New York City in the springtime, mid-40s to low-60s, Sol was convinced it was going to be polar cold. He instead requested packing every winter garment he still owned, including his ratty green and white New York Jets winter coat and matching green gloves.

Rather than traveling solo with Sol, the *stress inducer*, Myrna was able to convince her longtime tri-state friends Donnie and Barbara (and now fellow Miami Beach neighbors) to travel along, hoping to ease her anxieties and add some levity to the journey. Taking such a long flight to Eastern Europe, their destination to the central region of Transylvania in Romania, would certainly be a trip to remember. Myrna still had a few relatives there in Dumbraveni, a rural town bordering the Tarnava Mare River, lined with cobblestone roads, quaint shops, and oozing of old-world charm.

On the other hand, Sol had already convinced himself it was going to be like visiting Nowheresville, where flocks of sheep blocked traffic on main roads and you had to churn your own butter for your toast. The worst was that the town would be void of American beer. Myrna finally convinced her husband that yes, they did have electricity and indoor plumbing 'over there' but couldn't guarantee that livestock might occasionally hamper local traffic.

Myrna had always embraced her family lineage, despite moving to the United States in her late teens to further her education, earning a scholarship at St. John's University. It was a decision that both her parents had strongly encouraged, although at the time, she wasn't exactly sure why. She had extended family, cousins, and an older relative who resided in College Point, so the transition wasn't so traumatic. She especially missed her father, who had passed away under mysterious circumstances a decade prior. The last time she had seen her father was only a year earlier. Meanwhile, Sol's side of the family was filled with Olympic-medal complainers and competitors, specializing in squabbles over the most trivial of matters. The best was when Sol's two older brothers, Milton and Henry, actually agreed on a subject, yet still managed to turn it into an argument. That was a gold medal feat for sure.

Although Sol would have preferred to stay local, watching sports at the Cheeky Tiki Bar, his favorite watering hole owned by a fellow Queens native and die-hard Mets fan, lounging by the pool with a cold beer, or playing shuffleboard under the lights, he knew this trip meant everything to Myrna, whom he loved very much. He conceded, knowing at least he'd be traveling with Donnie, a fellow Mets fan, so that they would have something to sulk about.

After packing, Sol turned to Myrna, who was gathering up a few snacks, anything containing dark chocolate, for the flight.

"If you don't mind, I'm gonna play some shuffleboard with Donnie for a while." He sidestepped her as he reached for a couple of beers in the refrigerator. "Don't wait up."

"You're not playing for money again, I hope."

Sol grabbed his key off the dinner table and headed for the door. "Maybe," he replied. "Donnie says a couple of rubes from Michigan have been selling wolf tickets, so I may need to teach them both a lesson."

"My hero," smiled Myrna. "Win one for the Gipper."

Sol smiled, then closed the door and took the elevator down to the ground floor, where he met Donnie by the double glass doors of the recreation center.

"Hey, my friend. Ready to win some dough?" he said in a boisterous voice.

"To boldly shuffleboard where no man has shuffleboarded before," said Donnie, dressed in a New York Jets t-shirt and solid green shorts, bad rug and all. "Ironically, I think they're from Buffalo… or was it Detroit?"

"Buffalo? What does that have to do with it?" said Sol.

"You know that saying, shuffle off to Buffalo, the song from 42nd Street?" informed Donnie, sometimes a bit too clever for his own good.

"I'll take your word for it," said Sol, more engrossed in everything sports. That was his form of entertainment. A former soldier in WWII and amateur boxer, he also dabbled in politics, always fired up in full support for the red, white, and blue.

Sol handed Donnie one of the beers as they entered the recreation room, dimly hued in amber lighting. There was a pool table, the felt burnt orange, a deep mahogany wood bar, along with six black leather barstools. Donnie usually fiddled with the radio, tracking down some cool jazz station to listen to. When listening to the likes of John Coltrane, Dave Brubeck, or Miles Davis, Donnie loved doing his throaty impersonation of a jazz radio DJ. It cracked up Sol to no end. When the two went on a pool-playing binge during the day, they felt like a pair of moles when they exited into the bright Florida sunshine, each shielding their eyes with their hands.

Sol and Donnie cut through the building and approached two men who were sitting on a Kelly-green wooden bench by the lighted shuffleboard courts, four in all. The powerful corner lighting seemed to attract just about every palmetto bug in Dade County.

"Eddie Platt and Bob Larrabee, this is my friend, Sol Hirsch. And have sympathy 'cause he's a Mets fan like me."

"Ha, ha, Donnie. Pleasure to meet you guys," said Sol. The four shook hands, smiling politely.

"Hey, you guys were in the World Series in '73 and ten years ago your Mets won the World Series," said Eddie, a big-time Detroit Tigers fan, smoking a cigar. His team had captured the World Series over the St. Louis Cardinals in 1968, four games to three. He appeared quite dapper in his white and blue striped seersucker shorts and a white Lacoste golf shirt. Sol observed he was way too overdressed for shuffleboard; tennis, maybe. Both he and his sidekick.

"Bob here used to work for Budweiser in one of their big city plants, right?" asked Donnie.

"Yeah," replied Bob, almost a near replica of his friend Eddie. "Got a free supply of suds when I worked for 'em – too bad I don't like beer."

"You worked for Budweiser but didn't like the beer?" said Sol, in unbelievable surprise. "What a shame. Isn't there some sort of rule you gotta like the product?"

"Nah," Bob replied. "The pay was good and the perks even better, but I'm not really a beer person. Never was, never will be. Besides, I used to sell the free cases to friends and family for extra cash."

"So, what's your poison? Scotch, Gin?" prodded Sol, thinking any guy would love a gig like that.

Bob looked around like he was going to divulge a big-time secret, spilling his guts. "Vernors."

"Vernors? Never heard of it? Is that like Vemouth or something?" inquired Sol, completely unfamiliar with the name.

Eddie cut in. "It's actually the oldest soda on the planet, invented in the 1860s by a pharmacist. Really good stuff."

"It's a Midwest thing," said Bob. He, like Eddie, formerly resided in Michigan. "I add a scoop of vanilla ice cream for a float. But occasionally, a little Vodka don't hurt."

Sol laughed. "You had me worried." In his book, all

guys liked booze.

"It's effervescent and refreshing," said Bob. "Here, have a taste."

Eddie took a sip of his soda. "You have no idea how excited we were to find out Publix sells it right here in Miami Beach."

Sol took a whiff of the bottle, the bubbles tickling his nose. He hesitated for a moment, then took a sip. Donnie liked it, but could see Sol's face contorting in disapproval.

"Interesting flavor," said Sol as he quickly washed it down with his beer.

"To each their own, right guys?" said Donnie.

"So, who's ready for some shuffleboard?" said Eddie, sporting a Cheshire grin.

***

Two hours later and thirty dollars lighter, Sol and Donnie ambled towards the recreation room, tails between their legs. Sol reached into the refrigerator stationed behind the bar and pulled out a couple of emergency beers they hid in the crisper section. They slumped into the barstools and took prolonged chugs in defeat.

"Holy crap, were those guys good," uttered Sol. "They were like freaking pros."

"Kinda felt like we were the Mets and they were the Yankees," chimed Donnie, taking another gulp. "What a total beatdown."

"Please, no baseball analogies," said Sol, now yawning. "Maybe there's something in that ginger ale that gives you energy. I'm beat."

"Ginger soda," corrected Donnie. "Maybe we should hold off on the suds next time we play them."

"Maybe next time we should drink our Ovaltine," said Sol, his back and right shoulder aching.

"Well, it could be worse; we could be out thirty bucks," said Donnie.

"We are out thirty bucks," said Sol, missing those crisp ten-dollar bills in his wallet, now thinner. He glanced at his watch. Midnight. "Crap, we gotta get to bed. Big trip tomorrow."

Donnie nodded. The two headed for the elevator. As Donnie stepped off, he turned to his friend. "We'll get 'em next time."

Sol yawned again as the door closed. Yeah, next time."

CHAPTER 5

The group of four travelers flew out of Miami International Airport on a humid, overcast Monday evening, thunderstorms clearing up before takeoff. Thankfully, they had their tickets already and didn't have to wait forever in line. Sol slapped a couple of New York Mets bumper stickers on their matching luggage so he could easily recognize them from the other sea of suitcases. Myrna joked that no one in their right mind would steal them now.

As they sat at the bar waiting to board the flight, Sol turned to his wife. "You doing okay?"

"I'm fine," said Myrna, taking a deep breath and exhaling. "Just feeling the butterflies."

Sol held her hand. "Everything is gonna be fine. I'm here with you, Donnie and Barbara. We're a team."

Mryna beamed, nearly tearing up. "You have no idea what that means, thank you." She moved closer and gave her husband a kiss on the cheek. "I know you'll find something to complain about, but right now, you're the king of beers."

"I'm not sure how I should take that," smiled Sol, finishing up a Coke and nibbling on peanuts. "I'll try my best not to be a pain in the ass. Just let me know when I am."

"And I'll let you know too," added Donnie.

"Hold on, I think that's us," said Barbara, overhearing an announcement. "It sounds like we can board early."

"Right you are, honey," said Donnie. "And when we

arrive in Transylvania, we'll paint the town red." Sol growled. "White and blue," clarified Donnie with a chuckle.

"Better," said Sol. "No commies on my dime."

The four headed over to the American Airlines counter. The woman, tall and blond, inspected their tickets and handed back their copy. "Going to do some sightseeing in Romania?"

"Visiting family, mostly," replied Myrna, still feeling a bit uneasy about the expedition.

"And to Transylvania no less," said Donnie, adding, "I'm just hoping we don't come back as vampires."

"Well, in that case, better have lots of garlic on hand," said the employee. "Enjoy your flight."

"Only in my spaghetti sauce," joked Donnie. "And boy, do I love my garlic."

"Enough, honey," zinged Barbara. Her husband's comedic schmoozing always seemed to coincide with pretty women, and the curvy blond was no exception.

Sol and Myrna led the way onto the airplane, followed by Barbara and Donnie, a mammoth American Airlines Boeing 747, all silver with red, white, and blue stripes and the word, American painted in big, bold red lettering. Sol followed Myrna, clutching her oversized purse packed with an assortment of snacks as she made her way down the aisle. Myrna, glancing at her ticket yet again, spotted her seat, two rows up from the airplane wings on the left. She shifted over and sat down in the window seat, quickly buckling up. She glanced outside as she watched the baggage handlers loading the plane with a mountain range of suitcases coming in all shapes and colors. She managed to spot one of their suitcases, all plastered with New York Mets stickers. Ugh. Sol was less graceful, plopping down in his assigned seat. He peaked back at Barbara and Donnie as they settled in behind them.

"Fly me to the moon," crooned Donnie, cracking himself up as he buckled up. "I'm raring to go, people. I'm even looking forward to airplane food."

"You're the one," replied Sol with a smirk. "I remember the last time I flew, I got sick as a damn dog. Whatever you do, do not order the fish if it's on the menu. Trust me."

The pilot made an announcement welcoming everyone. A stewardess soon provided instructions to all passengers. Myrna's heartbeat ticked up when the woman explained using the seat as a floatation device, knowing they would be flying over the ocean.

Sensing her getting nervous, Sol caressed her hand.

"They have to give this spiel about safety and stuff," uttered Sol. "Don't worry, it's going to be smooth sailing in a flying sort of way." Myrna smiled at the humor. She took in a deep breath and exhaled, practicing her relaxation tips. It was helping.

***

For the first hour of the flight, Sol remained fairly quiet. He peeked over to Myrna, her fingers clutching the hand rests.

"It's all good, dear," said Sol, "You can unbuckle too if you want."

"I feel safer with it buckled," said Myrna, gazing out at the night sky.

Sol reached over and closed the shade. "Now, relax, and enjoy the flight.

Donnie spotted the stewardess walking by with a squeaky cart filled with trays of prepared meals. He rubbed his hands together. "Ah, here we go, dinner time."

Sol took a glance, his face wrinkling up, not thrilled

with the flight's scant offerings of either grilled chicken or fish with a side salad and baked potato. He wasn't a fan of either. And for dessert, a Styrofoam cup of strawberry-flavored Jell-O.

"What, am I in third grade here?" said Sol, raising his thick Queens accent. He was trying so hard not to complain.

"Then stop acting like a third grader," said Myrna.

"Just remember what I said about the fish," said Sol.

"What about the fish?" said the stewardess, hearing Sol's comments loud and clear. The experienced stewardess could spot troublemakers in a heartbeat. "You can be assured, sir, that our dinner menu is fresh and satisfying."

After she left, Sol turned to Donnie. "Notice how she said the menu was fresh and satisfying, but not the actual food?"

"Oh, Lordy, Sol. Just enjoy, okay?" Donnie received his dinner tray and gave it a once-over. He grabbed the back of Sol's seat, pulling himself towards his friend. "It doesn't look that bad to me."

"Then why'd you down a couple slices of pizza beforehand, huh?" quizzed Sol.

"Because I'm a sucker for Sbarros."

Sol grumbled. He opted for the chicken, but thought he should have eaten something beforehand, too.

Sol scanned his entire plate, thinking the meal would probably make prison inmates revolt. He immediately ripped open the minuscule salt and pepper packs and drizzled the contents onto his entry, already convinced it would have about as much flavor as John Stearns' catcher's mitt. Meanwhile, everybody else seemed quite satisfied with their meals. Two slices of pepperoni pizza didn't seem to hinder

Donnie's appetite as he dove right in. He even offered to lend a helping fork and eat Sol's chicken if he didn't want it.

"Be my guest," said Sol

"Why don't you try it first?" said Myrna, glancing over with peering eyes.

"Okay, okay." Sol struggled with the plastic utensils, snapping the fork in two, but managed to cut a chunk of chicken. Without saying a word, the former deli man took a bite. He posed a face of satisfaction and polished off the rest of his dinner, Jell-O and all.

"Not bad," he muttered. "And just the right hint of lemon."

"Always judging a book by its cover," scorned Myrna, who was used to her husband's occasionally stubborn actions.

"You're right, you're right," said Sol, apologizing. He ended up eating Donnie's dessert as well.

Myrna glanced at her husband. "Deary, you got a little schmuts on the right corner of your lip."

Sol took a napkin and took care of business. "Is it gone?" Myrna nodded in approval.

Barbara turned to her husband. "It's been a long time since we took an international flight," she said, peeking out the window at the darkening skies.

"Years," said Donnie, the cogs turning in his head. "Man, oh man, it was our trip to Italy. Worst pizza I've ever had. You'd think pizza in Italy would be the best, am I right, Sol?"

"Yeah, the birthplace of pasta," he smirked. "Nah, you want great pizza, you gotta come to New York City. Ain't no better than New Park Pizza in Howard Beach. Great brick oven pizza; thin and tasty crust every time."

"I prefer Bella Pizza on West 9th in the Village," said Myrna. "Huge slices, lots of mozzarella, and great sauce. And for the record, pasta was invented in China."

"Really?" said Barbara.

"Maybe someone spilled some tomato sauce on a bowl of Lo Mein noodles and thought… spaghetti!" joked Donnie.

"Oh please," replied Sol, almost repulsed. "Bella Pizza is for drunks heading back on the Path to New Jersey, or those rocker types that go to that weird club. What's the name?"

"That would be CBGB," said Donnie, who played acoustic guitar, mostly folk. "It's in the Bowery."

"For Christ's sake, why don't you just put some cheese and sauce on cardboard?" cackled Sol. "It's definitely New Park Pizza. And don't even pretend you know pizza, 'cause I know pizza."

"What you know is how to be a pain in the arse," countered Myrna.

It was Donnie's turn to add his two cents' worth. "As the only person that's one-hundred percent Italian, I firmly believe…"

"Drop it, dear," said Barbara, Irish and with fair skin and blond, graying hair.

Donnie leaned back in his chair as their friends of over fifty years verbally duked it out. He whispered to his wife. "Arguing over pizza. What a linguini brain."

Myrna changed subjects and instead, reached under her seat and pulled out a book from her purse about Romania, she had checked out from the local library. She had hoped it would spark some interest in her husband. He took little interest, thumbing through the pages. His bigger ambition was to find a quaint pub in town that served his favorite adult beverage, Rheingold. Donnie, peaking between the seats, asked to see the book.

"Here, Donnie," said Myrna, glancing at her husband with a grin. "At least you're curious."

Donie sat back and started flipping through pages before coming across a neat tidbit. "Hey, it says here the word "Transylvania" means "the land beyond the forest." He nodded in a rather interesting fashion.

Sol creaked his neck. "So, it's not all vampires and werewolves then?"

"Ah, no. And check this out," continued Donnie. "There's something called the Carpathian Mountains. Look how the highway meanders between those mountain ranges. That is amazing."

Barbara leaned over. "That kinda reminds me of the Colorado River running through the Grand Canyon."

"Now that was a fun trip," said Donnie as he kept reading. His interest piqued when he came across Bran Castle, also referred to as Dracula's Castle. "Ooh. It says here Bram Stoker based his novel, Dracula, on a Romanian Prince named Vlad Tepes." He looked up, eyeing everyone's full attention. "Shall I continue?"

"If you must," gestured Sol with his hand.

"According to this, Mr. Tepes had two nicknames: Vlad the Impaler." He cleared his throat as he scanned the text. "Jeez Louise. It looks like he found pleasure in shish kabobbing his enemies."

"Yikes," said Barbara. "And what was his other nickname?"

Donnie paused for effect, squinting his eyes before rolling out the name in dramatic fashion. "Dracula," he uttered, in a dead-on impersonation of Bela Lugosi. "Translated to English, the word Dracula means Son of the Devil. It adds that he was fearless about protecting his homeland."

"So, he didn't bite necks and drink blood like in the movies?" said Sol.

Donnie scanned a few more pages back and forth. "Nah. Nothing about taking shots of the red stuff."

"You're a regular Fodor's travel guide, aren't you?" said Sol. He leaned back in his seat before asking, "Uh, you mind if I take a gander at that?"

"Be my guest," said Donnie as he handed him the book.

Sol started flipping through the pages, then started reading intently. Myrna craned her neck around the other side and waved her index finger at Donnie. He leaned forward, getting close to her.

"How the hell did you do that?" she whispered, baffled. "I gave up trying to get him to take an interest."

Donnie, a friend of Sol's dating back to middle school, nodded. "You know how stubborn he is. You can tell him a hundred times to do something, but he's gotta do it on his terms. Plus, he doesn't want to be taken as a total ignoramus."

"I can hear you loud and clear, my friend," said Sol. He turned around. "But you're right."

Myrna glanced at her husband, totally engrossed in what Romania had to offer. "Check out this Armenian Cathedral right in the center square," said Sol. "It's something you'd see on a postcard. Did you ever see it?"

Myrna was close to pulling out her hair, having mentioned it at least a dozen times before. "No, never heard of it."

"Really?" Sol replied.

"Of course, I know about it!" barked Myrna, shaking her head. "It's in the town where my parents were born, for Pete's sake." She paused, reminding herself to take deep breaths.

"You musta mentioned it to me when the game was on," said Sol, apologizing.

Myrna got everyone's attention. "I remember it vividly when I was a child. Nearly the whole town had to cram inside the cathedral during a horrible tornado. It sounded like a bomb went off. There was so much destruction, but our town cathedral held. It was built like a fortress way back in the eighteenth century." Myrna inched closer to her husband and pointed to the photograph. "Notice anything peculiar about it?"

Sol glared intently at the image, but nothing immediate registered. "Looks like a beautiful old church. What am I missing?"

"The domes," she pointed out. "See? One of them is missing."

"How the hell did I miss that?" he said, rhetorically.

"What happened to the other one?" asked Barbara.

"There was a terrible storm in 1927 that destroyed the right dome. My mother said she and the rest of the community were devastated. The whole town wanted to contribute to get it repaired. And it didn't matter that some families weren't Catholic."

"Looks like an older picture. Was it ever fixed?" asked Sol.

"No, and I don't know if it ever will be, especially now that a communist dictator is running the country. Communists are not exactly the religious types," said Myrna.

"Government is their religion," said Sol, beginning to grind his teeth. "Schmucks."

"Who's running the country now?" inquired Donnie.

"That would be Nicolae Ceaușescu," snarled Sol, who followed politics with the best of them. "Took power in the 1960s; a real commie ass-hole. A good Christmas present for the Romanian people would be to see that guy get whacked."

"Wishful thinking, honey," said Mryna, staring at the image. "It would be a beautiful thing."

"Don't forget our own Big Apple is a trough of corruption," uttered Donnie. "That's why I stick with sports and music."

Sol cut in. "Hopefully, Ed Koch will clean things up. At least he's got chutzpah."

"If you're gonna survive New York City politics, you better have chutzpah," said Donnie. "Double chutzpah."

Myrna asked Sol to see the book for a moment. To lighten the mood, she asked if anyone could name the very first king of Romania. With everyone drawing a blank, she informed them it was King Carol I, original name Karl Eitel Friedrich from Germany. Sol and the Falcones waved the white flag.

The former teacher was a wealth of knowledge and loved challenging her husband and friends with trivia. She and Barbara even started a trivia night at the recreation center at their condo. Sol and Donnie stuck with what they knew best: shooting pool, playing poker, and losing money playing shuffleboard.

"I think I'm beginning to suffer from information overload," said Donnie.

"I'm sure you two would rather talk baseball all night,"

said Barbara.

"With the Mets, there's not much to talk about," said Myrna.

"Can't argue with that," sighed Donnie. He finished reading the March 1979 Spring Training issue copy of Sports Illustrated and tucked it in his coat pocket.

An hour later, Sol fell asleep with the book on his lap.

Myrna lifted the blind and peered out the window, seeing nothing but the night sky with whiffs of passing clouds. She turned to her husband, peeked back at their friends, all sound asleep, and followed suit.

***

Hours later, a pair of stewardesses paraded down the aisle with a cart full of covered plates of breakfast. Myrna lifted her shade halfway, taking a glimpse of beaming sunlight. Barbara lifted hers up completely, the sun hitting directly onto Donnie's face.

"Agh, I feel like a vampire at dawn," said Donnie as he shielded his squinting eyes with both hands. He stretched out both arms and surveyed the situation. Eyeing the approaching stewardesses, he was hungry for breakfast.

The tall, leggy woman with lengthy brown hair approached with the full cart of meals. "Good morning, sir. And what would you and your wife like for breakfast? We have a choice of French toast or scrambled eggs with bacon."

"Can't go wrong with bacon," said Donnie, perking up to the scent of his favorite pork product. Honey, you go first."

"French toast is fine," said Barbara. "Do you have coffee?"

"Yes, we do, and orange juice," she replied.

"I'll have what the misses is having with orange juice,

please."

The stewardess served their meals, even throwing in extra bacon for Donnie.

"Oh, Miss, how much longer do we have to go?" asked Donnie.

The stewardess confided with the co-pilot, who was passing by on his way to use the facilities. He walked over to greet the foursome.

"Should be about another hour, folks," he said. "We're actually ahead of schedule, so sit back and enjoy breakfast, it's on the house," adding with a wink. He tipped his pilot hat and headed towards the cockpit.

Both Sol and Myrna opted for French toast. Sol poured syrup and dug right in before taking a sip of coffee. "This ain't half bad," said Sol. "I may have to sing a different tune about airplane food."

After breakfast, with his lower back stiffening up again, Sol opted to take a walk down the aisle to loosen up his achy frame. He ended up at the back of the plane, chatting with a passenger wearing a Cincinnati Reds hat. He returned to his seat, feeling better.

"How was your stroll?" kidded Myrna.

"Short; about as much as you're gonna get at twenty thousand feet," said Sol. "How are you doing?"

"Good, good," said Myrna. "Having you all here was a tremendous help."

"I do what I can," said her husband. "By the way, your hair really looks terrific. People are gonna think I'm your father, you look so young now."

"They already do," grinned Myrna, batting her eyelashes, her hair now dyed a solid black. Sol couldn't help but laugh.

Soon after, the fasten seatbelts sign lit up. The pilot announced over the intercom that the plane would be descending in moments and to please return to your seats. The stewardess instructed everyone to fasten their seatbelts.

Sol sat back down and buckled in. There was a brief amount of turbulence before the flight found smooth sailing again. Myrna shut the window blind; the landing part always made her nervous. She took Sol's hand and squeezed it.

"It's okay, dear, we're almost there," said Sol, comforting her.

CHAPTER 6

The two couples arrived in the capital of Romania, Bucharest, mildly jetlagged and ruffled from their overseas journey. After schlepping their luggage from the airport, dwarfed in comparison by Miami International Airport back home, the four waited outside in the cool weather by the curb with forty-plus other people, young and old. Little did Sol realize they had another long trek into the heart of Romania, Transylvania.

Donnie took in a deep breath of the fall-like temperatures as he gleamed at the enticing sunny skies. "Looks like we're off to a good start here in Romania."

"Let's hope so," added Sol.

"That agent said here, right?" asked Sol. His hemorrhoids were starting to act up again. And when they did, he was not a happy camper.

"I think this is it," observed Myrna, as an approaching bus slowed down, the screechy brakes bringing the large vehicle to a complete halt in front of them. The driver offered up a hearty "good morning" as he stepped off the bus. In breakneck speed, the driver darted over and opened the side compartments of the bus, then loaded up each and every suitcase before securing the lock.

The passengers boarded the dingy white and orange-striped bus resembling a big popsicle on wheels. The driver, medium build with wavy black hair and a bushy mustache, lent a hand with some of the elderly passengers while managing to chomp down on a shiny red apple. As Sol boarded the bare-bones bus, he took a gander at the seats. To his dismay, it appeared that each and every one had barely any visible padding, definitely not good for a man itching to get over his bout of hemorrhoids.

"I bet this is a Russki bus," commented Sol to Donnie, who had little faith the bus would even fulfil its journey. The four plopped their weary bodies in seats nestled in the bowels of the bus as the rest of the travelers took their seats.

"It smells like livestock back here," uttered Sol. Myrna held her head, knowing the dike holding back the complaints was ready to burst.

"Don't start, please?" begged Myrna, tired and achy. She took a whiff and winced. "Maybe open a couple windows."

Sol obliged as he reached over his wife and lowered their window. "Better, thanks."

After everyone had boarded and gotten comfortable (except Sol), the bus driver, whistling a cheery tune, pulled away from the curb and headed straight and around the bustling city of Bucharest. After marveling at some of the distinctive French and German style architecture, the driver steered the two-toned dirigible on wheels out of the city. With his hearing affected by the high altitude of the flight, Sol started in with the complaining, and in a much too loud voice. Myrna shushed him.

"Sorry, but how in the hell is this rattling piece of crap gonna get us anywhere?" Myrna sighed, now gritting her teeth.

"It's not Greyhound that's for sure," added Donnie.

"Leave the complaining to the pros, okay, honey?"

said Barbara.

Donnie shrugged. "Sorry. Sometimes he rubs off on me."

"I know I'm a certifiable pain in the ass, but I'm dealing with a certain condition that's literally a pain in the ass."

"You fought in World War Two for Christ's sake," snapped Myrna. "You can handle a three-hour bus ride. Look out the window and sightsee, will you?" The full load of people started to take notice.

Donnie turned to his friend and smiled. "Come on, Sol, three measly hours aboard the Magical Mystery bus."

Sol grumbled. "Three-hour tour; how'd that work out for those folks aboard the SS Minnow?"

The two couples journeyed along on the timeworn bus, observing the vast pristine farmlands with rolled-up bales of hay, forests, and mountain ranges rounding out the beautiful vista. At the top of a winding hill, a flock of sheep decided it was siesta time. And what better place than in the middle of the road? A middle-aged herding man wearing a knit hat and thick black wool sweater, stocky build with a scruffy gray beard, seemed to be paying no attention to the rumbling metal blimp that sported tires smooth as dolphin skin.

"What the hell is this?" said Sol, poking his head out the window.

"Feels like we're stuck in traffic back in the Big Apple," observed Donnie. "The only things missing are the honking horns and screaming cabbies." And on cue, a parading family of ducks roamed past the bus, honking away.

Sol poked his head out the window and called out. "I'm starting to feel like lamb chops for dinner!"

The exasperated bus driver pleaded with the herder,

who finally got the message, with the help of a quick bribe. Soon after, the bus was rolling along again.

Sol kept twisting, turning, and complaining, trying to get comfortable. "If you don't sit still, I am going to beat you to a pulp with my purse!" The Falcone applauded. Locals on the bus who didn't know a lick of English cheered. Sol quietly moped, the bumpy ride not doing his achy body any favors either.

After a brief pitstop for a fill-up and bathroom break, the bus approached the town of Dumbraveni near dusk. The town was located just north of Sibiu County, smack dab in the heart of Transylvania. Splintered sunlight pierced through the trees, creating eerie shadows as the bus passed through the town square at a modest speed. The highlight was the towering Armenian Cathedral, an amazing spectacle for the two couples.

"Nothing like seeing it in person," overserved Donnie, sticking his head out the window like a blissful dog. The cool breeze invigorating him as he observed people fast-walking along the sidewalk, a mother and daughter hurrying as they got into a gray sedan. A handful of cars passed by along the worn cobblestone street.

"How far are we from your mother's house?" asked Barbara.

"It's a couple of miles from here, depending on traffic," replied Myrna.

"Thankfully, it doesn't seem too bad," said Sol. "Do things shut down early here?"

Myrna glanced at her watch. "It's Monday after 6PM, so yeah, most businesses usually close by now."

The bus driver dropped off a handful of passengers

just past a distinguished centerpiece fountain, a ten-foot-tall howling bronze wolf sculpture with water streaming from its open jaws, the circular base made of polished Westerly granite.

Donnie noticed a charming pub, tables set outside, people savoring their drinks in the dissipating sun. "Now there's a place we need to get to know better." Sol concurred wholeheartedly.

All four gazed out their windows, absorbing the Eastern European architecture. "This place looks real nice, Myrna," said her husband.

"Oh, we must see the cathedral tomorrow, if that's okay with you, Myrna," said Barbara. "Hopefully, the jet lag won't hit us like a ton of bricks."

"I've got my trusty Pentax K1000 locked and loaded," said Donnie.

"You remembered to bring extra film, right?" asked Barbara.

"Of course," said Donnie, recalling how he ended up having to buy a cheapo Kodak camera on their trip to Bermuda. "That was a complete suck. I could not find 35mm film anywhere."

Just in case, he rummaged through his black leather camera bag and took out two new boxes of Kodak 200 and 400 speed film, giving an exaggerated sigh of relief. "Hard to take pictures without film."

As they passed through the town lined with picturesque storefront shops, Myrna shifted towards the front of the bus to instruct the driver in her rusty native Romanian the address of their destination. To her surprise, the driver responded in English, and in a hearty over-the-top Texas twang to boot.

"Howdy, Ma'am. You like program show, Dallas?" he asked, posing a gargantuan smile that revealed crooked teeth. "I sound like real Cowboy, no?"

"Uh, no, I mean yes," Myrna replied, being polite.

Donnie, always the diplomat, called out with a bit of cowboy twang himself. "Sure do, partner. Could go for some of that famous Transylvanian barbeque right about now."

The man started laughing. "Silly man. Transylvania only famous for vampires!"

The driver rambled on and on about the Lone Star soap opera set deep in the heart of Texas in incredible detail, saying he watches the show when they are able to get a signal, usually late at night. He finally pulled up to the designated location. As the foursome got off, he added, "Ya'll come back, you hear."

The few remaining passengers glared at Sol, all equally irked by his cantankerous behavior, grumbling in their native language. As Sol exited, he swore he heard someone utter the word putz under their breath.

The weather was crisp and cool, not unbearably cold like Sol had imagined. He took in a deep breath of fresh country air.

"Feels like spring in the Big Apple." He approved, thinking he'd be up to his knees in snow and annoyance.

As the foursome picked out their luggage, Sol glanced back as the bus pulled away. He observed multiple people making the sign of the cross. He stared blankly.

"Come on," said Myrna, tugging at her husband's brown corduroy jacket sleeve. "Sol?"

"I'm coming, I'm coming," he replied. "No need to start nagging me on foreign soil."

They shuffled towards their destination, luggage in hand, a few blocks away down a long, gravel one-way street. Rather than imposing on Myrna's family, it was agreed they would all stay at a nearby motel.

Near dark, they came upon a perfectly bland, one-story motel where the rooms faced the parking lot, each fitted with past their prime air conditioning units. The motel was painted mostly white with red trim as waist-high shrubs encompassed the L-shaped building. It resembled one of those low-budget highway travel lodges where people go when either the big-name chain motels are booked up or you don't want to be found. Exhausted, they strode past a full line of parked cars and approached the front office.

"I'll check us in; why don't you sit and relax for a moment," said Sol. There was a wooden bench next to a bright yellow newspaper box. Myrna, Donnie, and Barbara sat down and sighed out in unison. Sol came out moments later, gritting his teeth.

"Well, it looks like some thimble-brain overbooked the rooms."

"What?!" answered Myrna. "So, we don't have a room?"

"Apparently not," replied her husband. "And the only reason I'm not going ballistic here in this parking lot is because I don't want to start World War III on our first day behind the iron curtain."

"So, what do we do now?" asked Donnie.

"The manager apologized and said he would take care of the reservation at another place close by. He said he will give us a ride there."

"Well, that was nice of him. Is it a motel similar to

this?" asked Myrna.

"He said it's a bed and breakfast inside a castle," said Sol.

"A castle?" said Barbara.

"As long as it's got comfortable beds, I'm all in," said Donnie. "I don't think I could walk another step."

The manager pulled up in an early-1970s blue Renault Dacia 1300 Break, a compact-sized station wagon, and parked out front of the motel office.

Sol checked out the car. "I'm thankful for the ride, but how in the hell are we all gonna fit in that?"

"Think slim, buddy," said Donnie.

The manager scampered about, opening the hatch first and placing their luggage inside before opening the doors for everyone to enter.

"Again, I apologize for inconvenience," said the man, middle-aged and pleasant, dressed in casual slacks, long-sleeved shirt, and suspenders. The four got in, and in no time, they were heading along a creepy stretch of rural road with no lighting whatsoever.

Past a clearing of overhanging trees, the man pulled up to the destination. As the two couples got out, the manager gathered up their luggage.

"Enjoy your stay," said the manager. He made the sign of the cross before leaving in a hurry.

"That's something you normally don't see," uttered Sol.

Donnie threw in his two cents' worth. "Hell, I made the sign of the cross anytime I took a cab in the city."

They stood there, gazing upon the three-story, barrel-roofed, blackened castle that had all the warmth and charm of the Addams Family place of residence. Donnie started whistling the TV theme song, complete with finger snaps.

"Oh, stop," chided Barbara, who shifted over to Myrna. "Well, here's home for the next seven days."

"When in Rome-mania, you… I'm too tired to be clever," said Donnie.

"Were you ever clever?" kidded Sol.

"Try not to think too much, dear," said Barbara, admitting they were all feeling a bit punchy. She reached down and picked up what appeared to be one of their brochures on the gravel walkway. She scanned the text and addressed the others.

"It's called Casa de Noapte, which means The Night House, and apparently, the castle is over three hundred years old. Wow."

"It better have plumbing," said Sol.

"What else does it say?" asked Myrna.

"It says Royal families have lived here for ages before being sold after World War II. It was purchased by the current owner, who converted it into a bed and breakfast. Donnie coined it a dread and breakfast.

Barbara continued. "Ooh. It also says the place was supposedly haunted years ago by mysterious creatures of the night. I like it already."

Donnie asked to see the printed trifold brochure. "Oh, I love this tagline, 'Dare to stay in our Lair.' It's creepy and catchy, and all in the same sentence. Not sure that would work for a Holiday Inn." He and Sol looked at each other and couldn't resist, singing the Addams Family theme song in unison.

"Oh, knock it off, you two," groused Myrna.

"Like dealing with children," added Barbara, smirking. "Let's try and be on our best behavior, shall we?" said Myrna.

With nighttime settling in and a bright yellow full moon appearing just above the encompassing pine forest, the foursome started down a long apricot gravel walkway leading to the entrance. To their right stood an imposing nineteenth-century black cast-iron gas lamppost that flickered a bright Halloween orange flame. The four-sided glass lantern mounted on top of the ten-foot-high post featured an ornate, copper wolf head ceiling cap.

The travelers jumped as a screeching sound rang out. Two large wooden doors slowly opened, and a tall, pencil-thin figure, clad from head to toe in black, paced slowly, taking measured steps as he approached the Americans. The man, possibly early-thirties, with a pale complexion and sharp-angled cheekbones, stopped abruptly, mere feet from the weary travelers. He glared intently, interrogating them with his piercing eyes.

CHAPTER 7

"I bid you... welcome, Hirsch and Falcone party," the man uttered in a patented Bela Lugosi intonation, brandishing his white, pearly teeth, his long black hair tied in a ponytail. "My name is Laszlo," he said, uttering his name like it was some swanky men's cologne.

"I've heard that line before," mused Donnie. The man's expression was stone cold before erupting into a booming laugh. He flailed his lanky arms wide open and gave them all a collective bear-like hug. "I love Americans!"

"And we love Romanians," gasped Sol, feeling like he was abruptly ensnared in a Venus flytrap. The man released his effervescent grip. Donnie and Barbara politely backed up a few steps in hopes of avoiding more of the strange man's awkward hospitality.

"I welcome you to Dumbraveni, coolest place on earth in heart of Transylvania," he announced with a boisterous grin.

"What's the story with this guy's second-rate vampire act?" whispered Donnie.

Laszlo, six-foot-five and tipping the scale at 170 pounds, gave Donnie a laser beam stare. Barbara got a sudden chill.

"Forgive bat-like hearing, but my 'act' as you say, beats working in factory," said Laszlo, with a wink. "I take pictures with tourists and make killing," he added, offering up a creepy, subtle laugh. "Since you stay at castle, you get fifty percent off retail price. Best deal in town."

"We'll think about it," replied Sol, raising a brow.

"You must think quickly, as I can only take pictures at night, you see," boasted Laszlo, whirling his cape up to his face almost like a bullfighter. "Or I turn into dust!"

"Of course you will," said Donnie, turning around and raising his brow, "This guy's one beer short of a six pack." Sol snickered.

"Oh, what the hell," said Donnie, reaching for his camera. "Let me take a picture with everyone with the castle behind you."

Laszlo put his arms around Myrna and Barbara, with Sol on the edge. "Okay, ready; say cheese," said Laszlo, brandishing a bright white toothy smile. Barbara, a former dental hygienist, took notice.

"I think that's my line," said Donnie as he snapped a couple of pictures.

"That will be five dollars," said Laszlo. Donnie, not wanting to upset the "vampire," forked over a crisp five-dollar bill.

"Now I take one with you; it's on the house," said Laszlo, borrowing the camera from Donnie, who gave him a quick tutorial. Laszlo directed the four over to the lamppost and clicked away. He handed the camera back to Donnie when everything got silent. Someone else was present.

The four turned as a middle-aged gentleman, bearded, tall, with broad shoulders, and sporting a black sport coat, turtleneck, and deep brown corduroy slacks, approached. He addressed the travelers, taking measured steps in his distinctive black boots as if he were in no hurry. He called out to the tall, slender man.

"Laszlo, please, that is enough," he said. "You are annoying our guests." Laszlo stepped aside as the man addressed the two couples.

"My apologies," he said. "My employee gets a little carried away with the Dracula act." Sol and Myrna offered up a nervous laugh, Donnie and Barbara too.

"Act, you say? It is not act," mused Laszlo. "To be or not to be, is act." He thumped his chest and grinned. "I am real deal."

"We will talk," he replied. "Forgive me, my name is Tibor, owner of Casa de Noapte. I understand you had a problem with your reservation. Rest assured, you will find it warm and comfortable here. Let me officially welcome you to my town of Dumbraveni, and to the beautiful country of Romania.

"Thank you," replied the four.

"I'm Donnie, by the way, and this is my wife, Barbara. And this grumpy guy over here is Sol."

"Pleasure to meet you all," said Tibor, his voice calming. He greeted each of the three, shaking their hands when he finally looked over to Myrna. Tibor paused, captivated by her petite and natural beauty, tanned with barely a wrinkle visible. She had at the last minute decided to visit the beauty salon to get her peppery hair dyed black. It made her look ten years younger with a hint of Annette Funicello of Mickey Mouse Club and Beach Bikini film fame.

"And you must be Myrna." Tibor stepped closer and kissed her hand gently with his thin crimson lips, eying her full-figured body from head to toe. "I can see the family resemblance clearly."

"Do you know my mother, Sabina?" asked Myrna.

"Oh yes," replied Tibor. "Your mother is quite the character in our little town."

"I'm sure she is," smiled Myrna, nervously.

Sol felt almost paralyzed at the stranger's gesture, not sure if he should slug him on the spot for being so forward towards his wife. Or maybe he should take it as a compliment for having a looker for a wife. He uncurled his balled-up left fist, Tibor noticing from the corner of his eye.

Laszlo cut in to break up the tension and commented on Sol's tattered blue Mets hat, interjecting with his effervescent personality. "I see, Mr. Hirsch, you are baseball fan?"

"Hell, yeah, I'm a baseball fan," bellowed Sol, a tried-and-true Mets fan from their inception way back in 1962. "Baseball's our national pastime. You know about baseball, here behind the Iron Curtain?"

"New York Yankees number one in my book," he replied. You know Reggie Jackson? He is World Series hero!" Lazlo offered up a meager left-handed swing.

"Not personally; sorry." Sol's smile evaporated, replaced by the sound of grinding molars. Even in the middle of Transylvania, there were Yankee fans. "Un freaking believable," he uttered under his breath.

Laszlo picked up three of the Samsonites with both arms. Tibor was about to reach for Myrna's suitcase when Laszlo slinked in and grabbed it as well. Tibor shot him a look. With two suitcases in each arm, the slender man headed up the walkway and approached the massive wooden Gothic-style castle doors, each one embellished with black, rusted spider web wrought iron. The heavy doors were held in place with large, golfball-sized metal bolts embedded into the thick, weathered brick wall.

The two couples stepped through the foyer and quickly gazed upon a massive fireplace to the right, complete with a pair of majestic twelve-point buck heads mounted above on each side.

"Cripes," said Donnie as he peered at the fireplace, "I could park my car in that thing."

The roaring fire instantly warmed both couples as they stood in the spacious room where an enormous rich burgundy rug patterned with intertwining black vines and forest green leaves covered a majority of the ancient oak-planked floor. Despite the cavernous interior, the room projected a feeling of warmth and comfort.

"Laszlo, please escort our guest to their room," said Tibor, addressing his employee. "I must attend to a matter in town. I hope you enjoy your stay at my castle."

Laszlo peered over to Tibor, then escorted the guests up the winding staircase. Paintings of past dignitaries graced the wall in a diagonal fashion. Donnie pointed out one of the men sporting a big bushy beard and handlebar mustache. The foursome dragged their weary, weighted feet up each step, making the trek feel like they were scaling Moldoveanu Peak, the tallest mountain in Romania.

Laszlo led them down the second-floor hallway that seemed to go on forever. The lanky man pointed out the artistic history on the walls as they ventured further along. He abruptly put on the brakes.

"Here is favorite painting of Count Dumitru, my great, great, great grandfather, with two of his most adorable pets."

The retirees gawked, absorbing the immense ten-foot by twelve-foot oil painting, the ornate oak wood frame painted in rich, vibrant gold. A distinguished man with fine facial features, clad all in black, sat with his legs crossed, relaxed in an 18th-century Claude-Louis Burgat chair, the cushioned upholstery graced in a lush crimson red. Bookending the gentleman were two imposing white wolves, the contrast striking as each animal displayed fanged expressions with penetrating orange eyes. The image of the ferocious beasts was disturbingly impressive.

Lazlo grinned as he gently stroked the canvas with his bony fingers, dragging his elongated fingernails as he turned his gaze to the weary travelers. "Feels like they could leap off canvas, no?"

"Let's hope not," gulped Sol.

"Look at those colors, they're so vivid," uttered Barbara, almost mesmerized.

"Kinda spooky if you ask me," conceded Donnie, whose taste in artwork consisted of Cassius Marcellus Coolidge's famous Dogs Playing Poker. "Aren't royalty usually painted with, I don't know, Dalmatians or something? These chaps don't look so friendly."

"It is said Dumitru could speak lupus – that is, wolf," replied Lazlo.

"I can speak wolf," yelped Donnie, offering up a mild howl.

Laszlo turned towards Donnie, his face etched in marble. "It is best not to mock wolves," replied Laszlo, "For in Dumbraveni, lupus will answer your call." His eyes narrowed before breaking into a hearty laugh. "Talking to wolves; how ridiculous!"

Sol and Myrna, now too exhausted to care, settled into the spacious bedroom across the hall from their friends.

Laszlo pulled apart the curtains. "You have best view

from castle."

Both Sol and Myrna stepped over and peered out at the panoramic view of the lake, visible with help from the full moon. A neighboring cemetery was partially hidden by a row of pines and leafless trees.

"In case you get cold," Laszlo said, pointing to the already lit fireplace located in the living room section of their home away from home. The two plopped down on the king-size mattress, masked in an ivory bedspread.

Laszlo sauntered over to the door entrance. "If you need anything, ring me, but not after midnight. Thanks to fearless Romanian leader, programming hours are limited. That is when I can watch favorite TV show."

"And what show is that?" asked Sol, with a weary expression.

"Fantasy Island!"

Lazlo proceeded to outstretch his thin, ivory pale hand and offered up a mild cough.

Myrna elbowed her husband and whispered. "Tip, Sol, he wants a tip."

Sol got off the bed and reached for his wallet tucked into his lined coat. "Oh, sorry. Here you go," said Sol, sliding a five-dollar bill between Laszlo's fingers. "I trust American dough is good here?"

"American dough is the best kind of dough," replied Laszlo, adding, "and lots of it. I bid you a pleasant evening."

Sol peeked between the half-closed door, watching Laszlo as he headed back downstairs with a spring in his step, and closed it. "Guy should be a Hollywood actor."

Sol headed for the cozy confines of the king-size bed when something caught his eye outside the window. He walked over and squinted out into the darkness. He searched for the handle and opened the tall window a crack.

"Some fog out there," observed Sol.

Myrna finished changing into her pajamas and brushing her teeth, then got into bed. She took notice of her husband peering outside from the large bay window.

"What are you looking at?"

Sol continued to stare at the landscape. "Thought I saw something running into the forest; probably a dog." He was about to shut the window when he spotted Tibor walking towards the woods, whistling a peculiar tune. A howl rang out from the forest. The window made a scraping sound as Sol attempted to close it. Tibor looked up, catching a glance of him before continuing on his walk.

Sol stared for a moment before shutting the curtains together. "Like I said, probably just a dog." He made sure all the other windows were locked, nice and secure, then went over to check the other large bay window before getting into bed.

Myrna sat up. "If that was a dog, then I'm Charro."

Sol got into bed and gave Myrna a kiss goodnight.

"And no cuchi-cuchi," said Myrna, who then put on her pink eye mask. Sol sighed.

CHAPTER 8

The next morning, Sol and Myrna awoke feeling refreshed to the sounds of barking dogs just outside their room. Sol got up and walked over to the window, and thrust open the heavy curtains, greeting the sunny morning with vigor.

"Yeah, definitely dogs." Both showered and changed before heading downstairs for breakfast. Donnie and Barbara followed in need of coffee. They all sat in the dining room located just outside the large kitchen, the solid dark oak rectangular table seating a dozen people. In the center was a large, two-foot-high ground crystal and gilt bronze vase full of blooming red roses. Donnie examined what resembled little paws at each corner of the base.

"Good morning, sleepyheads," greeted Laszlo as the four sat down. Plates and silverware were already set out for each of the guests. "I trust everyone slept well last night?"

"Like a rock," said Donnie. "Hey, did anyone hear howling last night? Maybe I was dreaming of werewolves."

"I heard it too, only I was awake," said Sol. "Ah, who knows?"

"There are wolves near castle, but it is rare they come close to people. They are cautious animals, not like in movies," said Laszlo.

"Where's Tibor?" asked Donnie.

"Grocery shopping, I believe," said Laszlo. "Sometimes, he goes to black market to buy special American foods for guests." Laszlo stepped back into the kitchen and opened one of the kitchen cabinet doors, and pulled out a cereal box. He showcased it to the Americans like it were a Christmas gift.

"This is one of my favorites."

"Oh my gosh, Count Chocula!" raved Donnie. "I love those monster cereals. Don't suppose you got any Boo Berry on hand?"

"Boo Berry is crap," interjected Sol, looking at his friend. "Now Frankenberry, that's what I'm talking about."

"Our husbands are perpetually ten years old," said Barbara. "Those cereals are nothing but sugar and artificial flavors. And as a former hygienist, I have to remind you."

"Yeah, I know, but they're so tasty!" said her husband, adding that getting a prize at the bottom of the box never got old.

"Oh, what's that funny line you used to tell patients about the need for brushing and flossing?" asked Donnie.

"Ignore your teeth, and they'll go away," said Barbara. "We even had a big poster of a smiling shark promoting it."

"I totally agree, Miss Barbara, about sugary cereal," said Laszlo, reaching back into the kitchen. "That is why I eat healthy cereal too, like Product 19!" He held up the box and studied it. "What exactly does Product 19 mean?"

"You know, I have no idea," said Sol, who dined on it regularly back home.

"Maybe it's some sort of secret government code," said Donnie, shrugging his shoulders.

"I'm not much of a cereal person," said Myrna. "Are there any other options?

"For you, of course," said Laszlo. "I make hearty breakfast for everyone. Be back in a jiffy."

Soon after, Laszlo appeared with a large plate of farm-fresh scrambled eggs, fruit, and thick-cut toast with a selection of homemade jams.

"All food you see here is from local farms," he said. "Nothing but the best for our American guests."

"Delicious, Laszlo," said Donnie. "My compliments to you."

They finished up and thanked their host before preparing to visit Myrna's mother, Sabina.

After breakfast, the two couples brought their plates into the kitchen, offering to lend a hand. Laszlo balked, stating he took pride in taking care of guests, solo.

"Tips are always welcomed!" smiled Laszlo.

Myrna placed her coffee mug in the sink and turned to the slender man. "Do you know if there is a bus that runs into town? I would like to visit my mother."

"Bus?" exclaimed Laszlo, almost insulted. "I will be personal chauffeur for you. It's one of the perks of staying at Casa de Noapte."

"If you don't mind," said Sol, appreciating the gesture.

After he finished cleaning up, Laszlo instructed everyone to wait outside near the entrance, saying only that they would be transported into town in style.

"So, what do you think?" asked Donnie, "A rusty old pickup truck with hay in the back?"

"Yeah, probably some jalopy left over from the war," smirked Sol.

Myrna caught a glimpse. "I think you're both way off on this one."

A royal maroon 1965 Lincoln Continental, complete with suicide doors, tinted windows, and white leather interior, pulled up. The passenger side window rolled down with the unmistakable sounds of Led Zeppelin's Rock and Roll blaring loud and clear.

Laszlo grinned. "Like I said, I give you ride in style."

"That would be an understatement," said Sol, his jaw dropping. He walked around the full-sized automobile, admiring the American-made craftsmanship. "What a beauty, Laszlo." The owner couldn't hide his beaming grin.

Myrna, Barbara, and Donnie got into the back seat with room to spare. Sol got in the front. The lanky man made a winding U-turn in the land yacht and headed for Myrna's mother's house.

Sol turned to Laszlo, who was singing along to the music. "You mind lowering the volume a tad? I don't mind music, but that stuff is gonna make my eardrums bleed."

"My apologies," said Laszlo, reaching for the knob and popping out the cassette.

Donnie, sitting in the middle, moved up closer to Laszlo. "You got any jazz radio stations here?"

Laszlo reached for the Led Zeppelin IV cassette, holding it up. "It's either this or propaganda radio. Which you choose?"

"I say we get the Led out," said Donnie.

Sol looked over to his friend and sighed. "Rock and roll."

Laszlo slid the cassette back in to rewind the song again. "I love intro!" He momentarily took his hands off the wheel, thrashing his spindly arms about, mimicking the frenetic drumming of John Bonham as he drove along, making the four visitors uneasy. Myrna politely asked him to rein in the theatrics so they would feel more at ease. Laszlo obliged.

After a picturesque drive along the rural road, much more scenic than at night, Laszlo pulled up at a stop sign next to a café, people were sitting outside drinking coffee and tea. Sol, still battling the long flight, yawned. "I wouldn't mind another cup of Joe. Anyone else?"

The four decided to get out there on the spot, grab a coffee, then walk to their destination. They stepped out of the car and thanked Laszlo for the ride. He called out, handing Sol a business card. "Call castle when you want to return; I pick you up." He cranked the music and sped off.

Sol reached up to his ears. "I think my head is going to explode."

The four entered the coffee shop. The aromatic scent of fresh roasted coffee permeated throughout. Sol approached the young cashier and asked for a large coffee. The person didn't understand. The owner, standing nearby, offered to take their orders instead. Unfortunately, Sol was told large coffees were off limits. Myrna played translator and chatted with the man, mid-framed, early thirties with long blond hair, and inquired why. The person spoke, and not in a pleasant demeanor. Sol quickly picked up on his annoyance.

Sol looked over to Myrna. "He seems upset. Was it something I said?"

Myrna translated. "No. He said because of commie sons of bitches, coffee is rationed. Best I can do is medium cups."

"I can live with that as long as it has caffeine," said Sol.

The owner spoke out again; Myrna continued. "He says most people must drink something called nechezol, a coffee substitute made from barley and chickpeas."

"Chickpeas?" she replied in Romanian, looking at the

man, puzzled.

"I know barley is in beer, so maybe that's not so bad, but chickpeas? That doesn't sound too appealing," said Donnie.

The owner served up their coffees and directed them to the sugar and milk. Sol, after hearing him refer to the commies as sons of bitches, took out his wallet and handed the man a ten-dollar bill. "You earned it, my friend." The man skated around the small counter area and gave him a hug, uttering "thank you" in English.

The four, armed with their precious coffees, stepped outside and drank them slowly, savoring every drop.

Sol, instead, took a gulp. "Wow, now that's a robust cup of coffee," he said, appreciating the pick-me-up.

They strolled along the sidewalk, admiring the array of shops and architecture. The weather outside was pitch-perfect, partly sunny in the low sixties. Between the hot coffee and the seasonable weather, Sol removed his coat, revealing a gray sweater with a small hole at one of the elbows. He gazed up at the morning sky and basked in its warmth.

"Good day, sunshine, huh, Sol?" said Donnie, uttering the title from a Beatles song. His good friend nodded in agreement.

From across the street, Myrna pointed out some of her favorite family-owned shops, including a corner bookstore, a new and used clothing store, a bodega, and a bustling grocery store that sold local produce outside in assorted wood bins.

The four approached the imposing wolf fountain they had seen the night before, its open maw and head pointed towards the sky. The attraction sat center stage at the roundabout, enclosed by a circle of manicured hedges and multiple park benches. Armed with his Pentax camera,

Donnie aimed, focused, and clicked away.

An older couple fed breadcrumbs to a group of pigeons as the two couples admired the landmark sculpture. The man got up and offered to take their picture by the fountain. Donnie set the camera up for him, explaining to press the button when he gave the signal. They stood at the base of the fountain and got in position. The gentleman peered through the viewfinder and waved his hand, asking them to shift closer together.

"Any closer, guys, and we'll have to get a room," kidded Donnie.

The old man gave the thumbs-up sign. He took the picture, then handed the camera back to Donnie, who offered up a big thank you and a couple of bucks.

"You two with your tips," said Barbara. "Everyone in this town will be following us for the rest of our stay."

"We're fortunate, that's all," said Sol. "To not be able to do and say what you want? I mean, getting a coffee here is a big deal. I'm not taking one Goddamn thing for granted."

"So maybe you won't sulk so much when the Mets lose," said Myrna. "There are more important things in life."

"That's debatable," countered her husband with a smirk.

"Anyone have any change?" asked Donnie.

Sol reached into his pocket and handed his friend a nickel. "What are you gonna wish for?"

"That our Mets will have a winning season this year," replied Donnie as he flicked it off his thumb.

"Technically speaking, if you reveal your wish, it won't come true," said Barbara.

Myrna couldn't help herself. "In this case, I don't think it'll make any difference."

Sol turned to his wife. "That was a fastball served right over the plate."

As they continued their walk, Myrna commented that many of the stores had been around for ages, adding that it made her feel nostalgic, like she had never left. After Donnie took a few more pictures of the surrounding landscape, they resumed their journey towards Myrna's childhood home.

After passing a large corner house textured in white stucco and trimmed in navy blue, they approached the neighborhood, about a half-mile away from the center of town. Similar homes lined the quiet streets, most close together. They seemed to alternate in color between white, beige, and light orange. Most had tile roofs hued in rustic burnt orange or white.

Despite the images in the book, the stereotypical Sol expected to see a bunch of ransacked, poorly constructed properties, but everything so far seemed as charming as a postcard.

"People seem to stare out of their windows a lot here, don't they?" observed Sol as the four strolled along the sidewalk, noticing all the gawking townsfolk. "What, do we look freakish or something?"

"We're New Yorkers," replied Donnie with a smirk. "People are bound to stare."

The four crossed the intersection as a modest number of cars passed by. "This way," instructed Myrna.

They continued walking four blocks when Myrna stopped in front of a waist-high weathered picket fence, some of the white paint peeling off. The house was set back twenty yards from the sidewalk, with sparse trees surrounding the boxy home. An orange two-door Saab 99 was parked out front. Sol eyed the car, having never seen one before.

"What the hell's a Saab? Is that a Romanian brand?"

"It's Swedish," said Donnie. "They're popular with the academic types in the northeast, front-wheel drive, good in the snow."

"So, only eggheads drive 'em," joked Sol.

"Well, this is it, guys, my mother's home," said Myrna.

"Looks appealing enough," replied Sol. "The yard could use a little sprucing up, though."

Myrna surveyed the patches of tall, straw-like grass and crawling ivy on the trees. A rusted shovel and rake lay on the ground near the walkway. "You're right, it does look a bit rundown. My mother is in her 80s, so I don't know if she has anyone helping her."

"When was the last time you visited your mother?" asked Barbara.

"Five years ago in the fall. Before that, it was for my father's funeral, God bless his soul," said Myrna, making the sign of the cross. She paused. "Almost ten years ago to the day."

"Looks like there's a mower in the garage," pointed Sol. "Maybe we can lend a hand while we're here and spruce things up." He then pondered his suggestion. "You know, I've never used a lawn mower before in my life. Hell, I've never had a lawn!"

"I'm sure your mother would appreciate that," said Barbara.

Myrna opened the latch on the front gate and entered first. Walking along a stone pathway, they approached the front porch featuring decaying flowers in terracotta pots on each side of the first step. In the detached one-car garage sat an early '70s red Dacia 1300. They walked up to the door, Myrna making sure she looked presentable.

"Hey kitty, kitty," said Sol, petting a large black and white tabby. "Is this hers?"

"Could be," she answered. "I remember there were always cats hanging around the house. My mother loves cats."

Noticing the fullness of the feline, Donnie commented. "I'm guessing your mother doesn't have a rodent problem. That is one plump puddy cat."

Myrna stepped up to the door and knocked. She was greeted by a young man in his early twenties, Florin Gherman, a family relative who oozed punk vibes with his disheveled blond hair, black leather coat, and torn blue jeans.

After greetings and handshakes, the two couples strode inside past the hallway. They stood momentarily by the tidy kitchen, simple, with aged appliances, the walls painted in light blue. An iron skillet and a pair of curved fish-shaped aluminum Jell-O molds hung on the wall. A tray of prepared snacks rested on the counter next to the sink.

Myrna spotted her mother sitting by the fireplace, a quilt on her lap, in a Jacobean oak rocking chair with a solid green cushion. Seeing her daughter, Sabina sprang from the chair.

"Myrna!" They embraced. Her mother teared up with joy.

She asked her mother in Romanian how she was feeling. Her answer surprised everyone.

"Not too shabby," said Sabina, in firmly pronounced English.

"She speaks English?" asked Sol. "Myrna, I thought you said your mother didn't speak a lick of English." Sabina strode over and gave her son-in-law a pinch on his cheek.

"It is not against law to talk English," she replied, feisty and apparently healthy as an ox at the tender age of eighty-three.

"No, no, of course not," said Myrna, "I think it's great. How did you learn English?"

"I watch American television when available late night," she added, "I read Sports Illustrated too. Don't care much for swimsuit issue, but your cousin, Florin, likes it. Maybe too much if you know what I mean." She glanced over to Florin, making him blush. "How are Cowboys doing? I like cute star on helmet!"

"The Cowboys are always good, but we're Jets fans," said Sol.

"For the record, I'm a Giants fan," said Myrna. Sol shook his head. Myrna introduced everyone. All exchanged handshakes and hugs.

Sabina offered the foursome cold beer and cigarettes.

"No thank you," declined Donnie. "I make it a rule never to consume suds before 10AM."

"I thought all Americans enjoy beer and smokes!" she said. "Hold on. Guess who I am. The Plane! The plane!"

The four looked at each other. Donnie spoke up. "Tattoo from Fantasy Island?"

"Bingo!" said Sabina. "It's my favorite show. By the way, I want next car to be Chrysler Cordoba with rich, Corinthian leather!"

Myrna, Sol, and Barbara politely declined as well, saying it was a bit too early in the day. Instead, they opted for tea and the tray of cheese, fruit, and crackers that Florin had prepared.

It reminded Donnie of a funny joke (at least in his mind). "Sabina, you should always buy fresh fruit, but if it gets too fresh, smack it."

Everyone went stone-faced, even after the translation. Donnie had told that joke at least a dozen times before, and he still never tired of it. After a moment of awkward silence, Myrna's mom burst into laughter. Florin offered up a polite smile.

"Forgive my manners," said Sabina. "You remember your cousin, Florin?"

"Yes, yes, or course," said Myrna. "You were so young the last time I saw you. I remember my father saying you were going to be an important figure in our town."

Sabina chimed in. "Florin executes his job well."

The young man raised a brow. "Your father was a good man. He taught me many things, like how to hunt down vamp-" Sabina quickly interrupted.

"For food," Sabina said. "Do you hunt, Sol?"

"Uh, only for bargains," he quipped.

"My father was a good man, Florin, and thank you for the kind words," said Myrna, taking her mother's hand.

"Sit, sit," ordered Sabina, full of zest. Florin went over to the fireplace and tossed a couple of logs on top. Despite the seasonable temperatures, Sabina enjoyed a good fire.

The two couples sat down, sharing a sofa and an antique love seat. "What have you been doing since I last saw you?" asked Myrna.

"I work at your favorite bookstore to stay active and earn money," said Sabina. "Mostly I play cards with friends and take walks with Scooby."

"Is Scooby a dog?" asked Donnie.

"No, Scooby is fish," smirked Sabina, before breaking into laughter. "Of course, Scooby is dog!" She snapped her fingers. From out of the bedroom lumbered a stocky four-year-old Alaskan Malamute with bright blue eyes and a mixed white, black, and gray coat.

"Meet Scooby."

The dog strode directly over and sat down next to Sol, eying him intently. "Is he friendly?" he asked, feeling a bit anxious.

"To humans, yes," said Sabina. She eyed Florin. Sol petted the dog behind the ears, Scooby approving with a gentle growl.

"He likes you," said Sabina.

"I must still smell of pastrami," kidded Sol.

Thinking Sabina was jesting, they shifted over to a folding card table and played poker before having a light lunch of sandwiches, iced tea, and homemade chocolate cake. With Sabina taking her customary post-lunch nap, the two couples decided to burn off some calories and take a stroll into town. First up was visiting the massive cathedral. Donnie went through a whole roll of 200-speed film as he took numerous pictures of the impressive exterior. He sat down at one of the back pews and inserted a roll of 400-speed film, better suited for taking pictures inside the impressive architecture.

There was a momentary chill in the air as the clouds shifted, partially blocking out the sun. Moments later, the sun reappeared, beaming brightly as they strode along the sidewalks, savoring the warmth. They checked out shop after shop, buying small items here and there, homemade candies, hand-crafted jewelry, and postcards. As the two couples approached a quiet street corner, one particular store caught

Sol's eye, a macabre bookstore called Infiorator. The brick façade was painted black with two large rectangular pane windows stationed on both sides. Each window featured distinctive displays of weird and wonderful books, papier-mache masks, fancy tarot cards, and other spiritual novelties.

Myrna beamed. "I swear this place hasn't changed in ages. I remember coming here when I was in my teens before moving to the States. We were told the owners dabbled in witchcraft. My parents forbade me to go, but of course, it made me want to go even more."

"What does I-n-f-i-o-rator mean?" asked Sol, as he peered through the rose-tinted windows. "Looks kinda creepy inside."

"That's what it means," said Myrna.

"It means what?" asked Sol.

"The name. It means creepy, frightening," she answered.

Donnie gazed at the assortment of oddities. "Yeah, there's a whole lotta that going on in here."

Sol eyed an assortment of devil-faced papier mache masks, varying in colors, but most painted in shades of red, yellow, black, and fiery orange. Each emphasized mischievous grins and diverse styled horns, some sharp and pointy, others elaborate and overtly creative. One that particularly caught Sol's attention was a flesh-colored model that resembled the famed actor and Frankenstein's monster, Boris Karloff. They entered. Sol ventured over to the counter and inquired about the mask. He was tempted to buy it when Myrna nixed the transaction. Even in Romanian leu, it was on the pricy side.

They browsed the assorted books, mostly non-fiction, postcards, and local maps. Behind the counter were a pair of black cats sleeping on an oversized maroon pillow with tassels at the corners. Sol inspected a spinner rack of paperbacks. One section housed a handful of local trifold maps. A book that caught his eye was titled *The Vampires of Dumbraveni*. He picked it up and thumbed through the roughly one hundred pages, all the creepy photographs captured in black and white. Halfway through, he stumbled across a striking image of what appeared to be the painting Laszlo admired of his way past great-grandfather from the castle. He paused, reading the caption before continuing. Another image suddenly caught his eye. He focused on the particular bearded face, then shrugged his shoulders before placing the book back on the metal rack. He walked over to the counter and purchased some locally made dark chocolate candy bars.

After leaving the store, Myrna spotted a new café across the street, the outside tables filled with mostly young adults.

"Chocolada Bakery," said Myrna, reading the bright yellow sign. "It must be new."

"Shall we check it out?" posed Barbara.

"I'm game," said Donnie. Sol nodded in agreement.

The four sat down outside at a round, black wrought iron table next to a thirty-something couple, their tan and white Welsh Corgie at attention, hoping for a morsel to fall. A plump waitress walked over and introduced herself as she handed them each a menu. After browsing the lists of desserts, Myrna recommended a Romanian favorite called dobos torte, a multi-layered Hungarian sponge cake featuring chocolate buttercream and a caramel glaze on top. All agreed.

Moments later, the waitress returned with four large slices of cake, each white plate accented with drizzled dark chocolate and a strawberry. Everyone relished their slices, each forkful sinfully delicious.

They walked off the calories in the seasonably warm weather. Soon, they approached Sabina's house, all a bit weary from walking on the uneven cobblestone roads, but still in good spirits.

"Holy moly, time flies when you're having fun," blurted Sol, noticing it was almost six PM.

Sabina, peeking through the living room curtains, spotted them. She opened the front door as they stepped up to the front porch.

"I am glad you return, but now you must go before it gets too dark."

"We just got back," said Myrna. "Can we at least catch our breath first? We just walked the whole entire city."

"Yes, of course, my dear, but it is important," she said. They stepped into the living room near the fireplace. Scooby came up to Sol, encouraging ear scratches. He obliged.

"Sabina, you have a lovely town. Very friendly people," said Sol. "We can't wait to eat at one of those local restaurants on the main drag and enjoy an adult beverage. Is Romanian beer good?"

"Romania beer is best," said Sabina. "Timişoreana, my personal favorite! Makes American beer taste like pee pee."

That quickly brought an unflattering expression on Sol's face. He composed himself, not wanting to ruin a perfect day, and anger Myrna's mother. "Well, Donnie and I are eager to sample some of Romania's finest brews."

Myrna was pleasantly surprised by her hubby's restraint. Normally, he'd get ticked off if anyone was critical of anything American-made. Although oftentimes, Sol would blow a gasket, and not because his problematic American-made automobile seemed to overheat any time the hot Florida weather passed ninety degrees. He was beginning to hear good things about Toyotas.

"I enjoy small talk, but you must go and catch bus. I see you tomorrow."

Myrna asked to use the phone to call Laszlo so he could arrange picking them up. She dialed, patiently waiting as the phone rang and rang.

"No answer." She turned to Sol and their friends. "Looks like we're riding the bus."

Donnie opened the front door as the two couples went outside. They stood on the front porch, saying their goodbyes. Sabina quickly retreated inside and locked the door. Myrna caught a glimpse of her mother, now appearing agitated as she conversed with Florin, who seemed to be doing his best to calm her down.

Observing them lingering in the yard, Sabina opened the front door and stepped outside again. "Please, I not want you walking late at night."

"Let me try calling the castle one more time. Maybe Laszlo was busy with something," said Myrna, walking past her mother to reach for the phone stationed on the wall.

"Castle? What castle?" inquired Sabina with a concerned expression. "I thought you stay at motel near main street."

"They overbooked us, so now we're staying at… what's the name of the place again?" asked Sol.

Barbara remembered. "It's called Casa de Noapte. It means…"

Sabina cut her off. "I know what it means… The Night

House. Nothing good comes from castles."

"Well, so far it's been comfortable, and Tibor has been a good host," said Sol, "Although we haven't seen much of him. Now that Laszlo takes the cake. Funny, and loves Americans."

"Laszlo is good man, but Vampire act kinda hokey," chimed Sabina, teetering her hands.

Myrna was able to get a hold of Tibor, who explained that Laszlo was having car problems, but that assured her the buses were running on time, approximately every other hour. He checked the schedule and said the next bus stopping in town should be in about seven PM.

Donnie and Barbara walked to the front gate, followed by Sol, waving as they left. Myrna hugged her mother.

"Had a great time, Ma; glad you're doing well. I love you."

"Of course, you do, my daughter," said Sabina. "What's not to love?"

Sabina glanced upward, noticing the darkening skies with a worried expression. There was a chance of rain, and it was officially the evening, now approaching 6:30PM. "See you tomorrow."

As they were leaving, Sabina called for Sol to return.

"Hold on, folks, your mother wants to see me. Hope I'm not in trouble," said Sol with a smile. He trotted back up the stairs and stopped at the door. Sabina ordered him to stay put for a moment.

Sol looked back at his wife and friends, shrugging his shoulders. She returned and placed an object in his calloused hands. Sol opened the palm and noticed a two-inch-long silver crucifix on a matching silver chain.

"Thank you, Sabina, really, but it's not my thing; I'm Jewish, remember?" said Sol, feeling slightly awkward.

"My Myrna covered. Barbara and bad joke teller Donnie covered, but you need also. I insist," said Sabina, stubbornly digging in her heels. "I take no for answer."

"Now?" asked Sol.

"Yes. Please, put on."

"Okay, okay," said Sol, his stiff, chubby fingers struggling to connect the chain. Sabina took the reins, hooking it together as she draped it around Sol's neck.

"Let people see! Tomorrow, we celebrate with Timisoara! Put hair on your chest."

"Gee, I hope not for your sake," grinned Sol. Sabina chuckled. "And thank you." He stepped off the front porch and joined Myrna and his friends by the gate.

"What was that about?" asked Myrna.

They started to walk away when the object caught her eye. "Uh, Sol, why are you wearing a crucifix?"

"I tried to explain, but your mother was very insistent," he replied.

Donnie reached inside his shirt and pulled out his crucifix, resting it on his shirt on full display. "Welcome to the club, Sol."

Myrna eyed her mother in the window, waving to her. "She knows you're Jewish, right?"

"Yes, but I'm not gonna argue with your mother," said Sol.

"Come on, folks, we gotta make that bus or we'll incur the wrath of Sabina," said Donnie.

"We're coming, we're coming," replied Sol.

A light drizzle began to fall. As they strolled a block

past Sabina's house, the blaring sounds of rock music filled the air. The four turned around, and there was Laszlo pulling up in his Lincoln Continental.

"I am sorry, but car battery went kaput," said Laszlo with his head sticking out the window, catching raindrops on his face. "Get in quickly, it is ready to…" A burst of lightning and thunder, followed by a deluge of rain, almost drenching the two couples as they piled inside the four-door.

"Laszlo, your timing is impeccable," said Donnie.

"You have dinner?" asked Laszlo, peeking in the rearview mirror.

"Not yet, but we're getting hungry," said Donnie, using his shirt to dry his face from the rain. "Any suggestions?"

"I know great pizza joint close by," said Laszlo, peering at Sol and company. Not wanting to hurt his feelings, they all agreed.

Fifteen minutes later, Laszlo navigated his behemoth vehicle, parallel parking with ease between two sub-compacts in front of the pizzeria. The four took a liking right away as it resembled some of the no-nonsense pizza restaurants they would find in the big city. After a brief debate, everyone finally agreed on toppings. Due to their soaked disposition, Laszlo volunteered to dash inside and place their order.

After a thirty-minute wait, they soon arrived back at the castle, the thunderstorms starting to subside. After drying off by the big fireplace, both parties sat down for dinner.

Donnie and Barbara lent a hand with the plates as Myrna brought out a new bottle of Recas Castle Pinot Noir, a Romanian red wine from Transylvania. Sol stuck his face in the refrigerator and retrieved a couple of bottles of cold beer for he and Donnie. Laszlo presented the two boxes, opening each like a game show assistant. Sol wasn't sure what to expect from Romanian pizza, but to his surprise, the pizza, topped with onion, green peppers, and black olives, appeared scrumptious.

"Dig in, my friends," said Laszlo.

Sol obliged and grabbed a slice for both he and Myrna. Laszlo, Donnie, and Barbara opted for the pepperoni.

Everyone eyed Sol, the so-called pizza expert, as he took a sizable bite. He chewed it and then washed it down with his beer.

"Well?" asked Myrna.

Sol beamed. "New Park Pizza in Howard Beach may have some competition. Absolutely delicious, Laszlo, excellent choice."

With Sol's seal of approval, everyone devoured their slices, and then some. They topped off the evening with another bottle of wine and then ice cream for dessert.

After cleaning up, Laszlo decided to sit and strum his acoustic guitar by the big fireplace. The four sat for a while, politely listening to his playing. They conversed about their sightseeing experiences earlier in the day while enjoying chamomile tea. After a round of yawning, the two couples said goodnight to Laszlo and then headed to their collective bedrooms.

While Sol was showering, Myrna heard what was becoming a nightly ritual: the sound of howling wolves that felt like it was coming from just outside their window. And like clockwork, there was Tibor, dressed in a long-length black trench coat and hat, whistling that peculiar tune as he approached the nearby forest in an encompassing fog.

Myrna couldn't resist and peeked through the curtains

to observe him. Tibor, taking measured steps towards the woods, suddenly stopped and turned towards the castle. His penetrating gaze caught Myrna off guard, his eyes zeroing in on her for what seemed like an eternity. She froze, unable to blink. Sol got out of the shower, drying himself off, and addressed his wife.

"So, what do you think of taking a little road trip and checking out Bran Castle tomorrow, home of Vlad the Impaler?" No response. He then saw his wife staring out the window. "Earth to wife?"

Myrna jumped, finally breaking from her stupor. She quickly shut the curtains. "Uh, I was just looking out at the forest, and…"

"And what. You see Tibor out there again? That guy digs his nightly walks. Maybe I should join him one of these evenings."

Myrna didn't answer right away, her mind still in a stupor. "I'm sorry, what did you say? A walk… at night?"

"Yeah, why not?" said Sol. "A stroll around that big, creepy lake would be a gas. I'm sure Donnie would love to join me; he's into monster movies and stuff."

"Just because one likes monster movies doesn't mean one doesn't embrace all things creepy crawly," replied Myrna. "And you know Donny. If he saw a spider, he'd jump up onto the nearest chair."

"You're probably right," chuckled Sol.

The two got into bed and read for a while. Sol zonked out from too much wine. Myrna read a little longer, her mind wandering intermittently before falling asleep.

CHAPTER 9

The next morning after breakfast, Sol and Donnie decided to take a walk around the lake, the weather feeling exactly like springtime in the Big Apple. Sol guessed the body of water was the size of the field at Shea Stadium, home of the New York Mets and Jets. The surrounding forest was made up of pines, oaks, and other towering trees. Although temperatures were warming, no leaves were visible on any of the tree branches. The two walked and talked, smoking Marlboros as they strolled along. Meanwhile, Myrna and Barbara sat outside, relaxing with cups of tea in hand and sampling pastries.

"Barbara and I are really glad you invited us," said Donnie. "And the fresh air seems to be doing wonders for you."

"Yeah, it has," replied Sol, zipping down his coat a bit. "It's really beautiful here. I know it sounds strange, Donnie, but I'm feeling like, I don't know, a real kinship to this place. And the pizza last night was actually pretty good. Maybe Myrna and I should buy a little summer cottage or something."

"You in a cottage? What's next, flyfishing along the Hudson River?" joked Donnie.

Sol scoffed. "You don't think so?"

"I know you dig it here and Miami Beach, but you'll always be a city guy through and through," said Donnie. "I mean, where the hell are you gonna get good pastrami in these parts?"

"Good point, but I guess I could adapt," said Sol, walking with a spring in his step. He leaped over a fallen tree. "I'm feeling spry, my friend. Wanna race?"

"Sure, to the nearest pub?" mused Donnie. The two ended up sitting down at an old wooden bench and rested.

"That Laszlo guy is some character, eh?" said Donnie.

"With that getup, he should be hosting one of those late-night creature feature programs," said Sol. "I do like how he's got that entrepreneurial spirit in him. I bet a lot of people here do. It's just being suppressed by those damn reds, and not the Cincinnati kind."

"You got that right," remarked Donnie. He reached down and picked up a flat rock about half the size of his hand. "Okay, how many skips do you think I can do?"

"Bet you a beer you can't do three," said Sol.

"You're on, buddy." Donnie took off his jacket and laid it on the bench. He stretched out his arms, whirling them in motion like he was getting the call from the bullpen.

"While we're young," barked Sol, shaking his head.

Donnie stepped closer to the water's edge and promptly drilled his throw straight into the water. He stood there, the water barely making a ripple. "Boy, that was really bad."

"An outdoorsman you're not," said Sol, poking fun at his friend. "Come on, fly fisherman, let's finish up our walk and join the wives."

Sol stood up when something caught his interest, a chirping sound coming from a large, rounded pine tree. He peered more intently through the branches, trying to decipher what it was. From what he could tell, it looked like a cluster of black birds of some sort, imbedded among the dense pine needles. Sol shrugged his shoulders, then joined his friend, and they headed back to the castle.

***

"There you are," said Barbara, standing outside with Myrna as they finished up their tea. The two had explored the old cemetery lined with an aging white picket fence, marveling at all the ancient tombstones, some standing six feet high and in various shapes and sizes, most dating back centuries.

"Imagine walking around out there at night," she added.

"That just gave me a chill up my spine," said Myrna. "If it's okay, I'd love to check out the town library this morning. It's not too far from the cathedral."

"A school teacher always," said Sol, giving Myrna a peck on the cheek. "Sure, why not?" He looked over and saw Laszlo tightening the bolts of the gargantuan front doors. He and Donnie strolled over to say hello.

"Good morning, Mr. Hirsch and Falcone," he said. "How was walk around beautiful lake?"

"Very enjoyable. Got in some much-needed exercise after all that delicious pizza and wine," replied Sol. "But please, call us by our first names; no need to be so formal."

"My apologies," said Laszlo. "I know you say that before. It is how I was raised. "Now my boss, Tibor, he is much too serious." The three men snickered.

"By the way, where is Tibor? We haven't seen much of him since we got here," questioned Donnie.

"He likes to visit markets early in morning to buy best produce and vegetables," said Laszlo. "He is happy you are enjoying stay at our castle."

"It's a lovely place, Laszlo," said Donnie, never

thinking he'd be spending the night in a European castle. "I know Romania is ground zero for Bram Stoker's Dracula. I guess that is your inspiration for your, uh, presentation?"

Laszlo grinned. "Romania is much more than vampires. We are a country rich in culture," he said enthusiastically. "But I enjoy playing up vampire image, and have love of old monster movies. Maybe Hollywood should call me."

"That they should," said Donnie. "In my book, there was no one better than Bela Lugosi. Now Christopher Lee wasn't too shabby in those Hammer films, but I'm more of a Universal monster movie guy."

"Oh man, The Mummy, Wolfman, and who can forget Boris Karloff as Frankenstein," said Sol, soon reminiscing about going to drive-ins and watching scary movies.

Laszlo, a horror film aficionado, corrected Sol. "Actually, Karloff plays Frankenstein's monster, not Frankenstein. Doctor Frankenstein is only Frankenstein in movie."

"That's a whole lotta Frankensteins," assessed Donnie.

Sol started contemplating, never having given it much thought before. "Holy crap, you're right, Laszlo," espoused the former deli man. "All these years…"

"Maybe the monster should be given a proper name, not just "the monster," you know what I mean?" said Donnie. "Let's think about this one for a moment."

All three stood around, wondering what a good name would be for Frankenstein's monster.

"I know," said Donnie with a sly grin, "How about Fergus, named after my late father-in-law, Fergus O'Connor."

"Fergus?" snapped Sol. "How the hell is a name like Fergus gonna scare people?"

"First time I met Barbara's father, he scared the crap out of me," said Donnie.

"How's that?" asked Sol.

"My first date with Barbara, he said I better bring his daughter home by 10PM, or he was gonna hunt me down and personally guillotine my privates."

"That would scare me," frowned Laszlo.

"Okay, so on this splendid spring morning at this splendid castle, Frankenstein's monster shall forever be known as Fergus," christened Sol, before pausing. "You know, I can't believe we just had this conversation."

"You two ready to visit my mother?" called out Myrna.

"Yeah," replied Sol. He looked over to Laszlo. "Are you available to give us a ride this morning?"

"At your service," said Laszlo. "I love to show off my hot wheels!"

Moments later, the familiar Lincoln Continental pulled up. Laszlo jumped out, the sounds of The Who now blaring from the automobile. Laszlo politely lowered the volume as the two couples got in.

Laszlo steered the Lincoln, making a wide turn before driving down the familiar road, giving a honk to a neighbor friend as he passed by.

The four arrived at Sabina's home. Sol handed Laszlo a five-dollar bill and shook his hand. Appreciate the taxi service, my man."

"Any time," said Laszlo, ready to pull away from the curb when he called out.

"Just in case I can't pick you up tonight, buses should be on schedule. Chao, my friends."

To their pleasant surprise, they saw Florin cutting the

grass and pulling up weeds in the front yard. "Looking good, kid," observed Sol.

"Florin, thank you so much," said Myrna in her rusty Romanian. "I'm sure my mother will appreciate it."

"I should have done much earlier, but mower was broken. It is now fixed," he replied. "Oh, your mother apologizes. She had to help out at bookstore, then pick up medicine later."

"Medicine?" asked Myrna, concerned. "I thought she was feeling well."

Florin assured her that Sabina was okay. "Beer and cigarettes are her medicine." He broke out into a miniscule smile. "She should be home in a few hours."

Donnie, overhearing the conversation, chimed in. "That's my type of medicine."

Sol glanced at his watch. "Hell, it'll be lunchtime in a couple of hours. What do you say we take a walk into town again, do some more sightseeing, then grab a bite to eat?" Donnie and Barbara seconded the motion.

Myrna called out to her cousin. "If my mother gets back early, tell her we'll be back by late afternoon." Florin waved and continued mowing.

At Myrna's request, the two couples checked out the local library first. They entered the half-century-old building, the façade unassuming, and painted in beige. Myrna offered up a hello in Romanian as they entered. The librarian replied the same. She and the rest observed a handful of people reading newspapers, all sitting in matching blue upholstered chairs.

"Hey, I wonder if they got the New York Post here?" said Sol, apparently a bit too loud as the librarian shushed him. He apologized.

"Apparently, librarians shush the same all over the world," observed Donnie.

"Yeah, the international language to put a sock in it," said Sol.

Both he and Donnie eyed the newspapers in hand, all appeared to be in foreign languages. "Looks like we'll have to catch the scores some other way," said Donnie.

To Myrna and Barbara's delight, there was a cardboard box with a handful of used books for sale to the right of the checkout desk. She and Barbara rummaged through the offerings. Both were browsing for some fresh late-night reading material. Barbara found a worn copy of Agatha Christie's "Murder on the Orient Express", featuring the famed Belgian detective, Mr. Hercule Poirot.

"You hit the jackpot, Barbara," said Myrna, still in search of a book.

"How about this?" said Barbara with a smile, holding up a book about Russian tanks. "Makes for some light reading."

The librarian walked over and placed a few more books in the bin. "Here. Enjoy bestseller about killer shark," said the librarian. She started humming the famous theme music.

"Jaws. Loved the movie; never read the book," said Myrna. "Thank you." Myrna took out a couple of dollars and gave them to the woman, thanking her.

Sol and Donnie walked over, the former noticing the book cover clear as day. "Jaws?" he inquired. "Loved the movie, never read the book."

"You and I both," said Myrna.

As they left, Myrna pointed to a restaurant that was

just around the corner, serving up soups and sandwiches. The four sat down outside, basking in the sunlight. They dined on ham and cheese served on fresh croissants. Sol and Donnie couldn't resist and decided to wash things down with a locally brewed lager on tap, crisp, golden, and satisfying. Myrna and Barbara shared a bottle of sparkling mineral water with lime slices. Afterwards, they visited a gallery and a few other stores. From across the street, they spotted a young street performer playing acoustic guitar, performing a Beatles song under the majestic wolf fountain.

"Who's in the mood for a concert?" said Sol. The four ambled across the street and sat down on the nearby benches. In the man's open guitar case was a handful of change, a few bills, and a schipperke, a cute black Belgian shepherd breed, snoozing away on the plush interior.

After finishing up an interesting rendition of Ob-La-Di, Ob-La-Da, Sol turned to his wife. "I wonder if he knows any Sinatra."

"If he does, you better give him a big tip," said Myrna.

"Absolutely, I will," he said. Sol stood up and shuffled over to the young man, slender, wearing jeans, a white long-sleeve shirt, and sporting a fashionable green Herringbone Harris tweed sport coat.

"Excuse me, but do you know any Frank Sinatra songs?"

The young man stared at Sol for a moment, then looked at his dog.

"Frank Sinatra?"

"Uh, yeah, you know, Ol' Blue Eyes?" said Sol. He turned to his wife and friends and shrugged. "I gave it a shot."

The musician thought for a moment, then nodded

his head, offering up a Cheshire grin. He started strumming away. Sol joined his wife and friends on the bench. They watched him play but couldn't detect what he was playing. The man played faster as if to warm up, when he abruptly paused before kicking into Fly Me to the Moon. It was Sol's favorite. He and Myrna had met the Italian singer when he was an up-and-coming talent on the streets of Hoboken, New Jersey, about the only thing Sol liked about the Garden State. Secretly, he liked their pizza, too, but that was strictly confidential.

After a couple more songs, Sol, who was singing along, was busting at the seams with gratitude, making his day. Already applauding like he was attending Radio City Music Hall, Sol gave the man a handshake and dropped a twenty-dollar bill into the guitar case. The young man bent down and nearly cried with happiness.

In a bold voice, he shouted, "I love you, America!" He gave Sol a monstrous hug before recoiling, dousing his enthusiasm just in case any police were hanging around.

"It's okay, kid," winked Sol. "You'll get there one day." He shook his hand, and the foursome headed back to Myrna's mother's house.

"Nice gesture," said Myrna, taking her husband's arm.

"That was so sweet," added Barbara, trying to hold back tears.

"You made that guy's year," said Donnie, who, not to be undone, walked over to the musician and dropped a ten-dollar bill before rejoining his wife and friends. "That's for the John Prine tune."

"We know behind that rough exterior, you're just a big, loveable pain in the toukus," said Myrna, giving her husband a kiss on the cheek.

"What should we do now?" asked Donnie.

Sol glanced around. "Oh, there was a book I saw yesterday at that weird bookstore, the one with those freaky masks on display. I'm hoping it's still there. You guys mind if I pop in real quick?"

Myrna knew the one. "Sure, it's just two blocks this way."

Catching raindrops, the four scuttled across the street, doing their best not to get wet. They walked inside the store, warm and dry. Sol strolled over to the metal rack just past the counter and started rummaging through the selections.

"Where is it, where is it?" he said, anxiously.

The bookstore owner, recognizing the American, asked what he was looking for in broken English.

"I'm looking for the book, Vampires of Dumbraveni, but I don't see it," Sol replied, "Damn, I should have bought it yesterday when I had the chance."

The bookstore owner, an older man with long, snow white hair and dressed like a low-budget warlock minus the hat, suggested the rack next to it. "Sometime customers misplace books."

Myrna sympathized, having dealt with that scenario on a regular basis while volunteering at the library in Miami Beach. Materials were always being misplaced.

Sol scrambled through the other pamphlets, brochures, and postcards, dropping a couple onto the floor. He quickly picked them up. "Bingo!" He rushed over to the counter and paid for the book. For being a returning customer, the owner threw in a small chocolate bar.

"Thank you, sir," said Sol, admiring the man's attire,

or at least, for wearing it out in public. "Nice outfit."

"I try," he said, dryly. "Come again."

After another full plate of sightseeing, they finally returned to Sabina's house, now early evening. Sabina stood on the front porch with her pooch, Scooby. She greeted them, but didn't seem particularly overjoyed. She pointed to her watch with an exasperated expression.

"It is evening. You should go and catch bus."

"Again, with the leaving?" answered Myrna in Romanian. "You weren't home, so we went ahead and did more sightseeing."

Sabina squawked. "It is now evening. I do not want you alone on streets at night. Go now to castle and be safe." She reminded each of them to display their crucifixes.

"Barbara, Donnie, you need?" asked Sabina, dangling a pair of crucifix pendants from her right hand.

Donnie and Barbara, who were both Catholic, declined, saying they were already covered, but thanked her anyways.

"What for?" asked Myrna, in Romanian. "Ma, are you okay?"

"Just show to anyone with fangs," instructed Sabina, whose mastery of English was on par with any New York City cab driver.

Sol interrupted. "Let's listen to your mother. We'll get a bite to eat real quick and then head back to the castle."

"You are smart one, Sol," said Sabina, pinching his cheek.

"Stay safe, my darling child; I see you all tomorrow, God willing," said Sabina, she herself making the sign of the cross.

"Don't be strangers." She abruptly slammed the door.

"That was peculiar," uttered Barbara to her husband as they stood in the middle of the yard, along with Sol and Myrna. They started walking down the sidewalk into town.

Sol turned to his wife. "Honey, is everything okay with your mother? You don't think she was mad because we did the 'tourist' thing again. I mean, she wasn't even home."

Myrna shook her head, not knowing what to think. "No, that wasn't it," said Myrna. "There's got to be something else."

"She said, fangs," snickered Sol. "We're not talking vampires, are we?"

"Of course not," uttered Myrna, but feeling puzzled. "I don't recall her acting like this before, ever."

As they headed back into the town square, Sol turned to his wife. "Not to be a jerk, but is your mother suffering from dementia or something?"

Myrna countered, her voice escalating. "We spent almost the whole day with her yesterday; did she seem off to you?"

Sol shook his head. "No. Actually, she seems sharp as a tack. And she's bilingual. That's no small feat."

"Precisely." Myrna glanced at her childhood home. "No, there's something else going on, and *that* has me worried."

"This place doesn't seem dangerous at all," observed Barbara. "Maybe because she's all alone? That might have something to do with it."

"She's got Scooby," said Donnie, "So at least she's got some company."

"And your cousin, Florin," said Sol. "Does your mother have any other family here?"

Myrna shook her head. "All of her siblings have passed away. She does have a few relatives remaining besides Florin. And they do keep an eye on her. You know, I really need to visit her more often. Life is too short."

"Here comes the Catholic guilt," said Sol. "We're here for what, four more days? Let's make the best of it for her sake." Myrna gripped Sol's hand. He turned to her. "Hell, maybe she could visit us in Miami Beach. Now that would be a hoot."

Myrna rolled her eyes; the mere thought of seeing her mother on the beach, beer and cigarette in hand. "You know, I never thought about her visiting us. Maybe because with her age."

"Well, we could pay for her airfare. She could stay at our place. We got the extra bedroom," posed Sol.

"If my mother is up to it, why not!" smiled Myrna, holding Sol's hand.

CHAPTER 10

Behind a tavern near a line of ghostly trees, a man grabbed the collar of a notorious hothead drunk, throwing him against a decaying brick wall. The drunk laid on his back, wincing in pain.

"This is second time I must speak to you about territorial infringement. You have cost me money yet again." The man's eyes grew large and penetrating. "Two strikes, Boris. Now, strike three."

The thuggish man spit at the much taller man, grazing his long black leather coat. "Piss off, old man," said Boris in broken English. "You've had your time; now I will run the show here." He shoved the tall man backward, throwing out his chest in defiance.

"I am alpha dog," boasted the short, stocky man, a tattoo of a raven on his neck.

The taller individual scoffed as he took out a handkerchief to clean off his coat. "You are not thinking straight, Boris; alcohol will do that to a person. A case of false bravado," he said, tucking the handkerchief back in his coat pocket.

"You have failed yet again to understand that I am the person that has given you an opportunity to exist in my world."

The younger man, rugged, bald, and in his early 30s, stepped closer. "Not anymore."

From his mouth came two razor-pointed canines. He pulled out a switchblade from his back pocket and attacked the man, slashing his arm. The taller man seethed. The thug attempted to stab him again. This time, the taller man responded quickly, gripping his hand tightly and forcing him to drop the weapon. The man then proceeded to snap Boris's wrist like it was made of balsa wood. He fell to the ground in agony.

"Augh, damn you!" He gnashed his teeth, eyes burning red. He picked himself off the damp ground and got to his feet. This time, Boris pulled out a revolver from his coat pocket and aimed it squarely at the man's chest.

"Are you really going to shoot me?" the taller man asked.

Boris, still in pain, steadied himself. "Right in God-damned heart, vampire bastard."

The tall man took measured steps in the thug's direction. "Takes one to know one," grinned the man.

Boris fired. Nothing. He fired again, and again, and again. And the tall man kept approaching. He clutched the man's gun and threw it aside.

"First off," said the tall man, "You should read up on your vampire lore. Guns cannot hurt me, unless of course they are silver. And even that's debatable." Before the thug vampire could think, he thrusted his hands around Boris's jacket collar, lifting him off the ground like he was a bag of mulch. He slammed him into the brick wall again. The thug grunted in pain. He underestimated the taller vampire's immense strength.

Boris made a last-ditch effort for survival. "Maybe we can make deal."

"A little too late for that, don't you think?" said the man, his eyes burning red. "Strike three."

The tall man pulled out a sharpened, solid wood spike and plunged it into Boris's chest. The instant the wood penetrated his heart, he knew he was dead. He cried out before dropping to the ground. The tall man watched as the man's body contorted, turning to ash before withering away.

He grinned. "This is a first for me, killing a vampire the old-fashioned way. What a pleasure."

He dusted off his leather coat and glanced back at the man's boots, the only thing left. "Alpha dog… please."

CHAPTER 11

The streets were relatively quiet, with only a handful of people milling about. The two couples were tired and hungry. They still had four more blocks to go before reaching the bus stop. All the storefronts had shuttered their doors. A bodega selling everything from newspapers to candy bars remained open. Two men stood outside smoking cigarettes, bantering back and forth with hand gestures. Across the street, a rustic tavern, Moartea, was bustling with locals.

"Wanna go check it out?" asked Sol.

"I'm game," said Donnie. "How about you gals?"

Barbara liked the idea. Myrna, on the other hand, was still mystified by her mother's odd behavior and absurd talk of vampires. She reluctantly agreed as long as they didn't stay out too late. They crossed the street and stood just outside the entrance. A young couple strode by and entered, the man holding the door for the foresome.

Myrna politely declined, saying they were still deciding. The man nodded.

"This looked like a cool joint," said Sol, looking up at the black and gold painted sign, sporting thorny blood-red roses at each end. "Honey, do you remember this place from the last time you were here?"

"Oh yeah," said Myrna. "The Moartea has been a staple here in town for decades. Good food and yes, good beer." Sol and Donnie perked up, already approving.

The wood-framed facade was painted in a dark forest green with a huge panoramic window where passersby could see the myriad of customers wining and dining. The front door had three rows across and four down of mixed crimson and orange-stained glass. Two gleaming wall lanterns hung from curled black iron stationed at each end of the building. The aroma of garlic permeated from a row of rectangular wooden flower planters stationed the length of the tavern. A nice added touch, thought Donnie.

"After another full day of walking and burning off calories, I'd like to think we've earned a few drinks and a hearty meal," remarked Sol, licking his lips with thirst. "It looks like a full house in there. I hope we don't need to make a reservation."

"I'm rather famished myself," added Donnie. His grumbling stomach singing out like humpback whales. "Yeah, it's dinnertime, alright."

"Maybe we should wait for the bus instead," said Myrna, her indecision making her feel uneasy.

"Laszlo said the buses are on schedule and run late, so we'll be fine," said Sol, in a cheery mood. "Come on, it's a beautiful day (or evening in this case) in the neighborhood, as Mr. Rogers would say."

Sol noticed people laughing through the windows. "It ain't Beefsteak Charlie's, but I'd say this joint looks appetizing."

"Ah, Beefsteak Charlie's," said Donnie, reminiscing. "Man, do I miss all that free shrimp and sangria deal."

Myrna was still thinking about her mother, but decided it was time to relax and enjoy the evening.

They entered the tavern, nearly full. There were a few

momentary stares, but for the most part, the locals were already aware of the Hirsch/Falcone party. On the wall, Sol noticed hanging papier-mache masks, along with what appeared to be paintings from local artists. Most of the younger clientele preferred congregating along the dark oak bar while the over-forty crowd sat at the heavily lacquered round, wooden tables, enjoying their meals, drinking, and conversing. Two older men sat in a secluded corner and appeared to be deep in thought as they played a game of chess, glasses of red wine stationed close by. Sol spotted an open table to the left of the fireplace as four people got up to leave, the formerly red bricks slightly blackened from perpetual usage. A tough-looking guy with a plastic bin and a towel draped over his shoulder came over and cleared the table.

"I'll be back with menus," he said.

The four sat down, adapting easily to the Dumbraveni way of life. With the temperature dropping, the warmth from the fireplace felt good.

"You know what?" said Sol, directing his question to his best friend. "We haven't talked baseball not once on this trip." His wife smiled, holding his hand. Minus the weirdness from Myrna's mother, the week-long trip was already an unforgettable experience.

The owner, a Bluto clone from the old Popeye cartoons, ambled over between the crowded room to take their order. He knew a handful of words in English, most of them of the cursing variety. He handed everyone a menu, basic and to the point.

"Look at menu; I come back to take order," said the owner.

Sol and Donnie hoped steaks were listed somewhere

on the menu. Myrna, her native Romanian improving with each passing day, helped translate the menu for everyone. The owner came back a few minutes later with a notepad and pen in hand. Myrna read off the menu and ordered everyone's meals, including drinks. He returned shortly with two glasses of red wine for Myrna and Barbara, and two drafts of locally made beer for the gents. Soon, both Sol and Donnie were enjoying their adult beverages fireside. Feeling relaxed, Myrna and Barbara leaned back in their chairs and sipped from their glasses of Cabernet Sauvignon.

"Barb, don't you think it was strange for my mother to worry so much about us getting back?" said Myrna. "It's not like I've never been here before."

"I'm sure it was nothing," replied Barbara. "But people change as they age. I think she's missed you."

Myrna took a sip of wine. "I guess you're right. Sol and I want to propose having her visit us in Miami Beach."

"I'm sure she'd love it," Barbara replied with a smile.

Sol came over and put her arm around Myrna. "I bet your mother will love Cuban food."

Myrna shrugged. Sol added his two cents' worth. "And we'll catch the bus after dinner, so no more talks of fangs, okay? Besides, we're all safe and sound here in this pub. So, let's enjoy the evening."

"Cheers, everybody," added Donnie, speaking for team Falcone.

Myrna sighed. "But what if the bus doesn't go to the castle?"

"Oy vey, Myrna, we spent our lives living in New York City," said Sol. "You think we can't handle a simple bus ride at night? No one is gonna mess with us." Sol's swagger was contagious as his wife deflated any anxiety she had built up.

"You're right, honey," said Myrna, who made a toast. "Here's to family and friends, both near and far."

"Now, that's the spirit," said Sol, as they clinked glasses again.

A slender man wearing a Rolling Stones concert shirt and mirrored sunglasses sauntered up to their table. "Good evening, my American friends!" The four looked up at the man, recognizing the voice and vigor.

"It can be the one and only Laszlo, am I right?" beamed Sol, standing up and giving him a hug. "What brings you to this neck of the woods?"

"Neck? Did you say... neck?" replied Laszlo with eyebrows raised, beaming. He shifted his sunglasses on top of his stringy, liquorish black hair, took a sip of red wine from a tall glass, and gleaned at Sol. "That sounds quite appetizing."

"You are such a kidder," replied Barbara, who was already halfway done with her second glass of wine.

How's the vampire business going tonight?" inquired Donnie, savoring his beer.

"Deliciously good," replied Laszlo, resembling a dead ringer for shock rock singer Alice Cooper. "I trust you are enjoying our hospitality, yes?"

"We like; yes," replied Donnie, "And these suds hit the spot."

Sol beamed. "Line 'em up, baby!" Both he and Donnie clanked mugs.

Laszlo took a sip of wine when he noticed Myrna gazing into the fireplace. "Myrna, you are in vexed state."

"I'm fine, Laszlo," replied Myrna. "I was just thinking of my mother."

"Ah, family; what exactly is problem?" he asked.

"She's been so insistent about us not getting back too late to the castle at night. Why is that?" posed Myrna.

"Why vampires, of course," replied the lanky gentleman with a wink. Sol choked on his suds. "Be careful with Romanian beer, it is much more potent than American counterpart."

"I think I'm figuring that out, my friend," said Sol, feeling a bit tipsy now, almost done with his second beer. "Whatever we're drinking is pretty damn good. Oh, before I forget, can we hitch ride with you tonight?"

Donnie gazed at his friend, amused.

"What?" asked Sol.

"You're starting to sound like him," laughed Donnie, sensing the beer was taking full effect on his friend, him too.

"No problem, my American friends," replied Laszlo. "Eat, drink, and be merry at Moartea; I take you back in style."

"Groovy," said Donnie.

"By the way, Laszlo, what does Moartea mean?" asked Donnie. "It sounds kinda regal."

"Actually, it means death," said Myrna.

"But no worries, dear people," said Laszlo, sensing their concern. "It simply means death to dull times. Now, let's rock on!" Lazlo dropped change into the antique juke box. Five seconds later, the sounds of *Miss You*, by the Rolling Stones permeated throughout the packed tavern.

Lazlo put on his sunglasses and started imitating the moves of the Stones' lead singer, Mick Jagger, accidentally bumping into a table, spilling his drink. The angular man apologized before wandering up to the bar for a refill.

"What the man said," said Sol. "Let's eat, drink, and

get our merry on!" He convinced Myrna to order another glass of red wine.

An hour later, the four travelers were schmoozing and enjoying their meals, four plates full of poultry, steaks, and fresh grilled vegetables. The local patrons reveled in their boisterous New York City accents, doing their best to imitate Big Apple lingo. After dinner, Sol conducted an impromptu class on how to pronounce tried and true city slangs and phrases, even sprinkling in a few Yiddish words along the way. They especially got a kick out of the words, schlep and fuhgeddaboudit.

After another round, they belted out a howling, albeit off-key, rendition of Frank Sinatra's signature song, *New York, New York*.

CHAPTER 12

The four were amazed as Laszlo finished devouring yet another T-bone steak, medium rare, before washing it down with what seemed like a pint of red wine. He strolled over to the 'Big Apple' table, as it was dubbed by the tavern owner, who with an employee, was wiping off tables and sweeping the floor.

"Looks like it's closing time," said Sol, observing the two cleaning up.

The two couples left a hefty tip and stumbled outside, basking in the effects of the potent alcohol content. "What a meal," exclaimed Sol, stretching out his arms and punctuating the evening with a playful howl. The cool, nighttime air invigorated the retiree.

"Not bad, my friend," offered Laszlo, "but I can do better."

"Oh yeah?" said Sol, always one to showcase his competitive nature. "How about a little wager, my Romanian friend?"

"Don't be foolish, Sol," said Myrna. "I'm sorry, Laszlo, but I think my husband's had a few too many pints if you know what I mean."

"Let us have fun, a wager between friends," replied Laszlo. "I say we bet twenty American dollars. If I win, I also get to sink my canines deep into Sol's neck." Patrons lingering outside got stone-cold quiet. "Just kidding, people. But if I lose, I must endure Donnie's bad jokes in closed room. No, just kidding, Donnie. You are funny man."

"That's debatable," smirked Barbara.

"Sounds fair to me," said Sol as the two shook hands. "Let the howling begin.

A few lingering patrons from the tavern gathered around to see the show. Sol took in a deep, passionate breath, burping first. "Sorry, folks." He closed his eyes and exhaled, letting loose with an uproarious howl. The patrons applauded, not thinking a total stranger would act so foolishly in public, especially in a visiting country.

"I didn't think you had it in you," said Donnie, patting Sol on his back.

"Oh man, I think I pulled a muscle from that one," grimaced Sol. "Alright, Laszlo, your turn."

"Not too bad," observed Laszlo. "Now, please, stand aside. It is time for the master."

The tall man limbered up, stretching his arms and legs, shaking his head from side to side. He pounced on all fours, growling, like he was going to run a track meet. The two couples stood back. They noticed many of the patrons holding their ears.

"Uh oh," said Donnie.

Laszlo blasted out a monstrous howl that rattled the windows of the tavern. Sol's face dropped.

The thirty-something man stood up, wiping away the road dirt from the palms of his hands. "That is how you howl in Dumbraveni."

"You've been practicing," admired Sol, mouthing the words, wow.

In the hills above the town, wailing howls rang out in

unison. "Sounds like you woke up the whole neighborhood," said Donnie. The few remaining patrons darted across the street with a sense of urgency to catch the approaching bus.

"The moon is my inspiration," said Laszlo, "That and making bets with tourists. I am true capitalist at heart."

"Well, let's get going, and I'll do my end of the bargain," said Sol, never one to welch on a bet. He took out his wallet and planted two crisp ten-dollar bills in Laszlo's hand. They walked a couple of blocks over, piled into Laszlo's Lincoln, and headed for the castle.

As they drove out of town, Donnie spoke. "By the way, Laszlo, where'd you get this automotive beauty?"

Sol, sitting comfortably in the front seat, caressing the dashboard. "They don't make 'em like this anymore."

"I win car in bet with big, wealthy car dealer from longhorn state, Texas," answered the slender man. "He even ship to me!"

"That musta been one hell of a bet," said Donnie.

"Never attempt to drink Romanian under table," boasted Laszlo with a wink.

The ride home was quiet and cozy, the heat set just right. Just then, Laszlo pushed in a cassette tape of Led Zeppelin's *Whole Lotta Love* and started singing off-key. He glanced in the rear-view mirror, eyeing Myrna, Barbara, and Donnie in the back seat. "You need coolin', baby, I'm not foolin!" The New Yorkers could only smile.

The car pulled up next to the detached garage, adjacent to a three-horse stable. The five piled out and started walking towards the mammoth front doors of the castle. They thanked Laszlo for a great evening as they entered.

"You know what?" said Sol. "I could use a good, hearty

stroll around the lake. Wanna join me, Donnie?"

"What, now?" he asked. "Are you crazy?"

"Yeah, now. We can work off the suds and steak," said Sol, prodding his friend.

"If you go, please, be careful," said Laszlo. "There are things that go bump in the night."

"You sound like Myrna's mother," said Sol.

"Maybe Laszlo is right. Let's just relax by the fireplace," said Donnie.

"Come on," replied Sol. "It'll be like walking around Central Park minus the muggers. Let's go, Donnie boy!"

"I really don't want to do this," he said, yawning.

"In no way, shape, or form do I want my husband walking out there in the pitch black," grumbled Barbara. Myrna seconded the motion halfheartedly, knowing that when her husband made his mind up, there was no turning back.

"Walk should not take long," said Laszlo, directing his assurance to the wives. "You and Donnie are in luck. There is full moon, so journey will be piece of cake. Unless, of course, you get lost." Laszlo walked back to his car and reached into the glove compartment. He quickly returned, handing Sol a flashlight.

"Maybe I should get some bread crumbs just in case," joked Donnie.

Sol gave Myrna a hug and headed down the path. Donnie lit up a cigarette and caught up to his friend, irked. "You owe me for this."

"Shall we sit by the fire and have drink?" inquired Laszlo, his voice snake-like, smooth like a lounge singer.

Both Myrna and Barbara looked at each other.

"Absolutely!"

After savoring the warmth of the fireplace and wide-brimmed glasses of brandy, the towering grandfather clock standing tall like a skyscraper in the vast hallway rang out like an ancient church bell.

Tibor called down from upstairs. "Laszlo, I need you to unclog a toilet on the third floor."

He glanced down at his watch and sighed. "The glamor of job," mused Laszlo, slightly embarrassed as he stood up from the comfy chair. "Let me take care of important business," he added with a wink. "Make yourselves comfortable and stay put."

"We aren't going anywhere," said Myrna. Both ladies were already fully relaxed in the soft matching pair of antique oversized felt-upholstered chairs. Barbara, taking a stab at her husband's style of humor, joked that her chair could probably fit a family of four.

The two ladies looked up as Tibor descended from the centered staircase, smartly dressed in a corduroy sport coat, black turtleneck, blue jeans, and black boots. He drew closer and picked up the empty brandy bottle.

"We need to rectify this situation," he said with a grin. "Give me a moment."

Tibor ventured into the kitchen. He began whistling his familiar tune as he gathered a full bottle of brandy and a glass for himself before returning. He poured the brandy into their glasses, his too, then sat down. He gestured towards Myrna with a sly grin. "For special occasions... and special people."

The three toasted. "Here is to the rest of your stay at Casa de Noapte," said Tibor. "I hope you are enjoying yourselves." He looked around. "By the way, where are your husbands?

"Sol wanted to take a walk around the lake, and he dragged my Donnie along with him," said Barbara.

"So, they are not here," said Tibor. "Then we must savor our brandy and drink to their health."

Each took another sip. Myrna sat up and addressed Tibor. "You said you know my mother? Did you know my father, too?"

Tibor shifted in his seat, somewhat awkwardly. "Uh, yes, I did," he replied. "A priest, I believe he was. He was a popular man here in Dumbraveni." He took another sip of brandy and politely smiled, eyes shifting towards the immense fireplace.

Sensing Tibor's awkward disposition, Myrna changed the subject. "Sol and I were wondering what that interesting tune is that you like to whistle."

Tibor moved closer to Myrna on the love seat, placing his hand on top of hers. "It is a bedtime song my late mother used to sing to me when I was a young child. It had such a calming effect on me. I have treasured it ever since."

"That is so beautiful," said Myrna, captivated by Tibor's grace and deep, soothing voice.

Tibor glanced at the grandfather clock and stood up. "My apologies, ladies, but I must check on Laszlo to see how he is progressing with our plumbing issues. It can be rather persnickety in a castle such as this. Enjoy the continued warmth of the fire while I am gone."

After watching Tibor ascend the vast stairway, Barbara shifted over and sat down next to her friend and whispered. "I think our host, Mr. Tibor, has the hots for you," she said with a boozy giggle.

"I think you're enjoying the brandy a bit too much, said Myrna.

"No, no, no," insisted Barbara, tipsy but persistent. "I see how he looks at you. Just be careful; that Tibor is very, very handsome and charismatic."

Sounds like you got the hots for him," joked Myrna. "If Tibor tries to get frisky, my Sol can take him out with a left hook. Remember, he used to be an amateur boxer when he was younger. Sol hits the punching bag set up in the exercise room at the condo. If only he would eat better."

"Donnie's has always played tennis, but now he's addicted to the treadmill machine," said Barbara. "I swear he can walk on that thing for hours."

"I'm just thankful not so many people use our condo pool, said Myrna, fit as a person half her age. "I love doing laps in the warm sun. Remember the pool at the YMCA in Queens?"

Barbara cringed. "Ugh, they used to use so much chlorine it started bleaching my lovely orange hair."

"Three cheers for retired living!" boasted Myrna. Both women sported hearty smiles and clinked glasses.

CHAPTER 13

Sol and Donnie continued with their midnight trek along the path surrounding the lake. The evening air felt cool as a light mist began to fall. A subtle breeze pushed the encroaching fog off the lake towards shore, the roundish body of water dark as oil with the moon reflecting off it like a Hollywood premier spotlight.

"See, this isn't so bad," said Sol, feeling vigorous and jaunty. "I bet we've already walked halfway; come on."

Donnie scoffed. "I should be back at the castle with a glass of brandy in my hand and hanging out by that colossal fireplace. Hell, I should be roasting marshmallows and making s'mores in that thing." He laughed at his own joke, which he tended to do most of the time.

"We will, we will," assured Sol, focusing on the task at hand. He didn't even mind the mist. They continued their journey, maintaining a solid pace along the rustic pathway through thick clusters of looming leafless trees, their extending branches intertwined like barbed wire.

"It's not like we're circling Central Park or something."

"Are you sure?" said Donnie. "It took me and Barbara over three hours to circle the park on foot. My dogs were aching for days."

"Next time, take a cab," smiled Sol.

Seeing his friend lagging behind, Sol spotted an old fallen tree and sat down. Donnie caught up and joined him, catching a breather. After a couple of minutes, Sol glanced up into the same rounded pine tree he had observed yesterday morning, the full moon above providing just enough visibility.

"Hey Donnie, you're a bird guy, right?"

"What?" he replied, puzzled. "Yeah, I'm a bird guy: fried chicken, Thanksgiving turkey, chicken parms. Whoa, why are you asking me such a weird question?"

Sol pointed forward. "Check out the chirpy flock of birds in that pine tree. I saw 'em yesterday morning when we took our walk."

Donnie peered upward in the darkness. The branches seemed painted in fluttering black leaves, accompanied by high-pitched squeaking that made the whole forest sound like an orchestra of mice. The wind suddenly whipped off the lake, replacing the subdued midnight calm.

"What the hell is happening?" balked Donnie, holding down his poodle black toupee from blowing off. "That wind came out of nowhere!"

The two men had started their walk around the lake at a leisurely pace, but now felt a sense of urgency. "Maybe we'd better pick up the pace a bit," said Donnie.

"It's unpredictability," reasoned Sol, standing up now. "I mean, who the hell knows what the weather is like here?"

Donnie finished up his cigarette and then flicked the butt into the lake as the two continued on their hike.

Sol looked up to see the shifting charcoal black clouds now blocking out the moonlight. "I can see the lights of the castle; we're not too far away."

Donnie side-stepped over a rotted log, but landed smack dab into a muddy puddle, his cordovan Hush Puppy loafers firmly entrenched in the muck.

"Will you look at this? This is all your fault, dunderhead!" Donnie slowly pulled each shoe out, both making a prolonged sucking sound. "You're paying for this!"

"Alright, alright, now shush," gibed Sol.

Donnie growled in annoyance. "You're starting to sound like a librarian." Donnie flung the mud from his shoes and sat down on a cut tree stump. He put his shoes back on, then lit another cigarette.

"What is it now, oh fearless leader?"

"I thought I heard something howl."

"I didn't hear anything," answered Donnie. He picked up a nearby stick and started to scrape the rest of the caked-on mud from his shoes when it snapped. He cursed.

"They don't make 'em like they used to," said the retired chiropractor, tired and annoyed. As he bent down to pick up another branch, a torpedoing trail of black bats spearheaded straight towards the retired deli owner.

Sol perked up again. "There's that chirpy sound again. Oh shit!"

A line of bats strafed the man like fighter jets. Sol frantically waved his arms, batting away the flying mammals. Stunned, Donnie rummaged for a bigger branch. When he turned, he gazed at a particularly large bat burrowing close into Sol's neck. He screamed. Donnie sized up the target and swung the branch like a golf club, sending the bat haplessly in the air before plopping right into the lake. *Kerplunk!*

"It's in the hole, baby," barked Donnie, enthusiastically. He quickly bent down to see how his friend was. "Holy moly, Sol, you, okay?"

"I'm fine, I'm fine; just help me up already." Sol placed his right hand on the left side of his neck. "What the hell?"

"What's wrong?" asked Donnie.

"I think I'm bleeding," said Sol. "Get your lighter, quick, quick." Donnie fumbled for his lighter tucked in the front pocket of his tan Haggar slacks. He ran his thumb along the top of the Bic lighter, producing a one-inch-high flame.

"Stop fidgeting," said Donnie, trying to see the injury. "I swear it's like dealing with a child."

"What do you see!?" begged Sol.

"Ah, it's nothing," Donnie replied. "A couple of tiny scratches on your neck, that's all, you'll be fine. Now let's get the hell out of here before we meet up with the werewolf or Fergus."

"Fergus?"

"You remember," said Donnie. "Our discussion to name Frankenstein's monster?"

"I'm trying to forget that." Sol rubbed his neck again, shaken, now especially anxious to get back to the castle.

***

Inside, the wives continued their relaxed vibe, now sitting closer by the fireplace, enjoying their drinks while listening to Kind of Blue by jazz musician, Miles Davis.

"I don't know about you, but I am savoring this fireplace," grinned Myrna, her glass of brandy nearly empty.

"Beats the hell out of watching the 'Yule Log' on Channel Eleven every Christmas Eve," said Barbara.

Tibor reappeared, coming down the stairs. "My apologies, but we had extended plumbing issues."

Myrna noticed Tibor rubbing his right shoulder. "Are you okay?"

"Oh, I must have strained it while removing the heavy sink." He ambled over to the fireplace and tossed a few more logs onto the fire from a pile of split wood, aged to burning perfection.

Tibor sat down on the sofa. "Hope I didn't miss anything too exciting."

"Nah," said Barbara, inebriated from too many drinks. She started cracking jokes about her husband's hairpiece.

"Did I mention I call him poodle head behind his back?" She blurted out in laughter, slapping Tibor's forearm. He offered her a courteous smile, then spoke to Myrna.

"And how was your family visit today?"

"Enjoyable," said Myrna. "Lots of walking around town. Sol especially liked the creepy bookstore on the corner block near the wolf fountain. He even bought a book there, *The Vampires of Dumbraveni*."

"Nothing but fiction, I'm afraid," replied Tibor, his levity appearing to drop a few degrees. "While I admire his writing skills, Bram Stoker's novel is an affront to the people of Transylvania and Romania. Unfortunately, your 'Hollywood' continues to perpetuate this myth in their absurd films. I'm afraid vampires do not exist."

The grandfather clock let out a boisterous, singular chime; it was one AM. It prompted both Myrna and Barbara to realize that their spouses were still out on their walk, possibly lost in the deep, dark woods.

"Shouldn't they be back by now?" asked Myrna, feeling anxious. Barbara, not so much, finishing up her drink.

After some mild conversation, the creaking front door opened. Both men appeared, Donnie looking disheveled, his shoes a muddy mess, and Sol rubbing his injured neck.

"We almost starting to worry about you," blurted out Barbara.

"Ha, ha, you and me both," Donnie replied before slipping off his ruined shoes by the front door. My new shoes are completely ruined!"

"No worries," said Tibor, seeing Donnie's dismayed state. "I will have Laszlo clean them up for you tomorrow morning."

"That would be much obliged," said Donnie.

"Sol, are you okay?" asked Myrna, stumbling a bit from too much brandy herself. She noticed her husband clutching his neck."Why are you holding your neck?"

"It's nothing," said Sol, trying to shrug off the incident. "What I could use is a stiff drink."

Tibor retrieved the bottle of brandy and poured Sol a glass. Suddenly feeling cold to the bone, Sol plopped himself down by the fireplace and swiftly consumed his drink. He thanked Tibor and asked for a refill.

Sol picked up the napkin used as a coaster and pressed it against his neck. He removed it, revealing two mildly pink marks about an inch apart.

Donnie and Barbara eventually trudged up to their second-floor room; one cranky, one blissfully inebriated. Myrna stayed with her husband, shifting one of the chairs closer to him. Tibor sat across from the Queens couple. Moments later, the castle owner appeared to doze off on the love seat.

Myrna yawned. "Sol, are you coming to bed?"

"I'll be up in a second. You go. I just want to finish my drink and watch the flames die down," said Sol, his eyes focused on the fireplace. It had been ages since he and the Mrs. experienced a real fireplace.

Sol finished off his drink. His eyes got heavy. Minutes

later, he dozed off, glass still in hand. Tibor, appearing sound asleep opposite of the retiree, opened an eye and peered over at Sol.

CHAPTER 14

For the last couple of days of their trip, Sol felt lethargic, like he had a case of the flu or a variation of the flu. Despite his sluggish state, he felt determined to prod ahead. There was no way in hell he was going to spoil Myrna's time... or that of his friends.

On their last day, the foursome stopped by Myrna's mother's house to say goodbye. After a lunch of pasta and salad, it was time to go. Florin was kind enough earlier to bring over a quart of hearty chicken noodle soup from one of the local restaurants for Sol. It hit the spot with the former deli owner giving it a thumbs up.

"I wish you all safe trip home," said Sabina, wearing a thick natural white wool sweater and long blue denim skirt. "Now don't be stranger and come back soon!" She gave Donnie and Barbara an embrace.

"I miss you already," spoke Myrna, tearing up as she hugged her mother. "Next year, we want you to visit us in Florida, our treat!"

Sabina loved the idea. "We go surfing!" She wiggled her hips, then peered over to Sol, who was rather subdued.

Florin arrived through the back door with Scooby after giving the big canine a brisk walk. The husky sauntered over to Sol like he'd done for the whole week for an ear scratch. He extended his hand, but Scooby suddenly appeared agitated, directing a low-volume growl towards him.

"Scooby, what is wrong?" said Sabina, holding the dog close to her. She looked at Scooby, then glanced over at Sol. Something didn't appear right.

"Myrna, your Sol don't look so hot. Come here, deli man, let me inspect."

With a cigarette dangling from the corner of her mouth, the feisty woman placed her hands on Sol's chalk-white face, tilting his head in every direction. She paused for a moment, placing the cigarette in the butt-filled ashtray, then gazed deeper into Sol's eyes before pulling away quickly.

"What is it?" Sol asked, unnerved by the unusual examination. He suddenly felt woozy.

"Where is cross I gave you?"

Sol felt around his neck. "Uh, I don't know. I think I might have lost it that night around the lake. I'm sorry."

"What happen around lake?" Sabina inquired.

"It was nothing; I'm fine now," said Sol.

"Ma?" shrieked Myrna, her bold Big Apple accent emphasizing her concern.

"Uh, nothing dear, nothing at all," replied Sabina. "Probably just flu bug. Now go before you miss flight."

Myrna eyed her mother with suspicion before giving her one last hug goodbye. Donnie and Barbara were already beside the front yard gate, patiently waiting. Sol felt cold. Sabina offered her son-in-law a quick shot of whisky before leaving the house. He politely refused.

"Feel better. Now go," said Sabina.

As he headed out the front yard, Sol looked back at Myrna's mother, who was now glaring out the window. He could read her facial expression that something wasn't kosher.

***

The long flight back to Miami Beach was thankfully non-eventful, yet Myrna was concerned for her husband. Sol slept most of the flight, waking up only to use the restroom, which he complained was the size of a phone booth. Dinner was passable. Sol reminded everyone about ordering fish on airplanes. He selected meatloaf with mashed potatoes and salad. Despite everyone's satisfaction, Sol barely nibbled on anything but thankfully kept his complaints to a bare minimum.

It was late evening as they arrived at Miami International Airport. As they stepped outside with their luggage, they were hit with warm, muggy weather. A friendly cabby named Nacho approached the four. He placed their luggage in the vast trunk of the Ford LTD sedan, then drove off to their condo. With barely any traffic, they arrived a half hour later. The cabby parked in front of the condo building and removed their luggage. He noticed the tags on the suitcases from Romania.

"Hope you didn't encounter any vampires!" he joked before Donnie handed him a tip. The cabby wished them a good evening, then drove off.

Sol remained sluggish as the four took their luggage and entered the warm, stale elevator, the air conditioning still not fixed. Sol and Myrna said goodnight to their friends as they headed up to the eighth floor. Upon entering their condo, the first thing Sol did was turn up the air conditioning. He kicked off his shoes, placed their suitcases in the living room, then headed for the bedroom where he quickly fell asleep.

CHAPTER 15

A week had passed, yet Sol was sleeping more than he was awake. He had tried an assortment of over-the-counter medications from the local Walgreens, but to no avail. Seven days now, and he still felt like crap.

It was half past twelve on a beautiful Saturday afternoon in Miami Beach, but Myrna had had enough. Beyond frustrated, she stormed into the bedroom and opened the blinds to their eighth-floor condo with a beautiful vista of the Atlantic Ocean.

"Sol Hirsch, it is absolutely gorgeous outside!" From the bedroom window, she could see the whole pool area. "Let's go for a swim. Maybe doing a few laps will make you feel better."

"The pool is probably crowded," he grumbled, his eye mask blocking out the sunshine.

Myrna peeked over again. "There's not a soul at the pool; we'll have it all to ourselves."

Sol pulled the blanket over his head and groaned. "No thank you." His daytime modus operandi now consisted of lounging in his La-Z-Boy with the blinds closed all day and occasionally getting up to nosh on snacks.

"The doctor said there was nothing wrong with you, so what's the story?" probed Myrna. "I'm frustrated here!"

He sat up and reached for his robe. "What the hell does Dr. Melnitz know?" said Sol, bitterly. "I have to fork over my hard-earned money for some quack to tell me I'm fine. Of course I'm fine!"

"Doctor Melnitz, your cousin by the way, is no quack," countered Myrna. "Look at you, we've been back a week, and you've barely even stepped outside of our condo. For God's sake, you're white as an egg, and beginning to look like one too!"

"You're getting on my nerves and staying there," snapped Sol. "Besides, it's too hot out; I don't want to burn my tender skin." Sol rubbed his toneless limbs, now white as bowling pins.

"Tender, my ass," snarled Myrna. "Then how about dinner tonight at Rascal House? There's no way in hell I am ordering subpar Chinese food or cardboard-flavored pizza again, all cooped up here for another night!"

"Alright, alright!" he answered. "Just let me be!"

Myrna went into the living room and retrieved her towel and book. "If you need me, I'll be at the pool."

"Enjoy."

Sol finally got up and went into the bathroom. He placed his hands on both sides of the sink. He gazed at his pale complexion and stuck out his tongue. "I look like shit."

Despite what his cousin said, he knew that something was wrong, but he didn't know what. He had the flu a bunch of times before living in New York City, but it never lasted more than a few days. Maybe it was time to put on his apron and whip up a great big batch of his patented chicken soup, the cure-all for aches and ailments. What was discerning was that he couldn't get the image of Sabina and her reaction out of his head. Whatever she saw in his eyes had unnerved both her and him. And now, the South Florida sun irritated the retired deli owner just as much as his wife.

Myrna returned to the condo, forgetting her bottle of Snapple. Sol was in the kitchen pouring a bowl of Product 19.

"If you're still in this malaise state tomorrow, I think we should go back to the doctor," said Myrna. "I'm sure your cousin can fit you in."

"Malaise? What am I, Jimmy Carter?" snapped Sol, in perpetual cranky mode. "I just have a touch of the flu, or some Commie strain. Who knows?"

"You used to work twelve-hour days in New York City, and you were always healthy as an ox. I've never seen you like this before. I'm worried," pleaded Myrna. "I hope you didn't catch anything infectious in Romania. Maybe I should call my mother."

Sol assured his wife he would not take his health for granted. "If I'm not feeling better by tomorrow, I promise to go see my cousin. I swear."

"And dinner tonight?" she asked.

"Yes, Rascal House is good." Myrna gave Sol a hug and grabbed her drink. "Join me if you can. See you soon."

***

It was nearing 7:00PM, the weather unseasonably cool for the middle March. The line for the Rascal House stretched outside the front door like a rock concert, no thanks to all the visiting snowbirds and tourists. But dinnertime was usually the busiest time at the legendary catery.

"I knew this was going to happen," proclaimed Myrna. "We should have been here at least an hour ago!"

"You know, we don't have to eat with the early-bird blue-hairs all the time," said Sol. "Besides, I wasn't hungry then." Donnie and Barbara were quite accustomed to their occasional verbal squabbles. Sometimes they felt like they were referees.

"If arguing is ever entered into the Olympics, you guys would capture the gold, hands down," said Donnie.

"That's enough," choired the Hirschs in unison.

"That's the first time you both agreed on anything tonight!" commented Barbara. "Here's to progress."

"Can we at least agree that we're all famished?" proposed Donnie, inhaling the smell of mile-high corn beef sandwiches and the roast chicken, his personal favorite. "Umm, savor that aroma, buddy. I know you're getting hungry."

"I'm working on it, I'm working on it," replied Sol. The line was finally starting to move; most of the early-bird folks were wrapping up their meals. One thing for certain, no one ever left Rascal House without a doggie bag filled with their patented fresh baked rolls.

Delores, the seasoned hostess, middle-aged, tough, and now sporting fiery orange-dyed locks, seated the two couples in a booth close to the bathroom.

"Sorry, Sol, it's either this or wait another fifteen minutes."

Sol was still feeling out of sorts and was in no mood for any confrontation. He simply shrugged. "This is fine, Delores. Just bring us the menus. Oh, I like the color of your hair." Delores squinted, not sure if Sol was poking fun at her or not.

Myrna and the Falcones turned with astonishment. The old Sol would never approve of sitting near the restrooms; that was reserved for rubes, he often stated.

"What?" replied Sol, feeling like he was on trial. "Do I have to complain all the time just to make you guys happy?"

All three were speechless.

"No dear, of course not," said his wife. "We're just not used to it, that's all."

A young waitress, an elementary school teacher supplementing her income by working part-time to earn extra money, petite with dark auburn hair, came over to take everyone's order.

Donnie and Barbara scanned the menu, not sure what to order. But as usual, Donnie ended up going with his tried-and-true order of roast chicken with baked potato, and house salad, topped off with Thousand Island dressing. Barbara opted for baked flounder. Myrna decided on a large bowl of matzo ball soup containing one lone matzo ball the size of a major league baseball and a side salad topped with vinaigrette dressing.

"And you, sir?" the waitress called out, and waited. "Sir?"

Sol finally looked up; his eyes almost popping out of their sockets. "Holy cow, you look like a young Jane Russell!" Myrna smirked at her husband, who finally showed a pulse since his return from Romania.

The ex-deli pro composed himself. "Hmm, sorry about that. I will have a New York Strip, medium, with a baked potato, and a large Coke, no ice."

"Will that be all, sir?" asked the waitress.

"I'm sorry, what's your name?" Myrna looked at her nametag, protruding outward more than most of the staff waitresses. "Uh, Helene? Make his broiled fish with steamed broccoli and a small house salad, lots of greens – no iceberg lettuce." The waitress crossed out the first order, breaking the point of her pencil in the process. She took out a spare from her red apron, a picture of the devilish Rascal House face sewn on the front.

"My apologies," said Myrna, "But my husband needs to eat healthy," she added in a subtle tone.

"I'm getting a steak!" said Sol, fully steamed that his wife would treat him like a child in front of the beautiful young waitress. "Helene, order me the biggest steak you got, only this time, make it medium rare, a side of French fries, and a side of slaw."

"With a Coke?"

"Yeah, a large Coke, no ice."

The waitress crossed out the fish order and jotted down steak again. "Are you certain this time, sir?"

"Oh, I'm certain," boasted Sol, defiantly. After the curvy waitress took their orders and left, Sol and Myrna verbally sparred like Ali vs. Frasier. Donnie did his best playing Mills Lane.

The waitress returned with their food fifteen minutes later. She reached inside her apron and pulled out four sets of utensils, all snug in tightly wrapped napkins. For Sol's meaty steak, there was a serrated knife, the tip sticking out an eighth of an inch. As she reached for it inside her apron, she nicked her index finger, drawing blood. Sol sniffed the air. His pupils gleamed big and wide as ping pong balls.

"Ouch," Helene uttered. "I am so sorry about that, sir. Sir?"

Sol became totally fixated, his energy level zooming from zero to sixty in a heartbeat. "Here, let me lend you a hand." He scooted out from the vinyl-covered booth and took out his seldom-used handkerchief, placing it on the cut.

"Oh, you don't need to do that, sir, I'm okay, really,"

she added, embarrassed as they walked away towards the restrooms.

"Are you going to let him do that?" asked Barbara, surprised by Sol's flirty behavior.

"Sol?" mused Myrna, glimpsing at her short, stocky, balding husband. "What could someone his age do with a young chippy like her?"

"You'd be surprised," said Donnie, exhaling a dreamy gaze. Barbara elbowed him right in the ribs. "Ow!"

Sol mistakenly followed the waitress right into the kitchen. "Uh sir, you're not allowed back here." The whole staff stared at him.

"Oh jeez, I am so sorry, folks. It's just that I have a soft spot for injured waitresses. I used to be a waitress. I mean, I used to be a waiter, and uh…" Sol, blushing like a tomato, finally composed himself before exiting the kitchen, thoroughly mortified.

Delores spotted Sol and gave him a stare and mouthing the words, "Nutball." He returned to the table, and the four dined on their meals in near silence.

Donnie did his best to break the ice. "My God, you inhaled that steak like you hadn't eaten in days. What's the name of that holiday where you guys fast? Yum Kippers?" He watched his friend lap up the rest of the meat juices with one of the fresh-baked dinner rolls.

"I'm sorry, what did you say?" replied Sol, his mouth full of food.

Helene returned with the check. Sol snatched it out of Donnie's hand even though it was his turn to pick up the tab. The two couples usually alternated the dinner bill, but Sol appeared zoned in on making a point.

"My treat, tonight," insisted Sol.

Sol had barely scanned the total bill; usually, he reviewed everything like a detective. He eyed the attractive waitress approaching and took out a crisp ten-dollar bill and plunked it down on the table for the tip.

"Nice job, honey," said the former New Yorker, then sauntered up to the cashier to pay the bill. He snagged a toothpick, whittling in between his teeth as he reached for his wallet, taking out a pair of twenties and handing them to Delores.

"Hope you left a hefty tip," said the hostess.

"I always do," said Sol before pausing. "By the way, I think the orange hair makes you look like Bozo the Clown's sister. Maybe stick with the pink instead." Delores growled.

***

After dinner, the four got into Donnie's 1971 Cutlass Supreme convertible, forest green with a white top and white interior. During the steamy summer months, Falcone kidded you could fry eggs on the broiling hot vinyl interior. Most of the time, he draped the seats with an oversized powder blue beach towel decked out with leaping dolphins.

With the top down, the two couples enjoyed a leisurely drive south along A1A. Seeing the familiar Dairy Queen, which they'd patronized many times before, Donnie asked if anyone wanted ice cream. With a resounding yes, he pulled into the parking lot and parked next to a butt-ugly bronze 1976 AMC Matador Brougham, the owner a resident at their condo building. The line moved quickly as they all ordered soft-serve cones dipped in chocolate. They sat down at the round, concrete, mosaic patio table with three matching curved bench seats, not exactly the most comfortable, but they were content to sit and enjoy their desserts in the mild evening.

"Ah, it's good to be retired," said Donnie, inhaling the ocean breeze coming off the Atlantic.

"I'll second that," replied Sol.

"Glad to see you showing some life, buddy," Donnie added, patting his friend on the back.

"Yeah, you and me both," replied Sol, catching drips of ice cream with his tongue. "It's been a couple of weeks since I felt this good." The four finished up their desserts and then headed back home.

Trying to work off their chocolate-dipped cones, the Falcones decided to take the stairs to their fifth-floor condo. Sol and Myrna decided to do the same. They followed their friends up to the fifth floor, said goodnight, then proceeded to trek up to the eighth. Despite being in good shape, Myrna was out of breath from the quick pace. Sol, on the other hand, barely broke a sweat.

CHAPTER 16

Myrna entered the condo first, placing her purse down on the kitchen table. Sol kicked off his Adidas Stan Smith tennis sneakers and went straight into the kitchen and grabbed a beer from the refrigerator. He looked for the magnetic opener shaped like a mermaid, usually attached to the front of the refrigerator. Hearing the commotion, Myrna said to check the side. Bingo.

The two sat down in their assigned recliners, both facing their twenty-four-inch Magnavox color television. Myrna kicked out the footrest and looked over to her husband. After a few minutes of silence, she finally spoke up.

"You were weird tonight."

Sol didn't debate his actions. "Yeah, I was kinda weird, wasn't I?" replied Sol, taking a sip of his Rheingold. It had been his first real chow-down since returning to the States.

"Kinda? That was some performance, but I'm glad you finally showed some life," bemoaned his wife.

"I know you're looking out for my health, honey, and I appreciate it. But tonight, I felt like I really needed a big, juicy steak," said Sol. "I promise to eat healthy the next time we go out."

"I swear you ate that steak like it was your last meal on earth," chuckled Myrna.

"That's an understatement." He squirmed to get comfortable in his favorite seat. He grabbed the TV remote off the coffee table and belched. "My apologies, but God, did I need that." He mindlessly flipped through the handful of channels, finding nothing but boring mysteries.

"You know what? I could use a leisurely stroll along the beach. Kick off our shoes, hold hands. Whaddya say?"

"Now, tonight?" said Myrna. She glanced at the clock on the wall. "It's after ten."

Sol took a gulp of beer. "Yeah, I know, but I finally feel like I got energy." He glanced around for his coat, which was normally hung on one of the dining room chairs. "Oh crap!"

"Oh, crap what?" said Myrna.

"My jacket! I forgot my Mets jacket at the restaurant! I gotta go back before someone steals it!" Sol reached for his car keys on the dining room table.

Myrna turned and called out from her cozy recliner. "Who'd want to steal a Mets jacket?"

"I heard that," uttered Sol as he closed the door.

Myrna turned back to the television and smiled, "Weird, indeed."

Sol ventured into the dimly lit parking garage and scurried over to his car, a yellow, four-door Oldsmobile Delta 88. He got in and then sped outside, emulating Jimmy "Popeye" Doyle's driving skills in The French Connection, the tailpipe scraping on the speed bump as he accelerated north on A1A. Low on gas, he stopped off at a Shell Station for a quick refill, then continued on his way.

It was nearing ten-thirty. Helene had wrapped up her busy shift and gathered her purse. She said goodnight to the manager and two other co-workers she was friends with, then exited through the back entrance. With the parking lot full earlier in the day, Helene was forced to park further away than she would have liked. The lamppost light by her car flickered as she approached her bright lime green 1973 AMC Gremlin X, marked with black hockey stick trim on both sides, in near darkness. Only a handful of other cars were visible. She recognized her friend's car right away, an orange VW Thing, parked close by the employee entrance.

Sol arrived and claimed his windbreaker from the lost and found bin. Before leaving, he asked the manager about a certain brunette waitress. After being informed she had just left the restaurant, Sol hopped back into his car and stealthily approached the back end of the lot, parking under a cluster of towering Australian pines. He stepped out of his car, hidden in the shadows.

He eyed the waitress and started to walk over to her when he abruptly reeled himself in, his heart thumping like a wild animal. "What the hell am I doing here? I must be out of my freaking gourd checking out that young broad."

Sol trailed back to his car, opening the door quietly. He was about to step inside his prized '88 when he saw another car driving recklessly towards the young woman. He stood motionless as the car closed in on the waitress.

A black, 1973 Chevy Camaro blasting the Doors, *Light My Fire*, pulled up alongside Helene, slamming on the brakes. A slim man, mid-twenties, with long black hair, jumped out. He strutted over to Helene and gave her a brazen kiss on the lips.

Helene shoved him away. "I told you we're through, Robbie, now go away," barked the waitress, as she attempted to unlock her car door.

The scene piqued Sol's interest. He shifted a few feet closer behind a sabal palm tree to hear what was going on.

"Oh, come on, sugar plum, I know you don't mean that," said the man, much taller than the five-foot-four waitress, a total rock and roll meathead. "I'll never see her again, I promise!"

"Go away, Robbie, or I'm calling the police this time," snapped Helene.

"You're not calling anyone, baby," insisted the pseudo-rocker. He grabbed her arm, squeezing it.

"You're hurting me! Stop it!" cried Helene. The man attempted to kiss her again.

Sol emerged from the darkness and called out. "Let her go, schnook." Sol's adrenaline surged. He balled up both hands into tight fists, anger engraved across his arched, lined brow.

"Snook?" he replied. "Who calls someone the name of a fish?"

"The word is schnook; it's Yiddish for jerk."

"Piss off, old man," shot Robbie, annoyed. The car stereo was cranking the wailing voice of Jim Morrison, the *Lizard King*, now crooning the song, *Back Door Man*. The young man bragged to Helene about how he learned how to play the tune on his Gibson SG.

The retiree stalked up to the man. "I said, let her go, or things are going to get messy." That's when Sol caught a whiff of the rocker dude's overpowering Hai Karate cologne. The guy must have showered in it.

"I know you, don't I?" asked Helene, surprised. "You were here tonight for dinner, steak, medium rare, overbearing wife, right?"

"Right on the button, sweetheart," answered Sol.

"Oh, so pops here is your new boyfriend?" snapped

the man, wearing a thin black pleather jacket, looking very much like a cheap imitation of the late Jim Morrison. "Why don't you take your walker and get the hell out of here?" He proceeded to shove Sol to the ground.

Helene screamed as she rushed over to help him up. "How dare you pick on an elderly gentleman like that!" Helene glanced into Sol's eyes, startled; they looked bloodshot. She helped him up off the pavement.

"I'm not elderly; I'm a successful retired business owner who is about to teach this punk a lesson in manners."

"Sure, you are, pops," badgered Robbie, "I bet you knew Moses personally."

Sol was boiling over mad. He couldn't remember the last time he had engaged in a brawl of any sort, but tonight, he was ready to throw some haymakers.

"You better go on home, Helene, I'll handle this prink from here."

She backed away, fumbling for her keys, then unlocked the door before getting in. The waitress turned to the retiree, unable to take her eyes off him. He was either her aging knight in shining armor or just another kooky snow bird.

Robbie came storming over to her car, slapping the hood with an open hand. The woman revved the engine and drove away, clipping the toes of Robbie's bargain JC Penny black boots.

"I'll get you for that, you bitch!" he yelled, as Helene zoomed out of the parking lot.

Hobbling in pain, the obnoxious man turned towards Sol. "You are gonna get a whooping deluxe, old man."

"I don't think so," replied Sol, as he stepped up to Robbie, tilting his head upward, eyes seething in blood red.

Robbie threw a wild right-hand punch. Sol ducked, catching nothing but breeze. The old man followed with a powerful left hook that cut the man down to size, breaking a rib in the process. Robbie grimaced in pain as he fell to the pavement, coughing and wheezing. Making sure no one was in view, Sol grabbed Robbie by the throat and threw him onto the hood of his car with a thud. The car stereo skipped briefly and then continued playing. It was the first time Robbie noticed Sol's reddened eyes.

"Ugh! You son of a bitch, I'll kill you!" Robbie bellowed, trying to fight back.

"Oh, I beg to differ." Sol then slammed Robbie's head again onto the hood. While stunned, the retiree launched his protruding canines into the man's slender neck, driving his teeth deep into the flesh. Moments later, strands of blood trickled down, reaching Robbie's black t-shirt. The dead man's car stereo was now playing the melancholy Doors tune, *End of the Night*.

Sol used the back of his hand to catch a trickle of blood. "How apropos." He looked around, making sure no one had witnessed him killing the rocker type.

He placed Robbie's lifeless body back into his own car and buckled him in the passenger side. Sol grabbed the keys and got in. He started the Camaro, revving the eight-cylinder engine.

"Ooh, nice,"

He adjusted the rearview mirror and sped out of the parking lot and raced north along A1A. He glanced into the rearview mirror and dabbed away a drop of blood around the corner of his lips.

Nearing North Miami, Sol made a left turn and drove

over the intercoastal bridge. He soon spotted a sign for Oleta River State Park, a rustic place he and Myrna had visited before to rent a canoe. He put on the brakes, then spotted a secluded gravel road that forked from the park entrance. The road was hidden by a canopy of sea grapes and palm trees. A half mile in, Sol parked near the end of a weathered old cement pier battered by decades of relentless hurricanes, the dense area now overgrown with thick tropical foliage. It was ideal, he thought, the perfect location to dump a car (and body).

Sol placed the dead man back into the driver's seat and buckled him in, even positioning his hands on the steering wheel and foot on the gas pedal. He placed the car in drive and pushed on the dead man's leg through the open window to get some momentum. In seconds, the car thrust forward before taking a nosedive into the brackish water, then sank like a 3500-hundred-pound car should sink.

"This is the end, alright." He wiped his hands and spat out a red goober.

***

Sol returned home nearly an hour later. He was able to thumb a ride back to Rascal House and then drove back home faster than an Oldsmobile '88 should really go.

He entered the condo with Myrna still sitting in her designated seat, asleep. She sprang up at the sound of the door opening and jangly keys.

"Honey, I was so worried about you. What happened?"

Sol quickly rushed to the bathroom to wash up. He returned to the kitchen, putting on a kvetching act for the ages.

"Myrna, it was a nightmare. First of all, it took forever

to find the coat. It turns out Delores had placed it in the manager's office and not in the lost and found," said Sol. "Then, I got a flat tire coming back. But to top off the evening, I got pulled over by a cop. I tell you, they enjoy harassing people like me, if you know what I mean!"

"Yeah, annoying New Yorkers," replied Myrna. I'd pull you over, too. Now just relax, and I'll make you a nice hot chamomile tea, or you can have the beer you didn't finish; it's in the refrigerator."

She prepared another mug and took out a bag of Pepperidge Farm Milano cookies. They let the teas cool a bit before drinking them. Sol, still agitated, polished off the cold beer first, quenching his thirst. He quickly showered and changed, then sat down with his wife.

"Cheers, dear," he said, kicking back in his La-Z-Boy chair. He glanced at his watch. "You know I should be exhausted, but I feel like a million bucks. Let's get cozy and catch the rest of the Tonight Show; that Carson is always a pisser." Myrna, finally seeing a spark in her formerly lethargic husband, smiled like a teenager.

As the two headed to the bedroom, Myrna picked up Sol's clothes off the bed to put in the hamper when she noticed something. "What's that on your shirt? Is that blood?"

Sol broke into a mini panic but covered up well, saying he cut himself while trying to change the tire. A near miss, but too close for comfort.

CHAPTER 17

The next day, Sol slept in like a rock, getting up at half past one in the afternoon. He peered out the window, eyeing the whitecaps of the Atlantic Ocean. The beach was already filled with an assortment of colorful beach umbrellas and sunburned tourists.

He peeked over to his nightstand and read the note Myrna left, saying she'd be having lunch at the pool with Donnie and Barbara. Sol ventured into the bathroom and turned on the light. Squinting his eyes and feeling a touch achy, he opted for an extended hot shower. He shampooed his balding head while belting out Sinatra's New York, New York. Suddenly, it hit him.

"Holy crap! I bit a man's neck last night and tasted his freaking blood." He shut off the water, begging to make sense of his actions. It wasn't working. "All that dieting is turning me into a God-damned cannibal!"

Sol dried off and wrapped the towel around his waist. He brushed his teeth forever before gargling with a half-bottle of Scope, hoping that would defuse his unpleasant breath. He shut the cabinet door, feeling more composed. He wiped off the fogged-up mirror from the steamy hot shower with his hand. He peered in closely when he took a double-take. He wiped it off again, this time with the hand towel. Something wasn't right. "What the hell?"

Sol pinched the bridge of his nose and rubbed his eyes,

then took another gander. His heart skipped a beat. "My reflection! Where the hell is my reflection?"

Although he never wore eyeglasses before, maybe it was time to invest in a pair. He expected to see his face like he did a million times before. Instead, staring at him was more like a watermarked version of Mr. Solomon B. Hirsch.

***

"So, where's Mr. Sleepyhead?" asked Donnie, wearing a straw hat and wire-rimmed mirrored sunglasses. "He can't still be getting over jetlag."

"He's coming down, eventually," said Myrna. "I swear all he does is eat, sleep, and a couple of other things I don't want to mention," she added slyly.

"You don't think he caught something in Romania?" asked Barbara.

Myrna looked at her best friend. "Something happened there, but I don't know what. I insisted he go see a doctor, which he has."

"Sol's cousin, right?" said Barbara. "What did he say?"

"Yes," replied Myrna. "The doctor said he seems perfectly healthy. Sol explained to him that he feels sluggish during the day and that the sun irritates his skin. But in the evening, he seems to pick up more energy."

"So, what, is he allergic to the sun or something?" said Donnie. "Not a good thing when you reside in the Sunshine State."

"Who knows," said Myrna, "But if this goes on any longer, I'm taking him to see a specialist."

"I wonder if it has something to do with that night we walked around the big lake."

"Sol didn't mention anything about the lake. What

exactly happened out there?" pressed Myrna.

Barbara added her two cents. "Donnie?"

"Now I'm thinking I should have said something earlier," confessed Donnie.

"What, what!" said Myrna.

"It didn't seem too out of the ordinary, but Sol got pecked by a bird or something," said Donnie. "Or was it a duck? I forget. Either way, I whacked it with a big stick."

"A duck?" asked his wife.

"A duck attacked my husband?" said Myrna. "You didn't think that was out of the ordinary?!"

"I don't know; it was black. It had wings and made a chirping sound," said Donnie. "I guess you could say your husband got stuck with the bill."

Barbara admonished her husband. "Buffoon."

"What you're describing sounds like a bat," said Myrna, speculating. "Oh no. I bet Sol's got rabies!"

"Has he been foaming at the mouth lately?" posed Donnie.

Barbara shook her head. "Maybe the doctor can give him a blood test to make sure."

"That's a good idea," said Myrna. "And no, Donnie, he's not foaming at the mouth, but I know fatigue is a symptom. So is restlessness and irritability."

"Sounds like Sol's had rabies all his life," quipped Donnie. "Sorry. If you want, I can accompany him to the doctor just so he doesn't try to skip out."

"That would be much appreciated; I know he'll refuse if I tag along," said Myrna. "Just keep an eye on him."

"I'll keep both eyes on him; it'll make it easier," added Donnie.

Barbara groaned. "You make being unfunny an art form."

***

Sol finished up a big bowl of Product 19 before washing it down with two cups of black coffee. He browsed the sports page of the Miami Herald; the start of the baseball season was still weeks away. He perked up when he read the Mets would be in Ft. Lauderdale to play the World Series Champs New York Yankees, in an upcoming spring training game under the lights.

The ex-deli man went into the bedroom and put on his bathing suit, then draped his body in a lightweight, blue-striped seersucker robe. He grabbed a Coke from the fridge, a bag of Lays potato chips, and placed the newspaper under his armpit, then headed for the pool.

While his wife, Donnie, and Barbara were at the beach, Sol dragged one of the beach lounge chairs and set up shop in the shade. It was true, the bright sunlight was irritating his skin, something that had never happened before. The doctor had ruled out common skin diseases like eczema, dermatitis, or psoriasis. He could still tolerate it as long as he was in the shade and draped in his robe and wide-brimmed beach hat. After browsing the comic strips, he dozed off with the newspaper on his lap.

The three returned. Donnie spotted his friend in the shaded corner, asleep. "Glad to see everyone's favorite recluse finally ventured down to the pool."

"I'll let him sleep," said Myrna. Maybe we can go out for dinner tonight." All three used the outdoor shower to clean their feet, then headed upstairs.

Sol finally woke up in the late afternoon, after 5PM.

Any sunlight left was mostly blocked by the towering condo building, ten stories in all. For his after-sunset ritual, he enjoyed chilling a Rheingold in the freezer then pouring it into his extra-large Harry M. Stevens souvenir cup, making him feel like he was enjoying a cold one at Shea Stadium.

To his pleasant surprise, Myrna had placed a small cooler by his side of the lounge chair. Sol opened it up and found a properly chilled Rheingold. "Bless you, wife," Sol uttered, blowing a kiss to the sky. Sol took off his shirt and cheap rubber beach flip-flops and entered the shallow end of the pool. The warm water smelled heavily of chlorine. The pool guy treated the pool water like a stew, adding blocks of chlorine as if they were bouillon cubes.

Sol took a healthy gulp of beer, setting it on the ledge, then waded into the deeper end in total peace and quiet. He dipped below the water and emerged refreshed.

"I'll work this thing out," he murmured to himself. "I swear on my mother's grave."

Myrna suddenly appeared, wearing a flowery pink dress and squeaky rubber sandals. "How's the water?"

"Refreshing, but way too much chlorine. What are you up to?"

Myrna pointed to her watch. "We're going to Rascal House for dinner. You want to join us?"

Sol thought about last night's altercation in the parking lot. What if someone saw him? Or if Helene asks about what happened to her ex? Sol thought otherwise. "Nah, I'll grab a burger at the Cheeky Tiki."

Myrna huffed. "Do what you want; I'll see you later then."

CHAPTER 18

After swimming some laps freestyle, Sol trudged back upstairs to change. He took a quick shower, put on his white shorts, and his favorite Hawaiian shirt embellished with pineapples and hula dancers. Taking the stairs for the first time, the seasoned citizen trampled down the eight flights with ease, then power-walked over to his cream yellow (officially omega maize), Fisher Body beauty. Feeling like a teenager, Sol turned on the radio and tracked down a rock station, and turned up the volume. *Let The Good Times Roll*, by The Cars, played loud and clear. Listening to all that rock music in Laszlo's car was rubbing off on him. He revved the car, then barreled out of the parking lot, driving south down A1A with one hand on the wheel.

He took a right at the Chevron station and drove up another two blocks. He found a parking spot at his favorite watering hole, the Cheeky Tiki Bar. The drinking establishment, bare-bones chique with accents of bamboo throughout the exterior and interior, was nestled right on the Intracoastal Waterway, a body of water approximately forty yards wide that ran parallel with the ocean along the east coast of the Sunshine State. Not exactly the yachting type, Sol sometimes enjoyed having a beer and watching the myriad of watercrafts parading back and forth, from Boston Whalers to 80-foot mega yachts, usually occupied with plenty of bikini-clad women.

He stepped out of the car and straightened his customary New York Mets hat, which he'd owned since the magical 1969 World Series season. He treasured it, having it autographed by lefty-hitting first baseman Ed Kranepool, whom he asked after a chance encounter in the players' parking lot.

The Cheeky Tiki Bar served up good, cheap eats, not to mention a respectable selection of booze. Manny Alachua, the owner, was a New York City transplant just like many of his thirsty clientele. Lately, to his dislike and Sol's, there was a disproportionate amount of Yankee fans to Mets fans, and they loved to bust balls, particularly those of the former deli owner.

"Hey Manny, extra cold Rheingold and a cheeseburger, medium rare, fries, pickles, and onions," instructed the retiree.

"Sol, why don't you just say the usual," said Manny, pointing to his head. "I got a memory like an elephant."

The bar owner was originally from Queens and a die-hard Mets fan to boot. He and Sol got along great. Both were still heartbroken when one of their favorite Mets players of all time, Tom "Terrific" Seaver, was traded two years earlier in the summer of 1977, shipping the righty fireballer off to the Cincinnati Reds for Pat Zachry, Doug Flynn, Steve Henderson, and Dan Norman. A year later, Seaver would throw a no-hitter on June 16, 1978, against the St. Louis Cardinals, blanking the Redbirds, 4-0.

It was going to be another brutal year for their beloved Metsies. Both men knew it, but die-hard fans are for keeps, for better or worse. And lately, it had been worse. It was only six years ago when the Amazing Mets nearly captured the 1973 World Series against the vaunted Oakland A's, losing four games to three. But maybe the worst part for Mets fans was their intercity rivals, the Yankees, the freaking New York Yankees, capturing back-to-back World Series titles against the Los Angeles Dodgers in 1977 and 1978. And 1979 was shaping up to be a trifecta.

A man, mid-sixties with dark gray hair, strolled in, pompous stride and all. He sat down next to Sol, patting him on the back. The familiar face, Walt Garvey, was a Yankees fanatic and loved reminding everyone in the Magic City that the Yankees were number one.

"Sol, you know we love you, but when are you gonna join the winning team?" said Garvey, a retired lawyer formally of the Bronx who donned his number seven replica Mickey Mantle Yankee pinstripe jersey like a proud peacock. He loved skewing Mets fans.

"How many games are those bums gonna lose this year, a 110?" joked Tommy Dwyer, joining his friend at the bar. Dwyer was a retired Staten Island police officer and part-time security guard at the Cardozo Hotel.

"Meet the Mets… in last place!" added Garvey, singing the cheery Mets jingle. Both men howled in laughter.

"Guys, don't push it, okay?" asked Sol, politely.

The mounted TV above the bar was showing Fantasy Island; no one was paying attention, although Manny mentioned on more than one occasion that he would love to drop-kick that annoying little Tattoo character into the Atlantic. Major League Baseball wouldn't start for real for another couple of weeks, and no one was interested in basketball. Unfortunately, the television networks didn't show spring training games. The two obnoxious Yankee fans were chomping at the bit to catch their beloved champion

Yankees against Sol's sad-sack Mets at the end of the week in an evening spring training game up in Ft. Lauderdale.

It was nearing 11:00PM. Nearly all of the patrons had gone home. The only people left were Sol and a pair of Manhattan-bred, New York City banker types still dressed in their near-matching Botany 500 gray suits. Each of the men was in their late 40s, overweight, and sporting flowery designer ties. To Sol's dismay, both were vocal Yankee fans and totally sloshed out of their minds. One in particular kept pestering Sol about the virtues of being a fan of the Bronx Bombers, slurring his words and busting his balls.

"We're da world chimps, and we're gonna win the World Series again!" spewed the drunk. "Reggie Jackson could bat right-handed and beat your sorry-ass team all by himself." He proceeded to let out a massive belch, spilling his vodka tonic on himself.

The other guy chimed in. "Don't feel too bad. You guys barely missed the playoffs last year by what, six touchdowns?" He exploded with laughter.

"They're an embarrassment to the greatest city in the world," the other man slobbered.

Sol bit his lip, seething, as he observed the two drunks rounding out the evening by downing a couple of shots of whisky, Manny secretly charging them double for being so annoying. The bar owner made his final announcement, ready to close up shop. Despite the ribbing, the ex-New Yorker offered to take the two drunks back to their hotel.

"No hard feelings, right?" said Sol.

The two loaded men stumbled into the back seat of Sol's Olds. The retiree pulled out of the parking lot and instead, headed north on Collins Avenue before making a left on 826.

He traveled west. Minutes later, he drove down the familiar secluded gravel road where he'd dumped the pseudo-rocker type the previous night.

Seeing all the palm trees instead of the string of beach view hotels, one of the men finally spoke up. "Hey, where are we?" asked the pear-shaped man. "Where's da hotel?"

"Oh, it's just over here," said Sol. "By the way, you guys ever seen live alligators before?"

One of the men perked up. "Hell no, but there's always a first time!" His speech was boisterous as he pulled out a small bag of peanuts from his pocket. "Got 'um on the plane." The other man was nearly passed out in the back seat, ready to throw up at any moment.

Peanut Guy stumbled out of the car as Sol led the way towards the dilapidated cement pier. "Over here," he instructed, as they reached the end.

"I don't see nothin," he slurred. The man wobbled a little, then realized he was out of peanuts. "Hey Mets fan, I want to go back to the bar."

"Nah, I've got something else planned for you."

"Whah?"

Sol surveyed the location, turning his head, then lunged at the man, digging his fangs into the man's neck. The drunken man cried out briefly, then slumped onto the damp cement surface carpeted with thick green moss. Sol wet his whistle just enough, then rolled the incapacitated man into the water and tucked him under the pier. The splash got the attention of a pair of alligators, each over ten feet long. Sol spit in the water, still tasting the booze from the man's intoxicating blood.

The other drunken man sat up in the back seat, hearing

his friend's muted cry. He fumbled for the door handle and spilled out of the car.

Sol turned and hissed, wiping away a few drops of blood from his mouth with his sleeve.

"Where's my friend, you son of a bitch!" slurred the man.

Sol flashed a mischievous Cheshire cat grin. "Swimming with the gators, you insufferable Yankee prick. And you're next."

The man staggered to his feet; his mouth was dry as beach sand. He took off, stumbling over and around the palm-laden scrub. The man yelled out for help, but his words ran together in a garbled mess. He dodged two coconut palms but smacked directly into a sturdy cypress tree.

Sol calmly sauntered over to the drunk, picking him off the waterlogged turf.

"You still think the Mets are a joke?"

"Kinda," he uttered, his eyes watery, his head achy from hitting the tree square on.

Sol clutched the man's shirt with both hands and lifted him up. The drunk noticed Sol's elongated canines. "Are those real?" The man watched as Sol scooped up a single missed drop of blood rolling down his lips, catching it with his tongue.

"You're going to find out how real they are," said Sol in a sinister tone.

The man was in tears, horrified. "I'm sorry, man, I didn't mean to be a jerk about your team, it's just our nature."

"This is true," replied Sol, with a smile. The man smiled back, weakly. Thirty seconds later, he was dead too.

Sol carried the husky man over to the end of the pier.

To his surprise, more alligators were patiently waiting.

"Feeding time." Although Sol was a city type through and through, he was beginning to appreciate the native swampy terrain of South Florida.

***

Myrna was already in bed when Sol returned home. He crept through the bedroom and went straight into the bathroom to examine his blood-stained pearly whites. His newfound pointy choppers had already retracted. A ring of dried blood surrounded his lips. He and his attire reeked of swamp and boozy, dead people. Sol gathered up his clothes and stuffed them into a plastic bag, then hid it under the sink. Sol showered quickly, then changed into his pajamas before nestling up in bed. Myrna was snoring away, although she denied the accusation every time Sol mentioned it.

Sol lay motionless on the bed, the blanket pulled up to his upper chest. He stared at the ceiling fan, catching the blades rotating in slow motion. He sighed.

"What the hell was happening to me?" he thought to himself. "Three people dead in two days."

This whole thing of killing people, tapping into their necks with his newfound extended canines, was completely insane. And yet, there it was. This was no Romanian flu. He tried approaching it with a logical frame of mind, but everything pointed to one thing: he was now a vampire, a blood-sucking vampire. But how?

That night at the lake, he thought. A bat, or something thereof, attacked him. The marks on his neck. What else could it be? Whatever was happening to him, he still wanted more.

CHAPTER 19

The next evening, Myrna, Barbara, along with two of her library volunteer friends went to see a movie. Sol and Donnie declined. Instead, they went to a clothing store next to Rascal House, where Sol picked up a brand-new leisure suit, black as Kingsford briquettes, that he had checked out recently while waiting in line for dinner. He completed his shopping spree with a crimson long-sleeve dress shirt and black dress shoes. He decided to ditch his casual threads and wear it out for dinner. Both men usually dressed casually in khaki shorts and Hawaiian shirts.

"Man, oh man," said Donnie, taken aback at Sol's fancy threads. "You're dressed to kill, my friend!"

"You could say that," said Sol with a smirk. The two walked a few blocks before stopping at their favorite Cuban restaurant, Old Havana. Both men sat outside at a table perfectly situated for people watching. Feeling thirsty, both men ordered a couple of Presidente beers, a refreshing pilsner from the Dominican Republic, perfect for the warm evenings in South Florida. The breeze coming off the Atlantic felt wonderful. There was no better place in the world to be than Miami Beach, thought the two retirees.

"You get a night like this, sometimes I can't believe we lived anywhere else," said Donnie.

"We'll always be New Yorkers, Donnie, but, yeah, Miami Beach is muy bien," said Sol. "Salud!" They clanked bottles and drank in unison.

The waitress, a recent arrival from Costa Rica, took their order in her broken English, good enough to get their order right the first time. Soon after, dinner was served.

"Oh man, I dig these plantains, said Donnie, who'd developed a frenzied zeal for Cuban cuisine. "And the shredded beef. What's it called again in Spanish?" snapping his fingers.

"Ropa vieja," replied Sol, dining on the same dish. "Not bad at all, and the black beans don't make me fart; that's always a big plus." The two laughed, shooting the breeze as they downed a couple more beers.

"You know, Sol, there are a hell of a lot of benefits being down here in Miami Beach. You kinda kick yourself in the ass for not doing it sooner, am I right?"

"I suppose so," Sol replied, "They're never gonna get the pizza right here, and I've given up on getting decent Chinese food." He was feeling good, but thinking what the rest of the night might bring.

After servings of flan for dessert, the two returned home to the condo building and got into the elevator. Donnie got off on his customary fifth floor. Sol waved goodnight, pretending to push the eighth-floor button. As the door closed, Donnie observed the light above the elevator. It started to go down.

"Maybe he forgot something in his car," Donnie shrugged out loud before heading inside his beach view condo.

Sol trekked back to his car. He took off his jacket, then topped his balding head with his worn Mets hat that had been resting on the dashboard. He pulled out of the parking lot in search of his next hemoglobin fix. As he drove south on A1A, he spotted a portly man, late thirties, buying a soda outside a gas station. Sol slowed down as he eyed the hefty man like an animal stalking its prey. The man continued his leisurely stroll along the beachside sidewalk. Sol made a U-turn then headed towards a darkened side street two blocks past the guy that led to the beach. He parked next to a corner public phone booth, the inside light flickering, the glass door busted. He turned off the headlights and rolled down the window, listening intently for the man's approaching footsteps. With his acute hearing, Sol heard the man whistling out of key. He leaped from his car like a big game cat. Since his transformation, he noticed his five senses were attuned like never before. Maybe this vampire stuff wasn't such a bad thing after all, he postulated. Still, the blood-consuming aspect he found disconcerting.

The obese man continued walking as he licked his index finger and thumb. Sol hid behind a wide sabal palm, surveying the scene in every direction as the man opened the can of Pepsi. He moved closer. The man took a healthy gulp then let out a monstrous, reverberating belch.

"Oh Christ, I needed that," said the obese man, thumping his burly chest. He'd just polished off two racks of succulent barbeque ribs from the Southern Pig restaurant. He dug his greasy hand deep into his front jean pocket and pulled out a Snickers bar. He tore off the wrapper, preparing to take a huge bite.

Sol approached, greeting him on the sand-blown walkway. "Hey mister, you got a light?"

"Sorry, old man, I don't smoke," he replied, as he discarded the wrapper on the ground, stuffing his face. "It's bad for your health, you know." He devoured the candy bar in mere seconds. Sol was getting sick and tired of being referred to as an old man.

Sol stared at the guy's jiggly neck; a blind vampire couldn't miss that thing from a mile away, he thought. "Oh, that's alright, I don't smoke. Never mind."

"Then why'd you ask?" he answered back as he wiped his mouth of chocolate residue. "That was kinda stupid. Oh, you're a Mets fan, I guess that explains it." The chubby man, from the city of brotherly love, Philadelphia, pointed at Sol's faded blue cap and let out a thunderous laugh, then strode right by him.

"No one makes fun of my Mets, and lives!" growled Sol, thrusting his finger in the air, the heated anger beginning to flow in his veins like erupting lava.

The portly man turned around and cackled some more. "That was pretty funny, pops. I bet you did stand-up in the Poconos." Then he sang the 'Beautiful Mount Airy Lodge' commercial jingle in a girly voice. Sol had had enough.

"It's Catskills, you schmo!" bellowed the retiree. "Catskills!"

The senior citizen with his newfound dagger teeth launched himself at the rotund man, tackling him to the ground before penetrating his jiggly neck with his needle-point teeth. Sol gorged himself. The man put up a brief struggle, flopping about before keeling over like a behemoth elephant seal. "And that's for littering too." Sol suddenly felt nauseous and hurled.

"Not kosher! Not kosher!" coughed Sol, spitting out red everywhere. The man's marinated blood had the full essence of barbequed pork running through his veins. Sol composed himself, praying no one saw his actions.

The man's dead body stood out on the boardwalk

like a beached whale, the skin pale as the full moon above. There was a nearby beach shower that Sol used to clean up his face and splattered blood. He dragged the man over to the edge of the boardwalk and dropped him with a thud. Sol jumped down and tucked the body stealthily underneath the wooden walkway. Clusters of sea grapes, tall grasses, and thrown garbage would help conceal his latest victim... at least temporarily.

Sol got back into his car, glancing into the rearview mirror to see if there was any dripping blood. His reflection was fading a little more each day. He strapped on his seat belt and headed north up Collins Avenue to go home. At a traffic light, he spotted a familiar vehicle going in the opposite direction, an antifreeze green AMC Gremlin, with an attractive brunette at the wheel.

"Helene."

CHAPTER 20

Sol made a quick left at the next light and shadowed the compact car. Traffic came to a screeching halt, the result of an accident up ahead. Sol was two cars behind Helene. He kept a low profile, making sure not to be seen. With traffic clearing, he tailed the waitress another couple of miles before she made a right into a nightclub called Boogie Beach. The parking lot was completely full at the premium South Florida disco, a mainstay for the entertainment crowd. Sol observed Helene as she parked her compact car between a pair of high-end sports cars. He continued past her and instead parked strategically in the shadows behind the building.

He peeked into the vanity mirror and patted down his disheveled hair and grinned. "I could go for a little swing music."

Sol grabbed his jacket as he stepped out of the car and put it on, hoping to conceal any blood splatter on his new shirt, which thankfully, was red. The retiree made a mental note never to feast on people coming out of popular rib joints ever again. He locked up the car, then strolled towards the entrance, a swagger in his step.

Before Sol even reached the front of the building, he could already feel the sensation of thumping bass under his feet. He marveled at the venue, a former warehouse now converted into the top disco club in Miami Beach. On the side of the aqua blue building was a huge painted mural of two disco dancing dolphins painted in silver.

Sol sensed he might be out of his league. "That doesn't sound like Benny Goodman to me."

Up ahead, he spotted Helene standing in line, looking gorgeous in a sparkling silver stretch dress. Sol bypassed a handful of people, then greeted the young woman.

"Helene, how are you?" addressed Sol. "You are the cat's meow!"

"The what?" said Helene, confused.

"Sorry," said Sol. "I'm showing my age here. It means stylish, appealing."

"Okay," said Helene, pausing. "Oh, you're the guy from Rascal House. What a surprise seeing you here… at a disco. I'm sorry I forgot your name."

"It's Sol, Sol Hirsch, and yes, I do remember yours. Are you with anyone on this lovely, enchanted evening?"

Helene politely smiled at Sol, being respectful. "I'm meeting a couple of friends of mine from FIU, but as usual, they're fashionably late. You know how it is."

"Not really, but I'll take your word for it," said Sol.

She pointed to Sol's chin. "Uh, you have a little spot near… it's just below your lower lip."

"Darn ketchup," he said. Sol quickly wiped it off with his handkerchief.

"By the way, whatever happened that night between you and my ex-boyfriend?" asked Helene. "Did he try to get into a fight? I should have thanked you for protecting me. Robbie has anger issues, which is why we broke up."

Sol began to sweat, but quickly weaved a believable story together. "Oh, he sucker-punched me and then drove off in his fancy schmancy sports car. He hasn't given you any problems, has he?"

"No, none at all; and that's just it, I haven't heard a peep from him. He's usually obsessed, calling me day and night. Whatever you did, I'm very grateful."

"Well, let's not dwell on your former boyfriend," replied Sol.

The line started to move as people exited the crowded club, appearing hot and sweaty. "Looks like we're next," said Sol as they approached the entrance. They were about to enter when a bouncer, a former pro football player towering six-foot-five, abruptly grabbed Sol's shoulder.

"No old people," said the bouncer, dressed in a tight-fitting black short-sleeve shirt that emphasized his bulging muscles and blue jeans. "You gotta hit the road, pops." Helene frowned at the man's disrespect, but wasn't surprised. Boogie Beach was the hottest club in town and not exactly a hotbed for retirees.

"The shuffleboard courts are down the street," said the man, emitting laughter from the burgeoning line of people, most decked out in bellbottoms, splashy dresses, and shiny, flowing shirts.

Sol, who stood chest high to the behemoth individual, gazed up at the man's ugly mug and flashed his boiling red eyes.

"You *will* let me in, right, Megillah?" The man stammered in silence, mesmerized, before nodding in a 'yes' motion.

"Welcome to Boogie Beach, sir. Enjoy your evening."

Sol tucked a dollar bill in the man's shiny black shirt pocket. "Thanks, and here's a tip."

Helene was in disbelief. "How'd you do that? I've seen

that guy throw out actors who didn't look cool enough."

"Hey, I'm cool," replied Sol, "In a Queens, New York kinda way." He patted down his flying comb over again. "He didn't know who he was messing with, that's all."

The two strolled in side by side as they approached the glowing dance floor, a sea of flashing colored strobe lights that knocked the socks off Sol. He felt like he had landed on another planet.

"Well, when in Rome," he quipped. The retiree began strutting to the pulsating music like he'd heard it a hundred times before.

Sol was floored by the reflecting lights from above. "Holy moly, what the hell is that?" asked Sol, pointing upward as if seeing a flying saucer from outer space. It looks like Times Square on New Year's Eve!"

"Oh, that's a disco ball," said Helene. "The lights bounce off it and create a laser-light show; it's pretty neat, huh."

Sol caught a blinding beam of light right in the eye. "I'll say." The bombastic sound of the Blondes' *Heart of Glass* filled the dance floor.

"You want to boogey?" asked Helene, as she held out her arms.

"Right here, in front of everyone?" kidded Sol, looking around. "Oh, you mean, dance? Sure, sure, why not!"

Sol did a slow-paced shuffle, holding his own in the middle of the dance floor. People were staring at him and the young brunette, but Helene didn't seem to care.

"I hope you got more energy in that body," yelled Helene, trying to be heard over the bombastic music.

"Oh yeah!" howled the retiree, who flung his suit top

off and hurled into the gawking crowd. He took Helene's hand and started swaying like a man half his age. The old man was dipping and jiving before settling down into a rhythmic groove. People were staring now in amazement, clapping in unison. The seasoned citizen was a well-oiled dancing machine.

"I love this song!" Helene blurted out as the music boomed through the speakers, reverberating throughout the building. Sol followed her every move, picking up the moves quickly. After the song finished, the two meandered through the crowd and over to a circular table to rest. Sol sauntered up to the bar and purchased two Cokes.

A waitress handed back his coat with a smile. "Nice dancing, mister."

"I do my best," he said with a wink before heading back to their table. He handed Helene her drink.

"I didn't know you had it in you," said Helene, taking a swig of soda, sweating like she'd just run a marathon. "I'm roasting." She waved a drink menu at her face, trying to cool off.

"That should be no surprise," said Sol, doing the same. "Your dress looks like it's made of aluminum foil!" Both laughed as they quickly finished off their beverages.

Helene's friends finally showed up; one took a seat next to her. Sol sat up like a perfect gentleman and offered his to the other woman.

"Good evening, ladies," said Sol, who picked up a chair from another table and joined in.

"Are you going to introduce us to your new friend, Helene?" asked Sofia, a plump twenty-five-year-old with dark hair and a distinctively Puerto Rican accent.

"Oh, I'm sorry, this is Sol. He saved me from my ex a few nights ago."

"Good for you, Sol," said Sophia, a stewardess with Eastern Airlines. "That Robbie guy was a first-class mierda."

"I don't think Helene will have to worry about him anymore," grinned Sol, who suddenly began to feel lightheaded. "Sorry, ladies, I think my blood reserve is running on empty."

"Oh, you mean low blood sugar," said Maria, a spunky blond dressed in a skin-tight red dress, snapping on bubble gum. "My grandmother's got that."

"Uh, yeah, that's it," replied Sol, standing up slowly, his face full of sweat. He waved for Helene to come over. "I hope you don't mind, but I need to get some air."

"What's wrong?" she asked, offering to walk with him to the entrance.

"I guess I got a little overheated there on the dance floor." He finished up someone else's drink at a nearby table by mistake. "Before I leave, I hope you don't mind me asking, but would you like to go to a baseball game with me and my wife this Friday night? My Mets are playing the Yankees up in Ft. Lauderdale. The game starts at 7:30PM. Our treat."

"The Yankees?" said Helene. "I have to work Friday, but maybe if I can get off early?" Helene was taken aback at the offer but appreciated the gesture.

"I'll cross my fingers then. See you around." Sol put on his jacket and headed outside, a much-needed cool ocean breeze hitting him in the face. The bouncer was there, standing alone, wearing a Yankee cap and sipping on a Fresca through a puny straw.

"Uh oh." Sol tried to walk incognito back to his car.

"Hey, pops, get back here!" said the beefy guy as he put the soda can down on his stool. Sol picked up the pace and fast-walked towards his car. The man caught up to him and gripped his shoulder tightly. "How the hell you'd get past me?"

"Hands off the merchandise, Megillah," growled Sol. The Miami Dolphin flunky attempted to grab him by the neck, but Sol swatted the man's arm away. He then squeezed the bouncer's thick left hand and then methodically snapped his index finger.

The man screamed in agony. "You fossil son of a bitch, I'll break your freaking skull!" The man swung wildly, clipping Sol in the shoulder. The retiree fell over on his rump. Staggering up, Sol tried a different tack, luring the brute into a dark corner of the parking lot behind a dumpster, hidden out of view.

"Over here, big boy," said Sol, taunting the monolithic man.

"Good, no one will see me whooping your wrinkled ass." The bouncer looked around. Anyone seeing him beat up an old man would not look good on his record. He paused.

"You know what, Pops? I ain't gonna waste my time on some retired asshole; I got better things to do," said the bouncer as he started to walk away.

"What, are you chicken?" said Sol, eyes bloodshot red, adrenaline flowing full-throttle throughout his body.

The bouncer stopped and rotated his massive frame, now facing the retiree. "I was gonna spare your life, old man, but if you want a major beat down, I'll oblige."

Sol got into boxing mode as the behemoth went for the kill. The bouncer uncoiled a left jab, striking Sol in the right shoulder. The retiree grimaced in pain. The bouncer attacked again, throwing a thunderous right. This time, Sol sidestepped the punch, then delivered a devastating left hook to the man's rib cage, breaking multiple ribs like dried spaghetti.

The man dropped to his knees, falling down like a freshly cut down tree. He gasped, desperate to catch a breath.

"Learned that personally from my friend, Smokin' Joe Frasier," said Sol. "Maybe you should stick to picking on guys your own age."

The bouncer coughed up blood as he attempted to stand up. Sol surveyed the parking lot. All clear. He landed another big punch to the jaw, knocking him out cold. A couple exiting their car close by spotted the two men. Quickly, Sol propped the man's arm over his shoulder, holding him like he'd had way too many. Passersby commented on how passed out the guy looked. Sol thought about stuffing him in the trunk, but instead, opted for the front passenger seat. He struggled to fit him inside the car.

"I need to stick to smaller people."

He buckled up the bouncer, then slowly drove out of the parking lot with the windows down, passing the club entrance. Helene came out in need of some cool air, but also to check up on her geriatric dance partner. She spotted Sol heading out of the parking lot. Helene thought she caught a glimpse of the bouncer's face riding shotgun, but wasn't one hundred percent positive.

"Sheesh, that was close," sighed Sol, directing his words at the brute.

He took the familiar route across the intercoastal and down the gravel-strewn road in North Miami and parked as close as possible to the end of the dilapidated pier. Even with his newfound strength, hauling around a 230-pound galoot was a real challenge. A congregation of alligators greeted Sol as he was about to dump the body into the water.

Sol looked at the unconscious man, now having second thoughts about serving him up as gator bait. He decided to place the man back in his car and headed in the direction of 163rd Street and pulled into the local McDonalds drive-thru. Famished, he ordered a Big Mac, large fries, and a soda. Sol parked the car in a corner space and devoured his food. With nobody around, he lugged the bouncer over to one of the outdoor tables and propped him up. He got back into his car then headed home.

"A vampire with a conscience," said Sol, "That's me."

CHAPTER 21

The next evening, both Sol and Myrna were watching the eleven o'clock news when the lead story blared out on their 24-inch color Zenith television screen. The stone-faced anchorman spoke.

"In Miami Beach, a young child stumbled upon a gruesome discovery this morning at a beach access walkway near Gleason Avenue. According to eyewitnesses, the boy was chasing after lizards on the walkway leading to the ocean when he peered through the wood planks and discovered the large, lifeless body of Fredrick Bunda, age 38, a stationary bike salesman visiting from Philadelphia."

He continued. "This also follows another story where three other people are missing, all adult males, possibly from the same vicinity. Miami Beach Police Detective Rex Keller, investigating the death, said in a statement that they have a few leads and believe there could be a common thread linking Mr. Bunda's death and the other missing people."

"That's horrible, and so close to us," commented Myrna. "What do you think? Hello, Earth to Sol?"

Her husband had a blank stare on his face. The murder he committed was now the lead story on local television and would no doubt make it squarely on the front pages of the Miami Herald tomorrow.

Sol went to the bathroom and peered into the mirror; his reflection was still visible but fading ever so slightly with each passing day. Guilt was rearing its ugly head. "What the hell am I gonna do?"

He sat on the bed, envisioning what would happen if he ever got caught. There would be Walter Cronkite, CBS Evening News anchor and the most trusted man in America, staring directly into the camera and introducing viewers to America's latest and most deviant serial killer ever, one Solomon Babe Hirsch. All serial killers go by three names, so now everyone would know his middle name, too. His father, a diehard Yankee fan, named him after Babe Ruth. Ugh.

Oh, this was the big leagues, he thought. And if they find the other bodies, what's next? He'd been arrogant, careless to say the least, with his disposal methods. Assuming that a bunch of four-legged lizards, close descendants to dinosaurs, were going to cover up for his horrid mess? Maybe, maybe not.

Sol turned away and went back into the kitchen, where he poured a substantial glass of scotch. He drank half, hoping it would help calm his nerves. The retiree placed his hands on the kitchen table out of view from his wife. He tried to find hope in his situation. Then his inner voice beckoned.

Hold on! Hold on! Who the hell would suspect a 66-year-old retired deli owner from Queens, New York, of being a serial killer? No one, that's who. He finished up his drink before placing the bottle back in the cabinet. Maybe it was just the booze giving him Dutch courage, but maybe this would all blow over. Sol even managed to poke fun, envisioning the wacky headlines the New York Post might plaster all over the front page, his favorite newspaper back home. There in bold black lettering: *The Kosher Queens Killer*, *The Matzo Murderer*, or better yet, *The Borscht Butcher*.

He snickered before giving himself a quick smack in the face to chill his thoughts. "Enough!"

"Enough what?" Myrna called out, still watching television.

"Nothing, dear, I was just thinking out loud," he replied. "I mean, a murder right here in Miami Beach. That's crazy."

"He didn't say murder," said Myrna. "They just found a dead body. She paused for a moment, thinking out the situation. "Then again, people don't normally die of natural causes and then strategically roll themselves under beach walkways."

Sol started to perspire, his ticker revving into high gear. "I think I need to go for a walk."

"At this hour?" said Myrna. "The mosquitoes are going eat you alive."

Sol quietly grabbed his keys. "I'll take the Off spray."

The last, and only time, Sol had made the news was back in the Big Apple when WPIX Channel 11 News did an entertaining feature on the deli owner back in the early '70s on his legendary chicken soup. He advertised that it could one hundred percent cure the common cold. An obnoxious customer, a Yankee fan to boot, tried to sue him for false advertising. It didn't amount to much, but it did make for good publicity.

Sol stepped outside and gave himself a healthy spritz of insect repellent. He placed his customary Mets hat on and headed out the door towards the elevator. He bumped into one of his fellow neighbors, a gentleman who was a couple of years his senior. As usual, they greeted each other cordially as both stepped into the elevator.

"Good evening, Sol," smiled Herbie Robinson, a former utility player who spent most of his six-year career with the Cleveland Indians back in the 1940s. "Always with your Mets hat on."

"A loyal fan through and through, but those hundred-loss seasons are testing me," said Sol. "You mentioned playing ball for the Indians, right? Not many people can say they were major leaguers."

"Had a cup of coffee, as they say, maybe two cups," answered Robinson, a humble man with a warm smile. "I was a utility player and pinch hitter for most of my career. I didn't play much, but managed to earn one of these." He held up his right hand displaying a gold ring with black onyx on the face and a large centered diamond with a golden emblem that read, "World Champions Cleveland Indians 1948.

"Holy moly," said Sol, impressed. "I might have to ask for your autograph. By the way, me and a couple of friends are playing poker for change in the rec room next Monday at seven. You wanna join us?"

"Sounds like some high-stakes gambling," said Robinson with a wink. "Might be too rich for my blood."

"Ah, it's casual," said Sol. "We hang out, talk baseball, and have a couple of cold ones. We could use another player."

"Sure, why not?" replied Herbie, adding, "But I'm not much of a card player."

Sol smiled. "Then you'll fit right in. By the way, what did you do after you wrapped up your baseball career?"

"Oh, I ended up owning a sporting goods store in Cincinnati, before retiring here in beautiful Miami Beach. And you?"

"Served up killer corn beef sandwiches in the city," Sol

replied.

"Sounds tasty," replied Robinson, a member of the condo committee and a shuffleboard sharp shooter. "And by 'city' you mean New York City?"

"Of course," boasted Sol. "Everyone knows 'The City' can only mean the Big Apple."

Robinson respectfully nodded as he zipped up his red windbreaker. "So, how do you think your Mets will do this year?"

"Spring training brings optimism; the regular season, reality," shrugged Sol. "The Big Red Machine should be in the hunt again as usual."

"Wish I could say I'm a Reds fan, but I've stayed loyal to my Indians, so don't feel so bad," Robinson replied. "They bite the proverbial hoagie every year; at least your team made the World Series twice in the past ten years. Cleveland hasn't been to the World Series since 1954."

"This is true, but it seems like a distant memory," sighed Sol, his gut telling him his beloved Mets were doomed for yet another last-place finish. "You know what really chafes my keister?"

"What would that be?" Robinson replied, a dignified man.

"The Yankees! Those damn Yankees winning the World Series the last two years, and now every transplanted New Yorker here in Miami Beach is rubbing it in my face. I could murder those bums!"

Robinson was taken aback by Sol's sudden rage; he tried to break the tension. "Oh well, it's just a game, right?" He could sense the intensity in Sol's eyes, which were turning bloodshot. "Are you okay? Your eyes — they look irritated."

Sol brushed it aside using the pollen excuse.

***

Meanwhile, Myrna went into the kitchen, poured herself a chamomile tea, and returned to the living room to finish watching the evening news. After the last segment, she got up and was about to turn off the television when a news bulletin appeared.

"This just in," said a thirty-something reporter, Cuban-American and dressed in a light blue pantsuit, a sudden gust tousling her hair.

"A gruesome discovery was made near an old pier near Oleta River State Park in North Miami Beach early evening, as two bodies were found, apparently mauled to death by a pack of alligators. Three fishermen from Hialeah who were fishing approximately thirty yards west of the pier noticed the large reptiles, some measuring over twelve feet in length, fighting over something in what turned out to be human remains."

"Sheesh!" said Myrna. She quickly turned off the television and sat down. She reached for her Times crossword puzzle on the coffee table but couldn't concentrate. "The news is worse here than in New York City…minus the alligators, of course." She got into bed to read a book. Dozing off after every other page, Myrna finally zonked out.

***

Sol simmered down, trying to sway the conversation. "Boy, is this the slowest elevator in the world or what?"

Robinson agreed, as both men stepped out on the ground floor. The former baseball player headed to his car, looking to buy milk and bread for tomorrow morning's breakfast. "Well, goodnight, Sol. And remember, your Mets will bounce back one of these days."

"I can only hope," he replied, waving goodnight.

Sol headed past the pool area and walked down to the beach, where he sat down on a blue and white striped beach chair someone had left behind. Nestling in, Sol quickly absorbed the rhythmic sounds of the crashing waves, taking deep breaths and exhaling to calm his frayed nerves. Thankfully, the annoying no-see-ums, the piranhas of the insect world, were nowhere to be found. The moon looked like it was resting on the water. After an hour of devising schemes and getaway plans, Sol fell asleep.

***

The next morning, Sol's eye slowly raised, awakened to the noise of cawing seagulls and crashing waves. He watched the sunrise, visible shades of purple and pink giving way to vibrant yellow and orange. It was glorious, thought Sol, something he hadn't witnessed in a long time. At least he wasn't frying up in an instant like vampires usually do in the movies. The early morning warmth made him feel like a million bucks, albeit briefly, before his skin started feeling itchy. In no time, the strange sensation intensified. He got up, taking one last glance at the rising sun, then headed back to the condo where Myrna was still sound asleep. He showered, shaved, and fried up a couple of eggs with an English muffin topped with marmalade. For the rest of the day, Sol lounged on the sofa with the blinds partially closed, reading a bit and snacking on pretzels. He was completely unaware of the latest news.

CHAPTER 22

Now early evening, Myrna dished out two plates of spaghetti and meatballs for dinner and poured two glasses of Argentine Pinot noir.

"This looks delicious," said Sol as he took a taste of the wine first. He split one of the meatballs with his fork and gobbled it up, leaving a spot of sauce on the corner of his mouth. "And how was the pool today? I hope they toned down the use of chlorine; it's making my eyes irritated and red."

"Much better. Uh, honey, speaking of red, you got a little spot right here," said Myrna, pointing to her lower lip.

Sol panicked. "Red? What red?"

"Relax, it's just some sauce. Here, let me dab it away for you."

Sol appreciated the gesture, but his nerves were frayed as old shoelaces. "Of course it's just sauce," he said, smiling weakly.

"You won't believe what was on the news last night," said Myrna. "Some fishermen discovered alligators knoshing on bodies at some old abandoned pier in North Miami. Sounds like a horror movie to me."

"Alligators? Bodies? Human bodies?" probed Sol, doing his best to sound surprised. He knew it was just a matter of time before his misdeeds would be exposed.

After dinner, Sol needed to clear his head, and what

better place than his favorite watering hole? Down a couple of beers at the Cheeky Tiki, talk baseball with Manny, and bitch about the rising price of gasoline.

After helping Myrna with the dishes, Sol headed over to the bar and parked next to an all-black Ford LTD with tinted windows. He'd never seen that car before. As he entered, Sol noticed a tall man in a ruffled charcoal gray suit interrogating his friend, Manny, at the bar. Oh no, thought Sol.

"What's going on, Manny?" asked Sol. "Hello, Officer."

"It's Detective," the man replied, with all the levity of a corpse. And what's your name, sir?" The gruff man, mid-forties, slender build with straight black hair slicked back, was a product of his old man, a top detective himself back in Boston for decades.

"My name's Hirsch, Sol Hirsch," he answered in a reserved manner. "What's the story here?" Detective Keller jotted down Sol's name, double-checking the spelling, phone number, and what time he arrived.

Manny butted in. "The police was here earlier today asking questions about the bodies found by some old pier. And get this, Sol, the police says the victims had one thing in common, and that's…"

"Zip it, numb nuts," snapped the detective.

Sol mouthed the word, "bodies?" Manny turned the channel from the Incredible Hulk to the local news. There, playing out on the mounted television was *the* story of the moment. Two people had been discovered, partially devoured by the largest reptiles in the United States of America. And another body had turned up under a beach walkway not too far from the Cheeky Tiki Bar.

"The 'story' as you like to put it, Mr. Hirsch, is we've got dead people turning up as gator bait," informed the detective. "And after speaking with Mr. Bar Owner here, it appears to be a strange coincidence that the victims had stopped off at this very drinking establishment."

"Really?" said Sol. "How do you know?"

"We found coasters with the cutesy Cheeky Tiki logo in their pockets. Probably took 'em as souvenirs."

"That reminds me I need to order more," chimed Manny.

The detective grumbled, then turned to Sol. "You recognize these two people?" asked Keller, holding up pictures of the two victims. Sol recognized the two dopes right away but preferred to play dumb.

"Doesn't ring a bell," said Sol.

"You sure, Sol?" interjected Manny. "Weren't they the two shit-faced Yankee fans who were busting your balls?"

"I think you're confusing Walter and Tommy with these two," answered Sol, wishing Manny would clam up.

"Yeah, you're probably right," said Manny.

The detective eyed Sol, then turned to the bar owner again. "I haven't confirmed the Yankee fan angle, so don't go all megaphone on me, capeesh?"

"Yeah, okay, but still…" countered Manny.

He shushed the bar owner. "Now, being originally from Boston and a dyed-in-the-wool Red Sox fan myself, I can certainly comprehend how obnoxious Yankees fans can be, especially after winning the God-damned World Series two years in a row, but to kill 'em off seems to be a little extreme."

"Yeah, uh, who'd want to kill people just because of who they root for?" replied Sol, his body temperature rising, his face flush.

"I see you're a Mets fan; tough couple of years for you, huh?" said the detective, mellowing a bit.

"Yeah, but hope springs eternal as they say," replied Sol.

The detective continued with the questioning. "You two notice anyone weird or suspicious coming in here lately?"

"Well, it's Miami Beach, so we get our share of oddballs, but for the most part, no," answered Manny. "Most of my clientele are repeat customers, from college age to retirees. I even got priests coming in here," laughed Manny. Sol took a sip of beer and nodded in agreement.

"If you see anyone out of the ordinary, you call me, okay?" The detective handed the two men his business card and walked out.

Manny watched the detective leave, then turned to his friend. "You sure you don't remember those two business types from the city?"

Sol put up a defensive front. "I told you I don't remember."

"Alright, alright," answered Manny, throwing his hands up. He walked over to attend to a group of spring breakers, then shuffled over back to his friend, not looking so chipper. "You okay, Sol?"

The retired deli man sighed before grabbing a handful of pretzels and washing them down with his beer. Manny waved his hand in front of his friend. "Earth to Sol. Hello?"

Sol snapped out of it. He finished up his beer and then hopped down from the barstool. "Gotta go... See you tomorrow." Manny revealed a perplexed expression as he watched his friend leave early, something that rarely occurred.

Sol walked over to his car and got in. He rolled down

the windows and sat for a moment, admitting the lies were piling up. Things were getting out of control. He needed help.

CHAPTER 23

The next day, as per custom, Sol slept in like he'd pulled an all-nighter at college. After a noon-time breakfast of Eggo waffles and coffee, he crept back into bed and read the latest Sports Illustrated. With their bedroom facing east, he had even started to pin up a black sheet to keep the bright morning Florida sunshine from penetrating through the two-inch wood horizontal blinds. It was irritating him more with each passing day.

Myrna returned from shopping and poked her head into the bedroom. As per usual, her husband was sound asleep. She went back to the kitchen and began pacing around the room, not sure if she should call her mother or not. But things were getting desperate. Two visits to the doctor proved that her husband was apparently fine and in good health. And thankfully, he didn't have rabies. She had contemplated ringing her mother in Romania for the last week, but always seemed to talk herself out of it. *He'll be back to normal any day now*, she said to herself. But he wasn't getting better. Each and every day brought the same results: sleeping late, moping around the condo, hitting the pool after 6PM, staying up late, and consuming steaks (medium rare). Whatever it was, there was definitely something askew with her husband, and it was up to her to resolve it once and for all.

Myrna tiptoed into the bedroom, making sure not to wake her husband. She then closed the door and walked over to the kitchen. She picked up the bright yellow phone mounted on the wall, finally making that long-distance phone call to her mother.

It was in the evening Romanian time. Sabina returned from walking Scooby, hanging up her leash by the front door. She sat down, ready to watch television, when the phone rang. She reached over and picked up the receiver. The operator put the call through, indicating it was from the United States. A thunderstorm of static shot from the receiver, then a clear voice spoke up.

"Who calls and interrupts me watching Love Boat!?"

"Hi Ma, it's your daughter, Myrna from Florida. Can you hear me?" She preferred conversing in her mother's native tongue to stay sharp, but Sabina insisted they speak in English so she could practice.

"Yes, I hear you. You hear me?" Sabina replied.

"Yes, clear as a bell," said Myrna.

"I hear you too, clear as bell. Everything okay in Disney World?"

Myrna shook her head. "That's in Orlando; we live in Miami Beach.

"Sorry, my boo boo. Now, why you call my precious flower?"

"I need to ask you something; it's very important."

"Shoot. What is problem?"

"It's Sol. The problem is with my husband," said Myrna. "Ever since we returned from our trip, all he does is sleep in late like he's doing now, and he's been acting all weird."

"Continue, my dear."

He said the day we left, you looked at him oddly. Do

you have any idea what that was about?" There was a long pause. "Hello? Ma, are you still there?"

Sabina remained silent, but finally spoke up. "Your husband, Sol, had look in his eyeballs."

"What?" replied Myrna. "Eyeballs? Something's wrong with his vision?"

"Deep in his eyes. I could see it; pupils black as night," she said.

"Pupils are black," said Myrna, exasperated. "What are you trying to say?"

"Your Sol is now among the living dead!"

"The living dead!?" answered Myrna. "I know he's not as energetic as he used to be, but to say he's dead is a bit overreaching, don't you think?"

"You not understand, sweet daughter. Sol is now a demon of the night!"

The connection momentarily dropped. "I'm sorry, did you say Sol's a demon of the night?" Myrna was practically pulling her hair out. She curled the phone cord around her index finger in a nervous fashion. "So, which one is it, Ma? Is Sol of the living dead or a demon of the night?" Myrna offered up an anxious chuckle.

Sabina cleared her throat and let the words out in dramatic fashion. "He is… a strigoi!"

Myrna was beside herself in frustration. The word didn't register with her. "He's stringy? I can barely hear you now. What did you say?"

"Oh, for Christ's sake, Sol is a vampire!"

On the other end of the phone, Myrna clammed up before bursting into laughter. "A vampire? Come on, Ma, Sol may like his steaks a bit on the juicy side, but a vampire?" She humorously pictured her husband decked out in all black, cape and all. "Are you serious?"

"Serious as heart attack," replied Sabina. "Put mirror over face to see reflection. Go now while the beast is at rest."

"Hold on for a second; I'm putting the phone down." Myrna put the phone on the kitchen table, then reached into her purse and pulled out her round compact mirror. She tiptoed into the bedroom and quietly moved over to her snoring husband and placed the mirror less than a foot away from his face.

Myrna shook her head. "I can't believe I'm doing this."

She positioned herself closer to the edge of the bed, bending down on one knee. Myrna looked at her husband, then glanced over to the mirror. Barely a reflection registered. She gasped. Myrna double-checked the mirror, wiping it with the end of her shirt. She maneuvered the mirror closer.

"Holy crap!" Myrna cupped her mouth to muffle her scream. Sol, sleeping on his side, opened one of his eyes slowly, spotting his kneeling wife.

"Huh?" he mumbled.

"Hi, Honey, just looking for my lost earring. Got it right here!" She raised her arm as proof, not holding anything. "You go back to bed, Dearie; nightly-night." Myrna patted her husband on the head before scuttling back into the kitchen. She picked up the phone, her knees wobbly.

"Hello, Ma?"

"What you see, my child?"

"Child? I'm sixty-two years old."

"You will always be my child. Now, what you see?"

"His reflection…it's like it was barely there. What does that mean? What do I do?" She sat down in the chair, back to twirling the curled phone line with her index finger again.

"If there is reflection, there is still chance he can be saved," said Sabina. "And I know just the person to solve your vampire problem."

"Who's that?" Myrna wondered with desperation in her voice.

"Laszlo," said Sabina. "I will send him on next flight."

"Whoa, whoa, whoa, Ma," countered Myrna, applying the brakes on their discussion. "Laszlo? The guy who thinks he's a vampire?"

"He is smart man. A lawyer. Very crafty too," said Sabina. "Plus, I like his taste in music."

"So, Laszlo can really help my husband?" asked Myrna. "Maybe I should think this through."

"Well, don't think too long," said Sabina. "With every day that passes, the strigoi in him grows stronger!"

"But how can this be?" asked Myrna. "How do you know so much about vampires? Hold on, does that mean there are actual vampires in Romania?"

"Vampires in Romania; who would of thunk," quipped Sabina. "The truth is, my dear, there have been vampires in Dumbraveni for quite long time. Your late father, he…"

"What, what?" barked Myrna. "Don't tell me my father was a vampire. If my father was a vampire, I'm going to need extensive therapy!" She thought for a moment, remembering the day her father had died. "What exactly happened to my father?"

Sabina finally found the courage to explain. "My Andrei, your father, was a brave man. He helped to keep townspeople safe from vampires. As you know, his name in Romanian means courageous, and he was. He protected our community his whole life. I never tell you this, but one late evening, you were still young girl. A strigoi broke into our home. He tried to bite you, turn our only daughter into vampire. But your father fought him, rammed spike straight into his heart. Bam! Pardon language, but your father took shit from no one."

"That might have explained that red stain on my rug," said Myrna.

"Blood stains very difficult to remove." Sabina continued. "It's the reasons we wanted you to go to United States, to be safe. Your father and I, we worried about you night and day. Mostly night when vampires lurk. For whole life he continued to hunt vampires."

Myrna interrupted. "Was my father the only one? Were there others?"

"Yes. There are many good people that fight to keep us all safe. Your cousin, Florin, is strong, dedicated fighter just like your father; his gardening skills not so much. Because of their courage, I am told only one vampire now exists."

"Do you think this vampire is the one that bit Sol?" asked Myrna.

"Yes," said Sabina. "That is why we must act now!"

Myrna paused for a moment, trying to absorb everything. "How did my father really die? It wasn't a heart attack, was it?"

"No," said Sabina. "I remember like it was yesterday. It was late in evening. I was asleep, but heard him as he opened bedroom door, that he had one more job to do. He kissed me on forehead, but never came home." Sabina did her best to hold back tears. "He was murdered in abandoned church where he was priest. Your father, I miss him so." Sabina held back tears.

"I am so sorry, Ma," said Myrna, she herself trying to hold back tears as well.

"It is okay, Daughter," said Sabina. "I call Laszlo and make arrangements. Good night, my peach. Stay strong; I love you."

"Night, Ma. I love you, too."

Myrna, stunned, hung up the phone almost in slow motion. She sat at the table, not moving a muscle, gathering her thoughts. She finally picked up the phone and called her best friend Barbara.

She stood up and walked over to the bedroom and peeked in on her husband. Myrna closed the door, then walked back to the kitchen. She took out the small silver crucifix she wore around her neck on a silver chain, rubbing it between her thumb and forefinger.

"Hi Barb, it's me, Myrna. Kind of a strange request, but may I borrow your crucifix? The big one?"

CHAPTER 24

Sol finally dragged his carcass out of bed. He put on his robe and wandered into the kitchen. Myrna eyed her husband's every move, clutching a fifteen-inch-long pale spruce wood crucifix.

"Hey, honey, did you buy more Product 19?" asked Sol. Myrna jumped, hiding the crucifix behind her back, gripping it tighter.

"What? Oh, yes. It should be in the cupboard," she replied, nervously. "Um, how are you feeling? You look good."

"I remember you saying I looked white as an egg," said Sol. He reached for a cereal bowl from the cabinet next to the refrigerator. He filled the bowl to the brim and poured milk, then sat down and started chomping away.

"You really like your Product 19, don't you, dear?"

"It's good for you," said Sol. "But you know what I could really go for?"

"What's that?"

"A heaping bowl of Count Chocula."

Myrna shrieked. "Count Chocula?" Oh, this is worse than I thought she muttered under her breath.

"Yeah, I know it's not exactly the healthiest, but hey, you only live once, right?" smiled her husband.

"Of course, honey," said Myrna.

The phone rang, startling her. Myrna slipped past

Sol and went into the bedroom to answer the phone on her nightstand. Sabina spoke.

"Laszlo arrive tomorrow night, American Airlines, 7PM Disney time. Stay safe, and watch your neck." Sabina abruptly hung up. Myrna reached for a notepad and jotted the information down.

"Who was that?"

"Uh, Barbara. She wants to go do some shelling at the beach."

"Where else would you go shelling?" said Sol with a smirk.

"My husband, the vampire comic," uttered Myrna.

"What was that?"

"Nothing, dear."

***

Laszlo's flight from Romania arrived the following evening as planned. Myrna was at the airport, alone, standing nervously at the designated arrival location for international flights. She knew this whole vampire thing was impossibly crazy, but something had to be done for her husband.

Myrna stepped to the front of the other people, spotting the angular gentleman right away. Dressed in his familiar black clothes and sunglasses, Laszlo easily stood out from the other passengers, resembling slender singer/guitarist Ric Ocasek from the band, the Cars. He emerged carrying a medium-sized black leather shoulder-strapped suitcase. He eyed Myrna, wearing a knee-length powder blue linen dress.

Laszlo approached her, giving Myrna a friendly hug. He took off his black coat and sunglasses, perspiring already. "This weather strictly for birds, wife of Sol."

"It's the humidity that'll kill you," she answered with

a slight smile.

"In my county, avalanche will kill you," said Laszlo. "It is good to see you again."

***

Sol had already ventured off to the Cheeky Tiki Bar when Myrna and Laszlo arrived at the condo. "Sorry, I didn't make anything for dinner, just leftovers," said Myrna.

She offered Laszlo a choice of Chinese food, pasta, or a frozen pizza. He opted for the former, Kung Po chicken with white rice. After reheating it for a minute, they sat down to discuss the situation. Myrna was a nervous wreck, despite Laszlo's assurance that everything would be okay.

"So, what exactly can you do for my husband, Laszlo?" said Myrna. "I mean, is he really, you know… a vampire?"

Laszlo finished up a forkful of food before speaking. "I will speak to husband Sol when he returns. I need to see what state of vampire-ness he is in."

"Of course," said Myrna, not having a clue what that meant. At this point, all she could do was pray that Laszlo knew what he was doing. She took a sip of her vino y sod and sighed.

Laszlo looked Myrna directly in the eyes. "Has husband Sol killed anyone?"

Myrna spit out her drink, now clearing her throat. "For God's sake, no! Sol would never harm a fly."

"I understand," he said. "But would Sol kill person and drink their blood?" He took a sip of red wine and looked at her. "That is million-dollar question."

CHAPTER 25

Sol got to the Cheeky Tiki in a state of vexation. Hanging out with his bar friend, Manny, was starting to feel like a therapy session as he sat in his customary bar stool.

Manny, a towel draped over the right shoulder of his light blue Cuban guayabera shirt, eyed his friend's lethargic demeanor.

"Sol, the last time I saw you moping around like this was last October when the Yankees clinched the World Series. What gives?"

Sol usually poked fun at his shirt, saying that with all those pockets, it made him look like a dentist. That evening, he wasn't catching a whiff of Sol's usual Big Apple braggadocio. Usually, he'd be firing off on the state of the Mets, Jets, or politics right off the bat, whatever was eating at him the most.

He reached for Sol's private stock of Rheingold's in the refrigerator and popped the top off with the bronze wall-mounted bottle opener shaped like a shark head.

"What's eating you?" asked Manny. "I bet it's all that healthy eating, right?"

Sol finally offered up a half smile. "I think you're right, Manny. Leafy greens will be the death of me."

"Then I know just the remedy," said Manny. "How's a double cheeseburger sound?"

"That, I could use. And load up on the toppings, if you don't mind.

"Coming right up." Manny reached for the remote and put on Dallas on CBS. "That JR, talk about a man with chutzpah."

After Sol finished up his first beer, Manny came over and placed a red oval basket filled with a grilled double cheeseburger, fries, and a side of slaw. For the perfect burger bun, he always added a schmear of mayo on each side, then placed it on the grill for a few minutes. Sol approved.

In better spirits after devouring his dinner, Sol took a healthy swig of beer and swiveled around in his barstool, taking a head count of the sparse clientele.

"Jeez, it's like a morgue in here."

The only other people in the bar were a couple of regular homegrown seasoned Florida coots. Both had matching sun-bleached scraggly hair and tanned wrinkled faces that made them resemble a pair of shar-peis.

Manny reached down and placed a bowl of pretzels on the bar. "You telling me. Whoever this crazy fruitcake is, he is literally killing off my business!"

"Don't worry; the police will catch the perp," replied Sol, noshing on the last of the crinkle-cut French fries.

During a commercial, Sol turned to Manny. "You have to admit, without all those Yankee fans, it's a helluva lot quieter in here."

"You know what's quiet?" said Manny, stoked. "My God-damn cash register, that's what quiet. As long as they're coughing up dough, you can root for any damn team on planet earth!"

"Sorry, Manny, poor choice of words," said Sol.

One of the Florida coots stood up, wobbling a bit, well-oiled, and proclaimed. "I know who's been doin the murderin."

"Really?" said Manny, both arms extended on the bar. "And who exactly would that be?"

"Who?" replied the old coot, a pencil-thin regular, pushing 60.

"The guy!" said Manny, exasperated. "Who's the murderer?"

The old coot, with two visible missing teeth, pointed at the television and proclaimed, "J.R. Ewing. He's roofless."

"Agh," waved Manny, annoyed.

The juke box kicked on with the song, Margaritaville, by Jimmy Buffett. The coot couple began singing loudly and off-key.

"Wasted again in Margaretville. Yeah, baby!"

"Understatement of the year with these two," uttered Sol. He got off his barstool, waved, and said goodnight to Manny. As he walked towards the door, the woman attempted to dance with him. He politely brushed her off and left.

Sol thought if he'd had tapped into the drunk woman's neck, he'd be pulled over for driving under the influence. He got into the '88 and headed home.

***

Sol arrived home near eleven o'clock and quietly placed his car keys on top of the dining room table. As he slinked towards the bedroom, he noticed the television set on, the volume set low, and his favorite recliner appeared to be rocking slowly back and forth. Myrna never sat in 'his' recliner. Sol inched closer. On the screen was the original Dracula, starring the one and only Bela Lugosi.

"What a ham!" blurted out a flamboyant voice, the Eastern European accent oh so familiar.

"Hello?" Sol called out as he inched closer.

A tall figure emerged from the comfy chair. "Sol Hirsch, my American friend, I am glad to see you!" said Laszlo as he wrapped his long, spindly arms around the shorter man.

"What the hell are you doing here?" replied Sol, taken aback.

"Myrna and mother of Myrna ask me to visit. They told me you are having… issues," winked Laszlo, zeroing in closer to Sol's face, inspecting his eyes. "You definitely are having issues."

Sol stepped back, now remembering Sabina's reaction when she looked into his eyes. "Are you here to help me?"

"As much as I can," he replied.

"That's good to know. I hope you don't mind, but I'm ready to hit the sack," said Sol.

"I understand completely," said Laszlo.

"Uh, you need a place to stay tonight?" asked Sol. "We have an extra bedroom."

"Appreciate hospitality, but I stay at Howard Johnson's close to beach. I hear sundaes are to die for."

"That they are," said Sol. "And how exactly are you going to help me?"

"In due time, my friend. After long flight, I must rest," said Laszlo. "Tomorrow, we discuss matter in full detail."

Sol walked Laszlo to the door, then to the elevator. Taking forever, they chatted. "Some weather we are experiencing," said Laszlo, wiping his brow. "Miami Beach is hot as wolf's breath."

Laszlo got into the elevator and added before the doors closed. "Stay strong."

Sol waved, then walked back to the condo and locked

the door. He turned, Myrna was standing right behind him. He nearly jumped.

"Sorry for the late evening surprise," said Myrna.

"So, our friend Laszlo makes house calls from five thousand miles away?" smirked Sol. "In New York, Dr. Melnitz wouldn't come ten blocks to see us. What gives?"

"I'm sorry, Sol. It's just that… I'm really concerned about you."

"And you called him?" Sol caught a glance of what was in Myrna's hand. "Uh, why are you holding an extra-large crucifix? The one on your necklace isn't sufficient enough?"

"It's Barbara's. She must have left it here by accident."

"Barbara now walks around carrying a crucifix the size of a tennis racquet?" posed Sol.

Myrna paused, then asked Sol to sit down for a moment. She held the wooden cross in her lap.

Sol shook his head. "Most Catholics I know prefer to wear the small variety around their necks."

"Well, you know, Barbara; she's really, really Catholic."

"Who called the string bean? Your mother?"

"No, actually, I called her," said Myrna. "After discussing the matter, she, um, recommended Laszlo for your 'problem'."

"Problem? And what exactly is my problem?" asked Sol, retreating into the kitchen, getting a glass of water.

Myrna shook her head, not exactly sure if she should come out and say it. "It's kind of funny in a Ripley's Believe It or Not kind of way," said Myrna. "The thing is… my mom thinks you could… you know, might be…, a creature."

"A creature?" Sol shook his head. "What kind of creature?"

Myrna hemmed and hawed. "Uh, a creature of the night variety."

Sol stared at his wife. "Maybe I should add scotch to my water."

Myrna sighed. "I think I could use one too."

Sol reached for the bottle and two shot glasses. He joined his wife at the table. Sol poured. Myrna took hers and threw it down.

"Since when do you drink scotch?" asked Sol.

She grimaced at the taste. "Since I found out my husband is a strigoi."

"What the hell is a strigoi?"

Myrna poured herself another shot. "In Romanian, it means vampire."

Sol gagged on his drink, coughing until he regained his composure. "A vampire? What the hell makes you think I'm a vampire? Oh, I get it. You musta caught me napping in the bedroom closet hanging upside down."

"Don't be ridiculous," said Myrna, miffed. "Look, you've been doing all these weird things lately. You can't stand the sunlight, you sleep late, you're lethargic... except at night when you seem to have all the energy in the world."

"All I have is some sort of Romanian flu, nothing more, nothing less."

"Look, I know it sounds ridiculous," said Myrna, trying to cover for making such a looney toon statement. "But the day we left my mother's house, she said you weren't looking so hot."

"So?"

"So, she said you had 'the look'"

"The look? And what does the "look" look like exactly?"

"My mother told me about my father, how he protected the town from vampires all his life. One probably murdered him. She also said there may be only one left."

Sol didn't refute what Myrna was saying. He knew he was a hot mess, but there was no way in hell he was going to divulge biting people's necks and imbibing human blood.

"Tomorrow I'll have Laszlo give me a once-over. If he diagnoses me as a vampire, you have full permission to drive a stake straight into my heart, medium rare with onions," said Sol, trying to bring levity to the dire situation. "Maybe I should make sure I'm up to date with my life insurance policy."

Myrna giggled nervously. "Yeah, when you say vampire out loud, it does sound kinda crazy."

Sol showered and got into bed, joining his wife. Both stared at the ceiling, unable to sleep. They slowly turned towards each other. Myrna had concealed the big crucifix under the blanket.

"Are you really going to sleep with that?"

"Is it too much?" she said.

"I promise not to bite your neck." Sol sniffed the air, then peered over to Myrna's night table. "Garlic?" He sighed, now noticing a line of garlic running the length of the headboard. "You're serious about this. Maybe I should sleep in the other bedroom."

"That might be a good idea," said Myrna. As she watched Sol exit the room, she placed the crucifix next to her in plain sight.

Sol went into the other bedroom and laid down. He exhaled and shook his head. "Sol B. Hirsch, loving husband, Mets fan, vampire." He yawned. "Christ, that's not going to look good on my tombstone."

CHAPTER 26

The next evening, before six PM, Sol and Myrna pulled up to the front entrance of the Howard Johnson, only a few blocks from their condo off of A1A. Both assumed their Romanian friend would be clad head to toe in his familiar black.

Sol kept an eye out for Laszlo as Myrna tweaked her makeup. "Oh man, take a look at this," said Sol.

Myrna lifted her head. "What? Oh, man is right."

Laszlo waved emphatically as he recognized the Hirsch mobile as he dubbed it. "So, what you think?"

Sol got out of the car and shook Laszlo's hand. "Miami Beach will never be the same."

The Romanian posed a striking image as he strutted outside the hotel in a vibrant red and orange Hawaiian shirt with printed hibiscus flowers on it, khaki shorts that went past his bony knees, and a pair of aqua blue flip flops. The cherry on top was his black Ray-Ban sunglasses and Gilligan's Island style white hat with the words Miami Beach embroidered in bright orange letters, the whole ensemble exposing his pale limbs.

Sol opened the back passenger door, and Laszlo hopped in. "Hello, Laszlo," said Myrna. "Looking very touristy. And how do you like the hotel?"

"Howard Johnson's is paradise," he exclaimed. "I even had sundae for breakfast!"

"Now all you need is a sunburn and you'll fit right in,"

said Sol.

Myrna added her two cents' worth. "Just remember to use lots of suntan lotion when you go to the pool or beach. You don't want to end up red as a lobster."

"I buy six bottles of Coppertone!"

"That should cover it," said Myrna.

"Where is Donnie and Barbara?" asked Laszlo.

"Barbara is a little under the weather, but Donnie will join us later," said Myrna.

"I miss Donnie jokes!"

Sol turned to his wife and grinned. "You're the one."

Sol drove north on A1A and soon turned into the Rascal House parking lot. They got out and approached the entrance.

"No one leaves Rascal House hungry, that's for sure," crowed Sol as he patted Laszlo on the back.

Most of the early bird crowd were wrapping up their meals, stashing the free bread rolls in napkins. Usually, the line was outside the door to get a table. The later evening hours attracted a younger clientele at the premier Jewish deli.

Sol was casually dressed in a white Lacoste polo shirt, red golf shorts, and Stan Smith Adidas sneakers, while Myrna wore a yellow linen dress (her favorite color) and black leather sandals.

After a short wait, the three were able to get a table near the back of the restaurant. With a day off from teaching, Helene was working back-to-back shifts, now handling the busy dinnertime crowd. After earning a much-needed break, she sauntered over to their table, doing her best to mask her aching feet. Recognizing Sol and Myrna, Helene greeted them with a friendly hello, then handed them the menus.

"How's school going?" asked Myrna, the former teacher now giving Helene tips on how to deal with problem students.

"Much better, thanks to you," said Helene, a relative newcomer to the profession. "Your advice on how to discipline problem children worked like a charm."

"What advice was that?" inquired Sol.

"Actually, I was inspired by the horrible news story about the bodies found at that old pier," said Myrna. "I said if any kids act up, tell them you're going to feed them to the alligators. Sometimes you've got to scare the crap out of them to keep them on their toes."

"So far, so good," said Helene, crossing her fingers.

Before she had a chance to read off the dinner specials, Laszlo stood up and greeted the young woman by taking her hand and kissing it. Helene was taken aback; that was the first ever hand kiss she had ever received.

"I am Laszlo. What is your name, my lovely orange blossom?"

"It's Helene," she replied, taken aback by the gesture. The only time she'd experienced something like that was in a movie. Truth was, she was getting full-fledged irked by every Tom, Ricardo, and Harry hitting on her. And it was usually by old, retired geezers with bad comb-overs.

"Pleased to meet you, Helene," said Laszlo. "Are all American women as beautiful as you?"

"Unfortunately, no," she replied with a wink. "I'll be back in a minute to take your orders." Sol excused himself to use the restroom and trotted over to the waitress.

"I apologize for Laszlo's weirdness. He's from Romania."

"That would explain it," she answered, glancing back. "He does seem awkwardly cute, though. Oh, about the baseball game, I'd love to go."

Sol broke out into an abbreviated Curley Howard stutter step. "Great, great. You'll have the time of your life, trust me."

"I've never seen a spring training baseball game here in Florida," replied Helene. "Just one thing, Sol. You need to know that we're just friends, okay? People might think I'm moving in on your territory, you know what I mean?" kidded Helene.

"Of course. Oh, by the way, Myrna says you're going to make a fine school teacher. And believe me, that means something coming from her."

"I love working with children," she added.

"Speaking of children, I hope you don't mind, but Laszlo will be tagging along."

"He seems like a nice guy," said Helene. "I'm off at 6PM; you can pick me up at the back entrance."

"Perfect," said Sol.

He went back to the table and sat down. He noticed Laszlo observing the elderly population dining at the popular eatery.

"Why people so old here? And what is with blue hair?"

"Lots of people who lived up north move here when they retire," said Myrna.

"And I'll tell you why, Laszlo," said Sol as he began counting off on his fingers. "You got the warm weather, the beach, the ocean, of course, cost of living, and uh…"

Donnie finally appeared, interjecting. "Don't forget Cuban food!" He sat down, greeting everyone, shook Laszlo's hand, then added. "I'll tell you what's the most important thing is."

"What's that?" asked Sol.

"No freaking snow!" They all agreed on that one.

"For me, I prefer seasons," said Laszlo. "Cold weather is invigorating. Warm weather all the time is how you say… flatline. You go to beach on Christmas?"

"We do," smiled Donnie. "There's nothing like building a snowman out of sand."

Helene returned to their table a few minutes later with her trusty notepad. "Is everyone ready to order? Oh, hi Donnie. No Barbara tonight?"

"She's got a cold, so I'm flying solo tonight."

Myrna opted for the grilled tuna, green beans, and house salad with vinaigrette dressing. Sol, feeling the itch to try something on the healthy side, stunned his wife by ordering the same thing.

"Good for you, Honey," applauded Myrna. Helene too.

"It's about time I take my health seriously," he answered. "Last night's double cheeseburger at the Cheeky Tiki didn't sit too well with me."

Donnie ordered next. "I'll have the meatloaf with mashed potatoes and green beans."

The waitress then turned to Laszlo. "And you, sir?" Laszlo was in a dreamlike state.

"My apologies," said Laszlo. "I shall eat big juicy steak, medium rare, with lots of French fries."

"And to drink?"

"Large Coca Cola, no ice," he gleaned, learning that trick from Sol.

Helene checked off her notepad and walked back into the kitchen.

"Hey Vicki," she called out to her co-worker. "You mind handling my other table?"

"Why, what's wrong?" replied the cagey waitress, short and feisty with blond graying hair. "Is that old guy hitting on you again?"

"No, no," said Helene. "Sol's harmless and actually kind of funny. His wife used to be a school teacher, so we've become friends."

"Well, ain't that just peachy," she said sarcastically. "So, what's the problem?"

"My feet are killing me; next time I'm wearing sneakers!" said Helene. "Oh, check out the tall, lanky guy in the Hawaiian shirt at their table. He's from Romania. A bit odd, but he seems sweet. Let me know what you think."

Vicky snarled. "If he tries anything weird with me, I'll karate chop his ass."

Soon after, Vicki came over with their orders. Laszlo asked where Helene was. She explained her co-worker was taking a much-needed break after working double shifts.

"So, what do you think of Miami Beach?" asked Myrna.

"Beach and ocean are beautiful," said Laszlo, perspiring despite the air conditioning. "Perhaps I learn to scuba dive!"

Dinner arrived; soon everyone was digging in. After minutes of blissful silence, Donnie spoke up. "So, how's the vampire business going, Laszlo?" Myrna and Sol eyed each other, remaining silent. "Was it something I said?"

Laszlo smiled. "Smashing, but October is when I make killing. I am all about Halloween!"

"I bet you are," said Donnie. "You enjoy watching

monster movies? I know I did when I was a kid. The Blob, that giant ant movie, The Thing, oh, and Jaws! Did you see Jaws? Now that was a film with bite." Sol and Myrna groaned in unison, even Laszlo.

"I see Jaws," answered Laszlo. "Maybe I not scuba dive."

"My strategy when I go swimming is always to make sure there's someone else farther out than you, that way they'll be eaten first," chimed Donnie.

"I take your advice, Donnie," said Laszlo, thanking him.

After everyone finished up. The other waitress approached, asking if anyone wanted dessert. Sol and Myrna decided to indulge a little and share a slice of chocolate cake. Donnie ordered a hot fudge sundae. Myrna suggested to Laszlo a slice of their signature key lime pie, a South Florida staple. Moments later, the waitress presented the slab of key lime pie, topped off with a dollop of whipped cream, planted in the middle, and a lime twist on top.

"That'll keep you busy for a while," joked Sol, taking turns with Myrna with their own dessert.

To everyone's surprise, Laszlo dug right in and practically inhaled the enormous slice of pie. "Best dessert I ever had," he said, brimming with satisfaction.

"How could you tell?" observed Donnie.

While they waited for the check, Laszlo noticed a middle-aged man, brutish, in a misfitting navy blue blazer with white slacks, cornering Helene. She was plainly flustered as the man moved in closer, sweet-talking her to no end. A little too close for Laszlo's liking.

"Excuse me," said Laszlo. "I need to use restroom."

He walked over and confronted the man, a foot shorter, his black hair slicked back. "Everything okay, Helene?" She eyed Laszlo, looking visibly upset.

"Beat it, Slim Jim," said the man, with all the appeal of a used car salesman. "As I was saying, doll face, I got a house with a jacuzzi right on the beach."

"Jacuzzi. Oh, that sounds like fun," said Laszlo, "When do we go?"

The man snarled. "Not you, idiot."

"Let's step outside to discuss plans in detail," said Laszlo. "Helene, I will return momentarily."

"Don't you hurt him," growled Helene.

"I promise," smirked Laszlo as he opened the door.

The troglodyte snarled. "She meant me, pencil dick."

The two stepped out of the back entrance. The shorter man confronted Laszlo. "No one interrupts me when I'm making my move, comprende?"

Whack!

In an instant, Laszlo gave the man a thunderous roundhouse kick to the head, knocking him senseless. While on the ground, Laszlo grabbed him by the collar and got in his face. "When you wake up, you will apologize to waitress, capeesh?" The man moaned, not sure where he was. Laszlo added a polite slap on his cheek before strolling back in. He eyed Helene.

She rushed over. "Are you okay? Did he hurt you?"

"I am fine," replied Laszlo as he walked back to the table. "Expect apology from little twirp."

The waitress walked over and was about to place the check in front of Sol when Laszlo intercepted it. "It is my treat."

After some gracious bantering back and forth, Sol conceded. "Okay, okay, you win, Laszlo, but leave a nice tip. That's how you get the good tables and service."

"Thank you, Laszlo," said Myrna. Donnie too. The four got up and headed out. Laszlo, catching the box of toothpicks at the register, grabbed one for the road.

CHAPTER 27

They returned to the condo full and contented. After changing into their bathing suits, Sol, Donnie, and Laszlo ambled downstairs and hung out by the pool with a few adult beverages placed in a small red cooler filled with ice. After swimming around for a while, the three set up shop along the deep end, dangling their feet in the refreshing 86-degree water.

"So, Lazlo, what are your impressions of Miami Beach, or did I miss that discussion at the restaurant?" asked Donnie, who, after four years of residing in the Sunshine State, already considered himself a Florida native.

"It is beautiful, but constant heat and sunshine is not my glass of wine," replied Laszlo, waving his hat. "I prefer forests and mountains; they are good for the soul."

"Romania is beautiful, that's for sure, Laszlo, but I gotta tell you, I don't miss the snow for nothing," said Sol. "I wish I had moved down here years ago."

Donnie took a swig of beer and then needled his good friend. "I told you you'd like it here," said Donnie. "Remember that winter when the heat went out all over our building for days and we froze our butts off? After that, Barbara and I called it quits and said we're migrating south with the birds."

"Life is a hell of a lot easier here, that's for sure," said Sol, "No winter clothes to wear, no trudging through snow at five in the morning to get to work. Now, when it comes to food, I do miss the city a whole bunch. All I can say is thank God for Rascal House."

Sol looked at Donnie and the new acquaintance from Romania with a smile. "Salud." The three men clinked bottles.

Donnie peeked at his watch and shrieked. "Holy smokes!" He jumped up and quickly dried off his feet.

"What's up?" asked Sol.

"Sorry, guys, I forgot there's a two-part 'Quincy' episode tonight. I'll see you both around."

"What's a 'Quincy'?" asked Laszlo.

"It's a television show starring Jack Klugman," replied Donnie as he gathered up his beach towel and sandals.

"Jack Klugman?" asked Laszlo. "He is 'Odd Couple' actor, no?"

"That's right," replied Donnie. "He even wore a ratty Mets hat like Sol here."

"Ha, ha," uttered Sol. He took a quick gulp of his beer, then set it down, now overflowing with suds.

"Hey, just like beginning of Odd Couple show!" laughed Laszlo as he broke into the familiar theme music.

"All right, all right, that's enough," barked Sol.

Laszlo observed Donnie getting on the elevator and the doors closing. After a few minutes of quiet, he turned serious and leaned closer to Sol.

"Now that we are alone, Sol Hirsch, we discuss solving your problem."

Sol swished his feet in the water, then slumped his shoulders and turned to his friend. "I've changed, Laszlo, and not for the better. I got a thirst for something and it ain't booze."

Laszlo tipped up his hat. "Strange thing happened to

you in Dumbraveni."

"Yeah, very strange." Sol took a sip of beer. "That night at the lake. Whatever happened to me is why I might be a, you know."

Laszlo contemplated Sol's recollection of events. "I think I know what problem is, Mr. Sol Hirsch. And if you have problem, we solve problem." He slung his arm around Sol. "You and me, together."

"So, what do we do?" asked Sol.

Laszlo then stood up before placing his hat on the round glass table. "I must think." He stepped over to the pool's edge and dove into the water, descending to the bottom of the deep end.

Sol peered down into the water, illuminated by the bright lights located at each end of the pool. Laszlo released a string of bubbles. He lay there on the pool floor with his eyes closed, looking like he was meditating – or drowning. Sol wondered if the guy could even swim. Suddenly, he shot up from the bottom, emerging right next to Sol's feet. The retiree almost rolled over on his back.

Lazlo's long, wet black hair trailed past his narrow shoulders. "This is what we will do. I have brought special potion from my country."

"Will it cure my, you know, urge?"

"It will pause your craving until we find root cause," reassured Laszlo. "There lies the bigger question."

Sol took a sip of beer. "I'm guessing you've done this sort of thing before back in your country?"

"Of course," he replied. "I have cured many people in my town, one way or another," he said slyly. "Did I mention I worked with Myrna's father?"

"Really? Doing what?"

"Let's just leave it at that," said Laszlo in a cryptic tone.

"You're the boss," said Sol. "So, when do we start?"

"We begin tonight!" exclaimed Laszlo, thrusting out his elongated index finger. "First, you must take on full stomach or it may lead to painful gas."

Sol sighed. "If gas is the only side effect, I can live with it. Hell, I eat rice and beans three times a week, so gas ain't a problem." Sol paused. "By the way, what exactly am I taking?"

"It is old family recipe, top secret. You must trust me." Sol nodded, although he was still felt skeptical. The two returned to Sol's condo. Myrna was downstairs watching television with Donnie and Barbara at their condo.

Laszlo walked into the living room and picked up a small black bag the size of a shaving kit. "Drink water first, then you will take medicine."

Sol went into the kitchen and filled up a glass with tap water, and drank it down. "Now what?"

"Fill up glass halfway." Laszlo selected a small blue glass bottle resembling something you would find at an antique shop. He walked over and removed the cork. He eyed Sol before pouring the contents in. It fizzed like Alka Seltzer tablets, the water now an effervescent turquoise. Sol peered at the glass, then sniffed around the edge before glancing back at Laszlo.

"This isn't gonna kill me, I hope?" asked Sol.

"Can't be worse than decades of pastrami sandwiches," snickered Laszlo. "Now, don't be baby and drink up."

Sol followed instructions and gulped it all down. It made his face pucker like he had sucked on a lemon.

"Interesting flavor, citrusy." He stood there for a moment, wondering what to expect next, when he started feeling lightheaded. Laszlo suggested he rest in his cozy recliner and let the mysterious tonic do its work.

"That's some kick, Laszlo." Minutes later, Sol was out like a light.

CHAPTER 28

A late evening flight from Romania arrived at Miami International Airport under clear skies. A bearded man, well-groomed in a long-sleeve black dress shirt, indigo blue jeans, and black leather Frye buckle harness boots, made his way off the plane. He picked up his suitcase from the luggage reclaim area and then stepped outside. A line of taxis jostled for position as travelers emerged from the terminal.

"Taxi, sir?" asked Ignacio Lopez, medium build, late-twenties, of Cuban descent with coarse black hair. His vibrant red guayabera shirt caught the man's attention.

He introduced himself like he had done a thousand times before with each customer. "Ignacio Lopez, Cab driver extraordinaire. But you can call me Nacho."

"Nice shirt," said the stranger.

"Gracias. It's perfect for Miami!" he grinned. "Where you need to go?"

"Howard Johnson's Hotel in Miami Beach."

"I know the place," said Nacho.

The taxi driver was about to pick up the man's suitcase when the man snatched it in front of him. Nacho was good at reading body language. Even with the shirt complement, there was something in the man's demeanor that struck him as off-putting. He pulled his hands away from the suitcase.

The man opened the door to the all-yellow Ford Galaxie 500 and got into the back seat, placing the suitcase next to him. The cabbie got in, clicked the meter, and sped away from the curb.

"First time to Miami, sir?" Nacho asked, always jovial and polite with his customers.

The stranger peered out the window, hoping for minimal interaction as possible; he was not interested in conversation, although that didn't stop the cabbie from trying.

Nacho drove east along MacArthur Causeway, explaining to the man that the stretch of road was named after General Douglas MacArthur back in the 1940s. Sensing it was a dead-end trying to converse with him, Nacho began singing a Celia Cruz tune at a low-key volume to pass the time.

"Please, no singing," said the man.

Nacho postured, gritting his teeth, irked. *Everyone loves my singing,* he thought. "Bien."

The cabbie had dealt with his fair share of unfriendly customers before, but with his effervescent personality, Nacho usually found a way to connect with even the surliest of individuals. In this case, he simply drove on, admiring the colorful city lights as he weaved in and out of traffic. He took a quick glance into the rearview mirror. He shook his head, not sure what he was seeing, or not seeing. Nacho offered up a meager nod to the gentleman. A shot of cold ran up his spine that made him quiver. The car swerved momentarily, almost approaching the other lane. Nacho righted the Ford and forged straight ahead.

"Everything alright, Nacho?" the stranger asked in a patronizing voice.

"Everything es bueno, sir," said Nacho, with a weak smile, not sounding too convincing.

The cabbie sped up to make it through the traffic light

turning yellow, then red. "Please, drive safely," said the man. "I would like to get to my destination in one piece."

Nacho didn't respond, only offering up a meager, 'si'. All the cabbie wanted to do now was drop off his fare at the hotel, then hit the nearest bar, pronto.

A few minutes later, Nacho recognized the familiar blue and orange Howard Johnson's sign up ahead and pulled up to the entrance, pressing on the brakes abruptly.

"Uh, here we are, sir," said Nacho.

The man inched up from the backseat of the car. "How much do I owe you?"

"It's free. Always a free ride with Nacho!"

"That is not a very good business model." The stranger handed the cabbie a twenty-dollar bill. "You didn't see me."

"No, senior," said Nacho, "I forget you already."

As soon as he saw the stranger exit and close the door, Nacho floored the gas pedal, the tires screeching as he rocketed out of the parking lot. He made a quick U-turn, and more screeching tires ensued, as he barreled south on Collins Avenue. His next destination would be with multiple cold beers at the Cheeky Tiki Bar.

CHAPTER 29

Myrna entered the condo having spent the evening at Barbara's. She placed her keys on the table and saw Laszlo noshing on an apple.

"Is everything okay with Sol? She asked.

"He is asleep like baby," said Laszlo. "More importantly, I have good idea what happened to your husband."

She peeked over to her husband. "That night at the lake?"

"Precisely," said Laszlo. "He was bit by bat."

"Donnie wasn't sure, but said it was black," said Myrna, "Was it a bat?"

"Correct."

"What can we do now?" said Myrna. "I mean, am I going to open the closet doors one day and find my husband sleeping upside down like… you know?"

"To truly solve issue, I need to find perpetrator. Meanwhile, I am little parched from hot, humid weather. "Would you join me for cold beer?"

"No thank you. I'm tired and ready to go to sleep," said Myrna.

"You recommend place for me?" asked Laszlo, itching to check out the nightlife of Miami Beach.

"My husband always goes to this place called the Cheeky Tiki Bar. It's right on the intercoastal, less than a mile from our condo. He says they've got good cheeseburgers and a good selection of booze.

"I am sold," he said. "Point me in direction."

"Let me find the address for you." Myrna reached for the Yellow Pages, almost as thick and heavy as the annual Sears catalog from a drawer in the kitchen. She looked up the address and wrote it down on a piece of note paper.

"Here you go," she said. "You can actually walk to it from here, about eight blocks south on the right. If you get lost, ask someone for help."

"I will do best not to get lost," smiled Laszlo. Thank you, Myrna. I will see you tomorrow."

***

With Sol out like a light and Myrna ready to go to sleep, Laszlo ventured out of the condo building and soon strolled along the bustling sidewalk along Collins Avenue. He marveled at all the towering condo buildings and hotels, bright lights everywhere. The night was busy with pedestrians and tourists driving and walking along the popular stretch of road. After walking for several blocks, he spotted a police officer exiting a 7-11 and approaching his car. Laszlo politely interrupted him as he was about to get in.

"Hi Copper. I am Laszlo from Romania. Where is Cheeky Tiki Bar?"

The officer, cherry slushy in hand, offered succinct directions to the lanky man.

"You go down two blocks. At the traffic light, make a right at the gas station, then walk straight ahead. You can't miss it." Laszlo thanked the officer and completed his trek.

Perspiring, he soon entered the drinking establishment, observing only a few people present. The bartender was conversing with a dark-haired gentleman at the bar, wearing a crimson red short-sleeved shirt. He appeared flustered as he chugged his beer from a glass mug. Laszlo moseyed up to the bar and sat down next to him. The man glanced over, nodding, then resumed drinking.

Manny finished up pouring a draft and then addressed Laszlo. "What'll it be, Mack?"

"That is good guess, but my name is Laszlo," he replied, correcting him. "And what is your name?"

"It's Manny, and I own the joint," he said, not exactly in a sociable mood. "So, what's your poison, Laszlo?"

"No poison, just ice-cold lager, please."

Manny shook his head. It had been a weird week at the Cheeky Tiki, and tonight was no exception. He handed the lanky man a bottle of Budweiser.

"Ah, the King of Beers," said Laszlo, proudly as he admired the bottle before taking a mouthful. "That hit the spot." He looked over and greeted the man sitting beside him. "I am Laszlo."

"Nacho," he replied with a gloomy expression.

"You seem vexed, Nacho."

"I am beyond vexed," replied Nacho, exasperated.

"And why is this?" asked Laszlo.

"Oh, you're gonna love this," said Manny, popping open one of Sol's Rheingolds from the refrigerator for himself. "Tell Mr. Laszlo here about what you saw tonight."

"Don't bust my bolas, Manny," said Nacho.

"What did you see?" asked Laszlo, "I promise not to bust bolas. What is bolas?" He observed nacho's irked state. "Nevermond."

Before the cabbie began, he asked Manny for another beer. Manny took his mug and refilled it, then handed it back to him. Nacho took a sip, giving himself a foamy mustache, and turned his head towards Laszlo.

"It's what I didn't see," he said. "Tonight, I picked up this guy from the airport. I was being friendly, but he didn't wanna talk, so I started singing. He didn't like my singing. Everybody likes my singing."

"You are gay?" asked Laszlo. "To each his own in my book."

"Am I gay? What the hell does that mean?" bellowed Nacho. "I'm a cab driver. I pick up people—customers, you idiota!"

"Thank you for correcting my mistake so bluntly," replied Laszlo.

Manny interjected. "Hey, Laszlo, it's best if you drink your beer and let Nacho finish the story." Laszlo nodded.

"So, I pick up this *customer* at the airport, and as I'm driving on the highway, I look in the rearview mirror. Only he isn't there."

"Person hides from you?" asked Laszlo, posing in a crouching stance. "Like this?"

"No, man," said Nacho. "I mean, I turn around and he's there, but when I look in the mirror, he's not there."

Laszlo put on his thinking cap. "Are you saying person made no reflection in mirror?"

"That's some strange shit, Nacho," said Manny, walking to the other end of the bar to attend to his thirsty clientele.

Laszlo leaned closer to the cabbie, who was already halfway done with his latest refill. "This person, what did he look like? And please, I need all details." The cabbie wasn't sure if Laszlo was being flippant with him or not.

"The guy had a beard, solid build, and he wore these real nice black cowboy boots with circular buckles." The cabbie noticed Laszlo's startled facial expression and got concerned. "What, what! You know him?"

"Possibly. Where you drop him off?"

"At the Howard Johnson's, about a mile north on A1A."

Laszlo pondered the situation, getting an queasy feeling in his gut. If his theory was correct, he'd have to play it incognito at the hotel. Laszlo finished up his beer, paid up, then handed Nacho a ten-dollar bill before leaving.

"Thank you, Nacho. You may have saved my friend's life!" The cabbie turned around on the barstool and watched him leave, then turned back to the bar owner, holding up the ten-dollar bill.

"Fill'er up, Manny."

CHAPTER 30

After settling in his hotel room, the stranger decided to take a walk along the cool sand by the waters' edge, the encroaching waves caressing the shore line in a slow, rhythmic pattern.

The man glanced up at the yellow-orange moon hanging low on the horizon, the reflective light leaving a trail on the Atlantic Ocean. He passed a drunk couple laughing as the woman kicked up water in the shallows. The man, beefy and brawny at six-foot-three with wide shoulders and wavy, black hair, clipped his shoulder, knocking the bearded man to the ground.

"You should be more careful, man," said the guy, strutting along the shorline with Neanderthal grace.

"You didn't need to do that, Joey," said his girlfriend, Maria, witnessing the altercation. "I'm sorry, sometimes my boxer boyfriend thinks he's sparring even on his off days."

"I must agree with your lady friend here," said the stranger. "You should be more careful." The woman rushed over and helped him up. He brushed off the sand from his clothes, thanking the woman. She suddenly noticed the man's irritated eyes in the moonlight.

"What, you got the hots for this joker?" said Joey, a jealous, hot-tempered meathead most of the time.

"Of course not, but that was unnecessary," said Maria, apologizing once again to the man. "He's just enjoying the beach like us."

"Yes, Joey. I'm enjoying the beach just like you," said the stranger. "Perhaps you should strive on improving your social skills; they're quite barbaric."

Joey gritted his teeth, seething. "What did you say?" He looked over to his girlfriend. "Maria, why don't you go ahead, while I sort things out with Mr. Prim and Proper here?"

"If you do anything stupid, I'm leaving you for good," said Maria, storming off. "I mean it this time."

Joey waved her off, then stepped up to the stranger. "Sorry, guy, I just like to hit people; it's my profession."

The stranger leaned in and stared at the oafish man. "I have a profession, too, Joey. I enjoy killing people and drinking their blood."

The boxer stammered. "You what?"

The bearded man seized Joey by the neck and hoisted him up, his canines visible. He peered towards the ocean, sauntered over, and tossed him in. Maria turned as she heard the splash. Stunned, and now soaked and extremely pissed off, the boxer emerged from the water with his fists up in a fighting position.

"Come on, you piece of shit," growled Joey as he lunged at the stranger, ready to throw some haymakers. The stranger stepped back, then countered by firing off a direct right cross that caught Joey square on the jaw, knocking him to the sand.

"I find your boxing skills quite amateurish, Joey. Perhaps you should go to the gym and practice more before you get hurt."

"Why, you son of a bitch," roared the boxer. "I'll punch your fucking lights out."

The bearded man countered with a true boxing insult.

"I believe in your profession you are known as a tomato can." The boxer charged at the man again. This time, the stranger grabbed the boxer's right fist and proceeded to crush the bones, squeezing it with vice-grip intensity.

"What's the magic word, Joey?"

"Fuck you," he bellowed, his eyes watering from the pain.

"I am so sorry, that is the wrong answer," said the man, "Let's try that again, shall we?" He proceeded to break his other hand.

Maria turned back, hearing her boyfriend scream in pain, then she saw that the stranger appeared to be giving her boyfriend a hickey. More screams ensued. She started running as the stranger dropped Joey's lifeless body to the sand, wiping his mouth with the back of his wrist.

He lifted his head, eyeing the terrified woman. He started after her and, in seconds, was upon her.

"Don't worry; I will not hurt you, but I'm afraid you will be in the market for a new boyfriend." He smiled, then kissed her hand, leaving a drop of blood on her knuckle.

"My apologies," said the stranger as he wiped away the spot. She staggered backwards before running away.

The man headed back towards Joey's lifeless body. Eyeing a a dorsal fin gliding along the shallow water, he lifted up the corpse like a bag of mulch, walked over to the waters' edge, and heaved the body into the ocean. Catching the scent of human blood, a bull sharks swooped in and enjoyed making a midnight snack out of the dead boxer's body.

CHAPTER 31

The next day, late afternoon, Sol and Laszlo hung out in the shade by the pool alone. After snacking on potato chips and sodas, Laszlo turned to the retiree.

"Do you feel better after taking potion?"

"Tell you the truth, Laszlo, it completely knocked me on my ass," said Sol. "What was it supposed to do, suppress the urge to, you know?" Sol made a comical vampire pose, turning his hands into claws and opening his mouth wide.

"Yes," winked Laszlo. "We suppress your cravings until situation is resolved."

Sol took a sip of soda and put the can on the round, glass table. "By the way, as a thank you for your help, you're cordially invited to attend the Mets/Yankees baseball game tonight. Myrna, myself, and Helene are going."

"Did you say, Helene?"

"Yes, Helene," said Sol. "I think she likes you, so you have to promise to be a perfect gentleman with her."

Laszlo found it hard to curb his enthusiasm. "To see baseball game with beautiful woman and friends. I am touched." Laszlo gave Sol a big hug.

"The game starts at 7:00PM, so we can stop by and pick you up at the hotel at 6:00," said Sol, glancing at his watch. "We should leave soon, though. I'll drop you off at your hotel."

"You must make it before six PM," insisted Laszlo.

They clinked soda cans. "It will be forgettable night."

"You mean unforgettable," corrected Sol.

"Yes, my mistake," said Laszlo. "My very first baseball game!" He started singing. "Take me out to ball game. Take me out with crowd. Buy me some things that I don't know…" Sol interrupted.

"Let's save it for the game."

The two got up and left. Sol dropped off Laszlo at the entrance of the hotel. He arrived back at the condo, showered, changed, and then put on his number 41 Tom Seaver jersey. He came out from the bedroom and saw Myrna in the kitchen, already set in her black Yankees t-shirt and khaki skort.

Sol, under his breath, grimaced as they left the condo. "Ugh, my wife, the Yankee fan."

CHAPTER 32

Helene finished up her shift and gathered up her belongings. She managed to sneak a couple bread rolls for Sol, wrapping them up in a napkin and tucking them in her purse. She turned to her co-workers.

"I can't believe I'm going to watch the New York Yankees play tonight!"

"And with Sol and his wife," said her co-worker, Nicole, a twenty-something waitress like Helene. "It'll be like going with your parents."

Another waitress, Andrea, chimed in. "Yeah, you're their adopted daughter!"

"Oh, stop it, you two," said Helene with a grin. "They're a sweet couple, not to mention excellent tippers. And don't forget their Romanian friend, Laszlo. It should be fun."

Helene grabbed her purse, pulling out her New York Yankee hat, and rushed through the back employee entrance where the Hirschs were waiting.

The retiree beamed at his prized Delta 88, sparkling clean after a fresh wash and wax from earlier in the day. He scurried over to open the passenger rear door like a gentleman, and Helene got in.

"Right on time," he called out.

"Hi, Myrna," said Helene. "Excited for the game tonight?"

"Any time I can watch Bronx Bombers clobber the Mets

is a good day," she said.

"Where's Laszlo?" asked Helene.

"We're going to pick him up at the hotel, then head on over to the stadium," said Sol. "Hopefully, we won't hit traffic driving up Federal Highway."

Sol closed the door and then shuffled around the front of the car. He spotted some dead mosquitoes on the headlights and quickly took out a handkerchief and wiped them off lickety-split before sliding back in the driver's side.

Noticing her husband's irritation, Myrna reminded her husband that friends of theirs on the west coast of Florida in Naples dealt with swarms of lovebugs two to three times a year that virtually plastered the whole front end of their car and a complete pain in the rear to remove.

"Maybe a few mosquitoes aren't so bad after all." He started the car, revving it a little extra, loving that V-8 growl. "Buckle up, everyone; it's my rule." They pulled out of the parking lot and headed north.

***

At Rascal House, Nicole was watching a breaking news story in the employee lounge. She called over her co-worker, Andrea, and pointed to the television.

"Oh, my God, check this out, quick, quick!" said Nicole, waving her over.

Images showed a tow truck hauling out a black sports car from the end of an old cement pier. A reporter standing in front of the Miami Beach Police Station spoke as the footage rolled.

"Today, the body of a man was discovered inside a submerged car at the end of an old Pier near Oleta State Park in North Miami, the same location where two men were mauled to death by alligators. According to reports, the victim, identified as twenty-seven-year-old Robbie Kroger of Hallandale Beach, was still buckled in the driver's seat." The waitresses gasped in unison as the story unfolded.

"That's Helene's ex-boyfriend, how horrible," gasped Andrea, one of her co-workers. "I bet she doesn't even know about it yet!"

Another reporter, part of the local NBC News team, stood ready as they televised the live feed of a press conference held inside the Miami Beach Police Station. A horde of reporters peppered Police Detective Rex Keller, who was working feverishly on the case, with questions. Despite his even-keeled tone, the detective appeared to be losing patience.

A twenty-year seasoned investigative female reporter from the local CBS affiliate, early 60s with black hair parted in the middle, pressed Keller.

"Is this discovery in any way related to the previous bodies found at the abandoned pier? Or the body of the man found under the boardwalk?"

"At the moment, we are not one-hundred percent certain," said Detective Keller. "What we do know is the victim was…"

The NBC reporter interrupted. "With the driver buckled in his seat, could this have been staged to look like a suicide?"

"That is, of course, a possibility," said Keller, "but if you let me finish, everything right now is preliminary. We are working with the North Miami Beach police department since these deaths could be related." The detective was agitated by yet another reporter who'd probably watched way too many

Sunday Night Mystery Movie episodes.

An eager reporter from the Independent News Service, late forties, dressed in a wrinkled blue striped seersucker suit, finally got his chance to question the detective.

"Were any particular wounds found on the neck of the young man, as with the previous two victims, and the other person found under the beach walkway? And if so, do we have a serial killer on our hands who thinks he's a vampire?"

"Bite wounds?" scoffed the detective, rhetorically. "I've never mentioned anything about bite marks on the neck. Who told you that!?"

"I have my sources," the reporter replied.

The detective sighed, recognizing who had asked the question. He offered a blunt response. "Number one: I am not going to engage in any type of wacko speculations, Mr. INS Reporter, and two, your sources are cuckoo bananas. Until I get the full coroner's report for each victim, I will not disclose if foul play was involved. At this point, that would be irresponsible on my part."

Nicole went over and turned off the TV. "I know they broke up and all, but she would never want anything bad to happen to him."

"What a horrible thing," said Andrea.

Delores, the restaurant's hostess and supervisor, noticed the congregation of waitresses by the television set. She stepped away from the kitchen and walked over.

"What's going on?"

"It looks like Helene's ex-boyfriend was killed last night," said Nicole. "She'll probably need some time off."

"For what?" Delores replied. "She already broke up with the guy; I'm sure she'll be fine."

"Thank you, Ms. Sensitive," growled Nicole, following up under her breath. "Tonta."

The host was walking away when she called out. "One, I have bat-like hearing, and two, I do understand Spanish."

"Muy bien," clapped Nicole.

***

To his amazement, Sol hit just about every green light as he eyed the Howard Johnson's Hotel sign. He glanced in both the rearview and passenger side mirrors, then turned into the right lane before pulling into the parking lot. He steered over to the front of the hotel entrance. Laszlo exited the glass doorway with a beaming smile, sporting a Yankees jersey and hat that he had purchased from a nearby sporting goods store.

"Hello, everyone," said Laszlo as he got into the back seat with Helene. "Who is ready for baseball!?"

"Our seats are so close to the field we'll be able to hear the players talk!" said Sol.

"Maybe I get Reggie Jackson's autograph!" said Laszlo, excited as a child. He turned to Helene. "Are you excited to see baseball game tonight?"

"Oh yeah, super excited," she replied, both sporting their Yankee hats proudly. "I'm originally from New Jersey; my whole family are Yankee fans." The waitress proceeded to rattle off some of the top players, names like Reggie Jackson, Jim 'Catfish' Hunter, Greg Nettles, Willie Randolph, and Goose Gossage.

Sol sighed. "Oh, I didn't know that." His insides stewed. Even a beautiful woman like Helene was a big-time Yankee fan. There was no escape from them. Ugh.

"We get hotdog and beer like Americans, yes?" asked Laszlo.

"Of course," said Myrna, "With mustard and relish!"

"I'll second that," said Sol, glancing over to his wife.

"I prefer ketchup on my hotdog," said Helene.

"Ketchup on a hotdog? Who the hell puts ketchup on a hotdog?" said Sol, horrified.

"Like everyone in my family," said Helene.

"That's New Jersey for you," he joked.

"To each his own, right, hubby?" reminding her husband that people have different tastes, especially from the Garden State.

Seeing that Helene was outnumbered when it came to hotdog toppings, Laszlo smiled. "I will order ketchup on hotdog, just for you."

Sol looked back. "What a gentleman."

***

The bearded stranger approached the front desk and asked the employee a question. "Excuse me, sir, would you happen to know where that fanatical sports fan was going?"

"Oh, you mean, Mr. Laszlo," he politely replied. "He's from Romania; the land of vampires!" The young man, a surfer type with long, sandy-blond hair, made a patented Bela Lugosi pose, arms raised, exposed teeth. "Isn't that cool?"

"Quite cool," replied the stranger. "Do you know where he was going? Some sporting event, I take it?"

"He and some friends are going to the Yankee/Mets game tonight up in Ft. Lauderdale. Oh, my gosh, he couldn't stop talking about it!"

"Is Ft. Lauderdale far from here?"

"About forty minutes, more or less," the employee replied. "If you're planning to go, I can call you a cab for you."

"That would be splendid," said the stranger.

The stranger waited at the entrance, people-watching in the meantime. Fifteen minutes later, a yellow Ford Galaxie 500 pulled up. Nacho parked the car and honked. The cabbie was preoccupied eating a Mars Bar bar when he heard the customer get in and closed the door. He looked into the rearview mirror but didn't see anyone. He slowly turned around…

"Hello, Nacho, long time no see," said the stranger with a wink.

Nacho froze before uttering under his breath. "The man who wasn't there."

"Relax, my friend," said the stranger, "Here's a pair of twenty-dollar bills to keep your mouth shut, again."

Nacho used the tips of his thumb and index finger and slid his fingers to the other side of his mouth. "I see nothing."

CHAPTER 33

They arrived at Ft. Lauderdale Stadium, spring training home of the New York Yankees, with time to spare. Sol pulled up to a bevy of baseball fans tailgating New York City style, ninety-nine percent sporting New York Yankee paraphernalia.

As they stepped out of the car, Sol and Myrna heard the boisterous accents of New Yorkers. It immediately made them feel at home. They approached the arched ticket booth sign, outdated with a hint of old-time Coney Island. Sol handed the tickets to a seasoned employee showcasing a vintage, number seven, Mickey Mantle jersey. He repeated the phrase 'enjoy the game' like an aging robot to each paying customer. They entered the eleven-thousand-seat facility, intimate and projected to be three-quarters full. The foul weather forecast predicted a better than fifty-percent chance of rain, having drizzled earlier in the day. Despite the threatening charcoal gray skies, Sol and company were optimistic. He was especially hopeful Yankee fans would choose to stay home. No such luck.

As they strode between rows of matching blue plastic seating, Helene was able to get close to the Yankees' dugout. The attractive woman took out her Polaroid camera and started pressing away, the camera spitting out picture after picture. Reggie Jackson, standing at the edge of the dugout while chatting with a fellow player, could not ignore the antics of one Laszlo, cartoonishly waving his slender arms, hoping to get his attention. He sauntered over.

"I'm guessing you'd like an autograph?" said Jackson.

"You are favorite player!" said Laszlo proudly in his boisterous Romanian accent. He took out a black marker and handed it to the star right fielder.

"I like it when fans are prepared," said Jackson with a wink, who proceeded to autograph the bill of his hat, top and underneath. He even autographed the back of Laszlo's Yankee jersey, signing it right below the number forty-four. Laszlo jumped up and down like a school kid.

"Thank you! Thank you!"

Jackson looked over at Sol, sporting his ratty Mets hat and Tom Seaver jersey. "I'm guessing you don't want an autograph."

"I'll pass, but my wife would love one," said Sol.

Eyeing Myrna, Jackson went back into the dugout and returned with a baseball bat. "And who should I make this out to?"

"Oh, my gosh, really? For me?" Myrna was flabbergasted. "Uh, my name... sorry."

Sol stepped in. "It's Myrna," he said, spelling out her name just in case. She was beside herself in glee. "Thank you, Mr. Jackson," said Sol. "That was really something special." He looked around, making sure no Mets fans were visible. "While you're at it, would you mind?"

"No problem," smiled Jackson. Sol handed the right fielder his Mets hat, and he signed it. "We're all New Yorkers tonight, right?"

"I might have to convert," grinned Sol, feeling almost as giddy as his lanky friend.

Myrna thanked Jackson again profusely, then asked

him a question. "Would Lou Piniella happen to be close by? He's my favorite Yankee.

"I feel slighted," mused the All-Star.

Myrna apologized. "But you're a close second!"

"No problem." Jackson called out for his teammate. Piniella emerged from the dugout, drinking from a can of Coke and smoking a cigarette. "You mind signing a bat for a lady?"

Piniella smiled. "I always have time for the ladies." He put out the cigarette and walked over. He took the marker and placed his signature above Jackson's, making it bigger and bolder. "Enjoy tonight's game."

Myrna nearly fainted, blushing with happiness. "Oh my gosh, thank you so much! We will, we will!" Both players managed to sign Helene's baseball cap as well.

The four, beaming with delight, headed for their seats stationed behind the Met's dugout along the third base side of the quaint stadium. One of the vendors offered to help them find their seats and pointed to the area five rows up from the Mets' dugout.

"A little sparse of Mets fans, honey," poked Myrna, still beaming at her signed baseball bat.

Sol addressed Helene. "Hey, how about taking a few pictures of me with some of the Mets players?"

"I only have a couple of pictures left and I don't want to waste the film," said Helene. "Oh, I'm sorry; I didn't mean it like that."

Sol shrugged it off, but couldn't blame her. "No harm, no foul ball." Helene gave a half-hearted laugh. To Sol's joy, she was able to take a picture of him standing next to recently elected Baseball Hall of Famer, Willie Mays, a real treat for the retiree. The four finally sat down, so close to the playing field they could smell the pristine Kelly-green turf.

"Hell of a view, huh?" said Sol. "I've never been this close to the field, ever. Usually, I'm smack dab in the nosebleed seats at Shea Stadium if you know what I mean."

It was fairly obvious where the fans stood in this particular Grapefruit League game, 99.9 percent with the Bronx Bombers. And most proudly wore their black pinstripe jerseys, t-shirts, jackets, and black hats with the intertwined N and Y insignia. As painful as it was to admit, Sol conceded their uniforms were classic, smart, and probably the best in baseball.

"Lots of New York transplants here, that's for sure," observed Sol. He spotted a few Mets fans, most appearing like they were ready for a root canal at their local dentist. Regardless, Sol was happy as a clam.

He spoke up. "Who's thirsty?"

Sol waved down a beer vendor and bought beers for everyone. Next on the evening's menu were hot dogs. A gregarious man hawking the classic ballpark cuisine sauntered over.

"What'll have, what'll have, what'll have," he called out.

The vendor appeared like he'd polished off many a hotdog in his day.

"Give me four red-hots, two with mustard and relish, and two with ketchup," said Sol. The vendor grimaced, Sol too. "Yeah, I know, ketchup on a hotdog."

Sol paid the vendor, thanking him with a tip. He held up his cup of beer, some suds dripping over the side. "Ain't nothing better than a Sabrett hot dog and a cold one at a baseball game. Now, that's America. Cheers, everybody!"

Before standing for the National Anthem, Sol informed Laszlo to yell "Play Ball!" afterwards, something he'd done since he was a little kid back in Queens.

A booming voice came over the loudspeaker. "We apologize for the slight delay, folks. There's a minor glitch with the field lights, but I'm told we'll have it up and running in just a few minutes. Sol glanced over his shoulder and noticed a section of lights along the left field line that were out.

The game finally started as Sol and company chowed down on their ballpark fare. Laszlo polished off his hotdog so fast he barely tasted it. Sol instructed him on the proper way to call out to the vendor. Laszlo improvised, standing on his seat, waving and whistling loudly. The vendor could only shake his head at Laszlo's theatrics. He bought two more, but this time topped them with mustard. His taste buds approved.

"You say Yankees are home team?" asked Laszlo.

"A sure sign is what hats and jerseys you see the most of," said Sol.

"Definitely Yankees," observed the Romanian.

"How long have they played in Ft. Lauderdale?" asked Helene.

"My friend Manny says the Yankees have been playing at Ft. Lauderdale Stadium since the early 1960s. My Mets, on the other hand, play on the west coast of Florida in St. Petersburg, near Tampa. Beautiful little ballpark they got there."

***

The first few innings were uneventful, no runs, a couple of scattered base hits, and two errors. A foul ball landed about ten rows behind them, adding a touch of excitement.

Sol turned to Myrna. "You know, after what Reggie Jackson did for you today, I might have to start rooting for him."

"He's not Darth Vader, you know," said his wife with a grin.

Sol asked to look at the bat again, inspecting it intently, "It's heavy, that's for sure."

"And coming up to the plate, number 44, Rrrrreggie Jackson!" said the announcer, booming with all the enthusiastic flair of a wrestling event.

The stadium erupted as the World Series hero stepped up to the plate, including Myrna, Laszlo, and Helene. Even Sol stood up and cheered. Jackson took the first pitch from the young left-hander for a strike. He didn't appear thrilled, thinking the fastball was a bit too high and away. On the second pitch, Jackson took a healthy cut at a curveball, drilling it foul down the right field line. The next three pitches were balls. A full count. On the payoff pitch, the pitcher threw a sneaky slider that fooled Jackson, striking him out.

Sol noticed Laszlo pouting. "I want Jackson to hit home run for me!"

"Don't worry," said Sol, "He'll get a couple more at-bats to hit one out."

While Sol, Myrna, and Helene were enjoying the sights and sounds of major league baseball, Laszlo's over-the-top zeal was becoming a tad grating. He cheered 'Go Yankees Go' on just about every play like it was the seventh game of the World Series. Sol finally had to tell him to reel in the enthusiasm. He bought another round of beers for everyone. Myrna, not normally a beer drinker, was savoring her adult beverage just as much as her husband.

The game was knotted up at 3-3 with one out in the top of the seventh, the Mets with a runner on second base. Sol explained to Laszlo that after the top of the seventh is over, that's when fans stand up to sing Take Me Out to the Ball Game.

"So many rules in baseball," said Laszlo.

The stadium lights on the left field side flickered for a moment. The evening sky was dark as midnight with ominous dark clouds rolling in. The evening weather forecast was now calling for thunderstorms, but so far, the baseball Gods had held any precipitation in check.

Switch-hitting center fielder Lee Mazzilli dug into the plate. "Come on, Mazz!" cheered Sol. "Little bingo!"

The Mets slugger came through, blasting a two-run shot over the left field fence off a lean, hard-throwing, righty minor league prospect. With the Mets now leading 5-3, Yankees manager Bob Lemon asked for time as he made a pitching change, touching his left forearm to bring in the south paw. After a dozen warm-up pitches, the crafty young left-hander with bushy hair stepped in to face utility player and former Cincinnati Red, Doug Flynn. The infielder hit a harmless pop-up to Willie Randolph, who backpedaled just beyond the infield dirt to make the catch for the second out.

The field lights flickered again. The announcer made a lame joke about not paying the electric bills on time, adding that they may need to call the game. With some of the crowd funneling out of the stadium, the remaining fans booed loudly.

"Just kidding, folks. Let's cross our fingers and hope the power doesn't short out again."

With everything righted with the lights, they resumed

the game. After third baseman Greg Nettles snagged a line drive to close out the top of the seventh, fans began to stand up in unison. With the help of the baseball announcer, everyone started singing a rousing rendition of "Take Me Out to the Ballgame," a Major League Baseball tradition dating back decades.

"I love baseball!" screamed Laszlo, as he mangled the words with off-key gusto.

Sol turned to everyone. "Anyone need to use the restroom?"

Myrna had used the facilities two innings prior, so she was fine. Both Laszlo and Helene elected to join him. "Let's hurry, we don't want to miss any action.

CHAPTER 34

Helene went off in one direction while Sol and Laszlo headed in the other. The two men went into the restroom, surprised that there were only a few people there to use the facilities. Both men stood at the urinals. A father and son finished washing their hands and left. An adult appeared at one of the sinks. Sol perked up at the sound of his whistling. He'd heard that tune before, but where? Sol turned his head ever so slightly, hoping to decipher it better. He peeked back and saw what appeared to be a familiar person washing his hands. To his amazement, the man made no reflection in the mirror stationed above the sink. Sol did a double-take, his heart skipping a beat.

He zipped up and made a subtle gesture to get Laszlo's attention. "Psst, behind you," whispered Sol, telling him to keep it cool and quiet. "Is that who I think it is?"

Laszlo craned his slender neck. He recognized the man right away. After all, he'd worked for him the past six months. It was Tibor.

The castle owner from Myrna's hometown finished up and dried his hands. Sol confirmed it again. There was no reflection in the mirror. Something wasn't kosher. He quelled his percolating anger and decided to play it coy.

"Tibor, what a pleasant surprise," said Sol, confronting the bearded man, standing mere feet away from each other. "Oh, it looks like you missed a spot of mustard on your beard.

But I guess you wouldn't know that because you're a vampire; no reflection, etcetera."

"Keen observation, Sol Hirsch," replied Tibor, coldly.

Sol couldn't suppress his anger any longer. "You son of a bitch! It was you, wasn't it?" he sneered, rolling up his sleeves, preparing to brawl. "You're the one that bit me that night across the lake."

"Yes, Sol, you are correct. And hello, Laszlo, everyone's favorite pretend vampire and dreadful handyman. And for the record, yes, I am the real deal."

Tibor's glaring eyes seem to blister straight through the former deli owner's chest. Laszlo had had his suspicions about his boss, but was in disbelief. A couple of drunken Met fans stumbled in to use the restroom. Tibor hissed and shot them a menacing glare. The two sobered up and ran off like frightened dogs.

Tibor calmly walked in a slow half circle, stalking the shorter man. Laszlo remained on the perimeter, processing the situation.

Sol steamed. "So, am I a vampire scum like you now?"

"You are in semi-state of vampireness," said Tibor. "Unfortunately, I did not get to sink my fangs deep enough into your flabby neck. If so, you would be dead now. Your friend Donnie, the bad joke teller, saved you when he teed off on me with that branch. By the way, he is chiropractor, yes? Maybe he can take a look at my achy shoulder."

"My neck is not flabby, pumpkin nuts," answered Sol. "And I'm sorry to inform you, but Donnie's retired."

"And so will you, Sol Hirsch, permanently." Tibor glanced at a stall door and punched a hole clear through with his right fist. A terrified man sitting on the toilet dashed out of the stall with his unbuttoned pants hanging around his thighs and scrambled outside.

Sol gritted his teeth, his pointed canines emerging. "So why the hell are you here besides wanting to kill me?"

"Why am I here?" asked Tibor, rhetorically. "Why, I am here to enjoy baseball, America's pastime, and to experience fun in the sun, Miami Beach style. Well, maybe not the sun so much. I was also intrigued as to why Laszlo would take such a sudden trip to the United States. The more pressing question is, what do I want? And what I want is your wife, Myrna. The first time I met her, I realized I must have her. She is a beautiful creature, and I will take her back home with me."

"Over my dead body," threatened Sol.

"I can (and will) properly arrange that for you," replied Tibor with a devilish grin. Tonight, Old Man, Mrs. Myrna Hirsch become a widow.

Sol seethed. "Don't call me old man."

"Oh, and I understand your sad sack Mets are horrible baseball team, unlike the Yankees, who are the best."

Sol became furious. "No one makes fun of my Mets, and lives!" Sol bore in towards the vampire, who took a wild swing at the shorter man. Sol ducked like a seasoned boxer and then followed up with a patented left hook, sending the taller foe to the ground, grimacing in pain.

"Just like Smokin' Joe Frazier, you blood-sucking putz." Tibor stood up, his complexion now a pale blue, teeth gleaming white and razor sharp. "Uh oh," uttered Sol. "Maybe we can call it a draw?"

Tibor picked up Sol by his jersey and threw him against the wall, smashing into the bathroom mirror above the sink.

Sol winced in pain as his back landed against the protruding faucet. Laszlo went over to help his friend up.

"Why are you doing this, Tibor?" asked Laszlo. "Sol Hirsch has done nothing to you."

"But he has," replied Tibor. "His wife is a charming and intelligent woman. Why she remains with this ogre, I do not understand. But she will live happily ever after with me in my castle... forever. And in order for that to happen, Mr. Sol Hirsch must die."

"What about me?" asked Laszlo. "Does this mean I'm fired?"

Tibor rolled his eyes. "Of course, you're fired, you incompetent fool. You can't even unplug a toilet. Do you think I should be unplugging toilets?!"

Laszlo put up his fists. "Then you must go through me first. Sol is my friend, and I will protect him."

Laszlo backed up as Tibor approached him. He blocked the vampire's initial attack and was able to strike Tibor in the chest with a straight right. Laszlo offered up a roundhouse kick, catching Tibor by surprise.

The vampire wiped the blood from the corner of his mouth. He sneered, "I didn't know you had it in you."

Laszlo attempted to kick him again, but it was blocked. The vampire threw Laszlo against the tiled wall, his head striking it hard as he fell to the floor. Tibor turned back and thrust his hand around Sol's throat and pinned him up against the wall, preparing to bite his neck. The vampire opened wide, his canines on full repulsive display.

Sol, in dire straits, cleared his head and shouted. "Hey, look, it's Christopher Lee!" Tibor turned, falling for the diversion. Sol thrusted his thick sausage-link fingers directly into the eyes of Tibor. He dropped him to the ground.

"I knew watching the Three Stooges all these years would pay off one day." A group of boisterous Yankee fans came in to use the bathroom. Tibor pushed them away and stormed outside.

Sol dashed over and helped Laszlo up off the floor. "You, okay?"

"I see little birdies like in cartoon," muttered Laszlo.

***

Myrna was about to take a sip of her beer when Tibor unexpectedly appeared out of nowhere, placing his sturdy frame beside her.

"Oh my gosh, Tibor, what are you doing here?" asked Myrna.

"My dearest, Myrna," he replied. "I am here to watch game with the most beautiful woman." He placed his hand on hers. Myrna blushed, then pulled her hand away.

"I'm sorry, Tibor, I like you, but I don't want to give you mixed messages. I'm in love with my one and only Sol." From the corner of her eye, Myrna caught an unsettling glimpse of the castle owner's lengthened canines. She trembled.

Tibor grasped her hand firmly, this time applying pressure on her wrist. "But, I insist, my love."

Myrna peered back, bewildered and frightened, desperately hoping to see her husband.

***

"We've got to get to Myrna!" Sol called out, Laszlo by his side. They sprinted out of the bathroom and into a crowd of people walking in both directions. As the two men headed towards their seats, they bumped into Helene.

She saw the trepidation in both men's faces. "What's

wrong? Is everything okay?"

"We explain later," said Laszlo, insisting she stay put.

Sol peered in both directions. "Where the hell is he?"

Laszlo ran ahead of Sol, gazing out into the crowd. "There!" he pointed. "He is sitting by Myrna!"

"Oh, God, no!" Sol raced down the stairs and saw Tibor clutching Myrna's arm tightly, pretending to be a loving couple.

Sol stepped forward. "If you…."

"Take another step, I will kill her," said Tibor, in a calm voice. Now sit down and let us enjoy baseball."

"At bat it's Mr. October, Rrrreggie Jackson!" said the announcer, exuberantly. The remaining crowd cheered. Manager Bob Lemon, sporting his tinted glasses, took a couple of steps outside the dugout, clapping his hands. The World Series hero took a huge cut at a high fastball from the Triple-A southpaw, whiffing completely, now taunting the superstar. Jackson seethed.

"So, what is your plan of action, or nonaction, Sol?" asked Tibor. Myrna was in tears, frightened as the man gripped her arm tighter. He ran his pointed fingernails across her neck.

"You better not hurt her, you bastard!"

"Tough words coming from rumpled shrew of a man," he replied, smirking. The announcer called out strike two as Jackson chased a breaking ball low and away.

"I mean it, wacko." Tibor pressed his nails firmly against Myrna's throat.

"You know, I have no patience for baseball; it is a boring game. We must leave, my love," ordered Tibor. The two got up from their seats.

People started booing as Tibor blocked their view, Myrna in tow. Sol eyed his wife. She nodded.

Myrna, also a fan of the Three Stooges, tried a different tack. "Honey, what's the rush?" in a lusty voice, caressing Tibor's hand. He returned with a smile.

That's when Myrna, with her painted red manicured fingernails, jammed them directly into the vampire's eyes. Tibor cried out in angst, releasing his grip momentarily. She scrambled up the stairs and into the safety of Laszlo, now with both she and Helene by his side. Seizing the moment, Sol drove onto the vampire like a blitzing linebacker, forcing him to the ground, punching him repeatedly. The remaining crowd erupted, chanting, fight-fight-fight!

"Ball one," called out the umpire.

A light mist began to fall. Tibor emerged with both hands clutched around Sol's jersey, lifting him completely off the ground.

"Ball two," called out the umpire.

"Hey, down in front!" yelled a handful of drunken fans.

"Gotta love New Yorkers," squeaked Sol, eyeing the crowd, his back to the field. Tibor opened his mouth wide, ready to bite Sol's neck.

"Get a room, you two," barked another fan. The hot dog vendor chimed in as well. Sol attempted to jab Tibor in the eyes again to escape, but the vampire was ready this time.

"You've tried that trick once too many," raged Tibor. "Now you die."

Just as Jackson ripped an outside fastball foul down the third base line, all the lights cut out, leaving the ballpark in total darkness. Jackson's Louisville Slugger splintered in two, the heavy barrel piece sailing in the direction above the Mets team dugout. Tibor heard Myrna scream out for her husband. Tibor momentarily loosened his grip to look. Sol dropped to the ground.

Thoomp!

The jagged section of wood impaled the vampire's heart, penetrating straight through the flesh. Tibor staggered, his eyes wide open in disbelief, as he peered down at the lethal section of Louisville Slugger. He dropped to his knees. Sol froze, now eye-level with the vampire's shocked expression.

Tibor slumped over on his back as blood oozed from the mortal wound. He gazed at Sol, his outstretched arms attempting to grasp him around his throat, gnashing his fangs with full-fledged hatred in his burning eyes.

Sol swatted his feeble limbs away. He bent down and grabbed the vampire by the shirt collar, staring him straight in the face.

"Zol er krenken un gedenken." Tibor offered up a blank expression. Sol raised his balled-up fist. "Let him suffer and remember." Sol then unloaded with a powerful left hook to the vampire's jaw, breaking it. The vampire wailed in pain.

Sol stood and backed away as the vampire's agonized face contorted into a flurry of colors, first ash white, then into darker and darker shades. The body started deflating, withering like an old, burning newspaper. His limbs turned bony; his body dissolving before Sol's eyes. The section of the bat then toppled harmlessly over onto the cement floor.

"Take my wife…please," huffed Sol. "Like I said, over my dead body."

CHAPTER 35

The lights popped back to life, revealing nothing more than a pile of tattered clothing and ash. Sol gawked in amazement at what was once a person, or at least something that resembled one in human form.

The beer vendor called out. "Hey, where's that prick who kept blocking the view of the game? I wanna kick his ass!"

"Sorry, my friend; Reggie Jackson beat you to it." The vendor sported an odd expression before scurrying off to sell more beer.

Sol immediately sensed the bountiful energy in his body evaporating. He slumped over in his seat, his knees creaking, and his lower back throbbed in pain. He felt like he'd been through the Thrilla in Manila against heavyweight champion Muhammad Ali.

Fearing his wife might have been injured, he sprang up, desperately calling out for her. A few rows back, Myrna answered. She hurried down the steps and embraced her husband.

"Oh, Sol, I was so scared. Are you alright?"

He gazed at Myrna in the eye and gave her a hug when his lower back seized up. "My back!" She helped her husband into a seat. "I could really use something for the pain."

"Aspirin?" asked Myrna.

"Beer," begged Sol.

Myrna shuddered in her seat. "Oh, my God, where's that horrible man, Tibor? Did he get away?"

"Nah," grimaced Sol. "He caught a souvenir then flew the coop." Without going into details, he assured his wife that Tibor the vampire was indeed no more. He eyed the ash, now fluttering away in the South Florida breeze like dead leaves.

Myrna peered at Tibor's black leather coat, then trailed her eyes. "Oh, my God!"

"What? What?" pleaded Sol.

"Those boots." She started tearing up, pointing at the distinctive buckles. "The round hoops; I would recognize those boots anywhere. They belonged to my father."

"Your father?" said Sol, stunned.

Myrna bent down and fanned away the ashes with a game program. She used a napkin and picked up the distressed black leather boots, inspecting the size 10s more intently. Inside, under the tongue of the shoe, were her father's initials etched in the leather. It became clear that it was, in fact, Tibor who had murdered her father all those years ago.

"I remember how my father treasured them, the oldest brand of boots made in America, he would say. He thought he was an American cowboy." Myrna offered up a tear-filled smile.

Sol asked the nearby hotdog vendor if he had a bag. The man obliged.

"Here, Honey," said her husband, Sol, patting her shoulder gently. Myrna picked up the boots and then dropped them in the bag.

"You know, they would probably fit you," said Myrna.

"It would be an honor to wear your father's boots, but I'd have to find a local cobbler to do a full-fledged disinfecting;

I don't want my feet touching any vampire residue."

Myrna took his hand. "Understood."

Despite his back pain, Sol was able to reach over with his arm and retrieve the broken piece of bat, the barrel displaying the signature of one Reggie Jackson. Sol used a handful of napkins to wipe away the remaining blood from the splintered wood.

"I think I'll keep this as a memento."

"But he's a Yankee player," said Myrna. "What would all of you Mets friends say?"

Sol grinned. "After tonight, I'm buying a number 44 jersey in those classic pinstripes. Just remember to keep it confidential."

Myrna got the attention of the beer vendor and asked for two. "Enjoy the suds, lady," said the portly vendor. "They're on the house."

Laszlo greeted his friend, Helene, standing beside him. "Sol Hirsch, vampire killer!"

Sol waved his index finger at Laszlo, signaling for him to come closer. "You had no idea that Tibor was a vampire?"

"I suspect, but never certain," said Laszlo. "That is why I worked at castle; to find out."

"I mean, no hints?"

"Vampires not broadcast they are vampires."

"Good point," replied Sol.

"And you?" said Myrna, directing her question at Laszlo. "Never a vampire?"

He smirked. "Only on TV."

"Is my husband officially cured now?" Myrna asked.

Laszlo addressed both her and Sol. "Yes, main source is kaput." He patted him on the shoulder with a bit too much zest. Sol winced in pain. "Ooh, sorry."

"My choppers," said Sol, "What about my choppers?"

Laszlo inspected. "Teeth back to normal, my friend, but your breath. It is quite bad."

"Bad breath I can live with; fangs not so much."

"What about Sol's reflection?" posed Myrna.

Sol addressed his wife. "You got your compact?" Myrna dug around in her purse but came up empty.

Helene, hearing the conversation, stepped over. "You said compact? I have one." She took out a gold, butterfly-shaped compact and handed it to him. "What do you need it for?"

"Uh, I got something caught between my teeth, damn Cracker Jack," said Sol. He flipped it open and gazed into the mirror. There, before his very eyes, he saw his face, wrinkles and all. He then dabbed away the touch of deli mustard near the corner of his mouth,

"I can see myself! I can see myself!" pronounced Sol, joyfully dancing around.

"So can everybody else, asshole, now sit down, so we can watch the game!" said a burly Mets fan with sideburns, sitting a few rows back.

"God bless you, New York fans," cried Sol. He polished off the rest of his beer, wiping away the foam from his lips. "Man, does this taste like heaven." Not wanting to sit down where Tibor the vampire just got vaporized, the four found open seats directly behind the Mets' dugout.

Helene turned to Sol. "Um, can I ask why you're all talking about vampires?"

"Next time we're at Rascal House, join us for dinner and I'll give you the full skinny," said Sol.

After a slight delay, the lights finally popped back on. After a few warm-ups from the pitcher, Jackson, armed with a new bat, stepped into the batter's box and swung at the very next pitch, launching a mammoth three-homer over the right field fence, putting the Yankees in front by a run. Fans, young and old, standing outside the fence, scrambled for the prized souvenir. With the Yankees now up by a run and the drizzle intensifying, the game was officially called. Yankees win.

CHAPTER 36

Sunday morning, Myrna finished up breakfast, then changed to get ready for church. She grabbed her purse hanging from one of the yellow vinyl kitchen chairs and headed for the door when Sol emerged from the bedroom, smartly dressed in a white Lacoste polo shirt, navy-blue khaki shorts, and black penny loafers.

"Are you going somewhere?" Myrna asked her husband. She was joining Donnie and Barbara in the lobby, then heading over to St. Patrick's Catholic Church in Miami Beach for 10AM Mass.

"You mind if I tag along?" asked Sol. "I think I could really use a moment of reflection, especially after what happened to me last night. Maybe I can do that confessional thing."

Myrna glanced at her watch. "Well, let's get going, or we're going to be late."

They arrived at St. Patrick's Catholic Church; the parking lot near full. Donnie managed to squeeze his Cutlass Supreme convertible into a partially hidden corner parking space nestled between a cluster of coconut palms on one side and a late 1960s mauve Cadillac El Dorado on the other. Donnie looked up, noticing an overhanging group of coconuts dangling over his car.

"Oh crap, none of those coconuts better land on my convertible top," said Donnie.

"They're too ripe to fall," observed Sol. "When they turn brown, then you gotta watch out."

"I read in a magazine that more people are killed each year from falling coconuts than from sharks," said Barbara. "Probably wouldn't make a scary film."

"I'll take my chances with the coconuts," chimed Donnie, "They got less teeth."

As they approached the church, Sol was immediately taken aback at the beautiful Spanish Mission Revival place of worship, the building's exterior fashioned in white stucco, the roof covered in orange barrel tiles. The bookish Myrna stated that St. Patrick's was the first Catholic parish ever in Miami Beach.

They entered through the front arched doorway, arriving a few minutes after ten. Despite the full house, Donnie spotted an empty pew in the back and they sat down. Sol surveyed the diverse group of parishioners, lots of families, adults, and seniors. On rare occasions, when Sol attended the aging Beth Jacob Synagogue, also located in Miami Beach, he often joked that he felt like a teenager whenever he attended, as a majority of the congregation were north of seventy years of age.

As the Mass continued, Sol kept an eye on his wife and friends, following the appropriate time to sit and stand. When it came time to kneel, Sol grimaced, hearing his achy knees ring out in a chorus of snap, crackle, and pops.

The priest then offered parishioners the sign of peace. Myrna turned to her husband and gave him a hug. Sol followed suit and then proceeded to shake hands with Donnie and Barbara. People in the pew in front of them offered handshakes as well. One person in particular turned to shake

Sol's hand. It was Detective Rex Keller. Sol had hoped he'd never encounter the detective ever again. But there he was, now face to face.

Sol's frozen expression quickly thawed, now displaying a passable smile. "Peace, Detective Keller."

As the detective shook his hand, Keller moved closer and whispered. "We've solved the case," he said with a wink. Sol's pulse went into overdrive.

Oy vey, I'm going to get cuffed right here in a Catholic church!

After the service, the detective approached Sol at the entrance lobby. "Mr. Hirsch, thought I'd let you know we've chalked up these recent deaths as 'self-inflicted' as they say."

"Self-inflicted? What do you mean?" he asked.

"The coroner wrapped up the autopsy on those two Yankee fans turned gator bait. Turns out their blood-alcohol level was through the roof. Why they were there, we'll never know, but I suspect they fell into the water, panicked, then drowned. The gators did the rest."

"That's great news!" exclaimed Sol, showing way too much enthusiasm. He swiftly dialed it back. The detective raised a brow. "I mean, that's good news that you've solved the case. Wasn't a young man found dead in his car by that old pier?"

"Classic suicide in my book," said Keller. "Coroner found marijuana in the guy's system. Probably stoned out of his gourd as he drove his car into the water. Musta thought it was a car wash."

"Suicide? You're certain?" asked Sol.

"We spoke to the ex-girlfriend, who said they had recently ended their relationship. Died of a broken heart, I guess you could say. Very sad." He continued. "As for the fat guy found at the beach... heart attack."

Sol addressed his wife, "Oh, my apologies, honey. This is Detective Rex Keller of the Miami Beach Police Department." She shook his hand.

"Nice to meet you, ma'am," said Detective Keller. I was just telling your husband here that we've resolved the recent deaths, so rest assured, the people of Miami Beach can sleep with ease tonight."

"Take care, Detective," said Sol. He watched him leave the church, then gazed up at the ceiling. "There is a god. Thank you, thank you!"

Pondering his good fortune, he turned to Myrna. "Can you talk to the priest now about me doing confession? I really need to get things off my chest; it's important."

"Let me talk to Father Gleeson," said Myrna, explaining that confessions are generally scheduled on specific days and times.

As they exited the church, Myrna approached the priest. He was finishing up, shaking hands with parishioners, wishing them all a good week.

"Hello, Father. Do you have a quick moment?"

"Yes, of course, Myrna," said Father Gleeson with an Irish twang, late 60s with thick white hair parted on the side. "Is everything okay?"

"Never better, but my husband would like to know if he can do confession now. I know it's rather last-minute, but he says it's very important." Myrna then offered a little background about her husband.

The priest glanced at his watch. "I have a baptism later this afternoon, but I think I can squeeze him in. Give me five minutes," uttered the priest. "Tell your husband I'll be in the third confessional." Father Gleeson then walked up the steps and headed back inside the church.

Myrna waved Sol over as he, Donnie, and Barbara chatted by the front entrance.

"So, what did he say?" asked Sol. "Can he see me?"

"Father Gleeson said it was fine," said Myrna. "I'll show you where to go when he's ready."

"Do I need to do anything special to prepare, or can I just go in full tilt?" asked Sol.

"Relax, and just say what you need to say to the priest," said Myrna, reassuring her husband. "He's not there to interrogate you." Sol sighed in relief.

"First wearing a cross in Romania, attending Mass today, and now confession," observed Donnie. "Holy smoke, I'd say you're well on your way to becoming a Catholic."

"I'm playing it by ear," smiled Sol as the four trailed back inside.

The two couples sat in the back pew, patiently waiting. Moments later, they noticed Father Gleeson entering the third confessional.

"That's your cue," said Donnie. "Good luck, my friend."

Sol stood up, but hesitated. He turned to his wife. "After I make my confession, can the priest, you know, rat me out to the cops?"

"No. Your conversation is strictly between you, the priest, and God," said Myrna.

He sighed. "That's good to know," said Sol, feeling a bit more at ease as he sauntered towards the confessional.

Myrna suddenly got concerned. "What exactly are you

confessing to?" she called out. Then she thought about what her mother had asked on the telephone, and Laszlo, too. *Did Sol actually kill anyone?* Myrna gulped.

"Well, here goes nothing," uttered Sol as he stood in front of the confessional. He paused, took a deep breath, then went inside. The retiree sat down and closed the door. In the darkness, he heard a calm, reassuring voice.

"Good morning," said Father Gleeson. "I usually don't get many people of the Jewish faith for confessional, but I like to say we are all God's children, and that no one is perfect."

Sol wholeheartedly agreed, thinking even his favorite Mets player, all-star pitcher, Tom "Terrific" Seaver, wasn't so terrific on rare occasions. "Uh, hello Father Gleeson," said Sol, his voice a little nervous. "I really appreciate you seeing me on such short notice. And yes, I am kinda new to this sort of thing too. Usually, when I have a problem to sort out, I talk to Manny."

"Manny?" said Father Gleeson. "Is that the name of your rabbi?"

"Rabbi? No, no," replied Sol. "Manny owns the Cheeky Tiki bar right off the intercoastal. He's a great listener when I need to get things off my chest. Plus, he serves up cheap cold beers."

"Sounds like everyone should have a friend like Manny," chuckled the priest, who acknowledged he knew of the place, having consumed a lager or two there. "After hearing hours of confessionals, sometimes I like to sit back and savor a cold one. Despite my Irishness, I'm a Rheingold lad."

Sol concurred, but then he turned somber. "Father, I, um... got a sea full of remorse that I'm dealing with right now."

"Take your time," said the priest.

"Before I spill my guts, my wife says that anything I tell you is in strict confidence. Is that true? Because I don't want to end up in a slammer, if you know what I mean."

"That is correct," replied Father Gleeson. "What we discuss does not leave this confessional."

"That's good to know, Father, because I've done some bad things. I should preface that I was under the influence when I committed these sins."

"You were intoxicated?"

"Not on booze, but something worse," expressed Sol. "I was a vampire."

Father Gleeson cut him off. "Vampire?" he repeated. "Did you say vampire?"

"Yeah. See, I got bit by this vampire bat. And as a result, I turned into, albeit briefly, a vampire. I noshed on a few people, and the results weren't so pretty." Sol paused. "I'm sorry, this is really difficult for me."

"For you and me both," replied Father Gleeson, caught off guard. He peered at his Seiko luminous watch. "Before we go any further, do you repent what you have done?"

"Absolutely, one hundred percent!" exclaimed Sol, beginning to feel the guilt weight slowly evaporating from his shoulders. "You know, Father, I really dig this confessional stuff and appreciate your understanding. I tell you, if I had gone to my rabbi, he'd have said I was meshugeneh."

I bet," said Father Gleeson, mystified at Sol's extraordinary confession. He fumbled with the proper penance for such a peculiar confession. "Well, um, under these unique circumstances, let's make it… a hundred Hail Marys and another hundred Our Fathers. If you're not familiar with either prayer, I'm sure Myrna can lend you a hand."

"Ooh, a hundred each?" contemplated Sol. "Small price to pay, I guess. Thank you, Father Gleeson. Maybe I'll see you around at the Cheeky Tiki, first round is on me!" There was a light creaking. "I know you're pressed for time, but boy oh boy, if I could tell you the whole story, inside and out." Sol giggled. "There was this real fat guy that I…" Everything was quiet. Sol tapped his knuckles on the wall. "Hello, Father Gleeson? You still there?" *Maybe he's contemplating everything I said*, he thought. *It was a hell of a lot to digest.*

Sol waited for another minute, then began whistling. He knocked again. He eventually opened the door a sliver and poked his head out. He immediately saw his wife and friends standing just outside the confessional with their mouths agape.

"Hey, I think Father Gleeson ditched me."

"He made a straightaway for the Cheeky Tiki," said Donnie, "Something about happy hour. You musta said a mouthful."

"More like he was shell-shocked," said Myrna. "What exactly did you confess to? Never mind, I don't want to know."

"I just told him the truth," Sol replied. "I tell you, I'm so relieved I could fly."

"Like a bat?" joked Donnie.

Sol smirked. "Hahaha, very funny. Who's ready for lunch?"

"So, what's your penance?" asked Myrna.

"A hundred Hail Marys and another hundred Our Fathers," answered Sol. "Is that a lot?"

Donnie cringed. "That's not a penance, that's a punishment!"

CHAPTER 37

That evening, Sol and Donnie ventured downstairs to play shuffleboard with the two guys from Michigan. Sol, still achy from last night's events, played especially poorly. Ten games and another thirty dollars lighter, they headed for the pool area to relax and hang out.

"Jeez, another beatdown from the Michigan Boys," said Donnie. "Maybe we need to find another sport."

"Shuffleboard, a sport?" said Sol. "What's next, skateboarding in the Olympics?"

Donnie laughed. "So, how was the game last night? I thought for sure you'd get rained out."

"The weather cooperated just enough," said Sol. He took his Mets cap off and placed it on the table, scratching his head.

"Hey, you still got Ed Kranepool's autograph on the bill of your hat?" Donnie picked it up and inspected it. Sol tried to intervene, but was too late. Right there in bold black script was a fresh new signature.

"Reggie Jackson?" barked Donnie. "You got Reggie Jackson's autograph? On your Mets hat? How could you!" exclaimed Donnie, calling out his best friend as a traitor.

"Yeah, well, the truth is he was a totally gracious man," said Sol, also noting he did get a picture with Willie Mays. "Jackson not only signed my cap, but he gave Myrna a signed baseball bat."

"Are you serious?"

"As serious as a dog on a boat," said Sol. "He might be my new favorite player."

"For Crist's sake, Sol, don't tell me you're gonna start rooting for the evil empire," said Donnie.

"Nah, I'll die being a Mets fan, but after last night, I will forever be in debt to Mr. October."

"What exactly happened last night? Besides, you becoming a turncoat?"

"Let's just say I'm done with vampire movies." Sol took a sip of his Coke and snacked from a bag of Bugles.

"By the way, it was nice of you to join us at the beach today," said Donnie. "I was getting tired of hearing about Bundt cake recipes from the gals."

"Now we can get back to talking sports and checking out women in bikinis," said Donnie.

"I'll toast to that," said Sol.

Sol sat back on the beach recliner. He paused for a moment, his eyes suddenly becoming fixated on the pool lights and the gentle movement of the water.

Despite the confession at Mass today, the memories were still imbedded in his mind that he had killed multiple people, and tapped into their veins with the help of long, pointed canines. Sol had been a vampire, well, temporarily. Not exactly something you want to shout from the rooftops. Yes, a lifetime of professional therapy would definitely be on the itinerary for one Sol Babe Hirsch. Then it got him thinking. What if Detective Rex Keller realized the errors of his ways and reopened the cases as new clues emerged? The bite marks on the necks? He'd be arrested just like that. Nah.

***

The next day, late afternoon, Sol walked out of the local sporting goods store with Laszlo, who extended his stay for another week.

"You and I are now like twins!" crowed Laszlo, as both men sported identical Yankee jerseys with the number 44 pasted just below the name, Jackson.

As they strolled down A1A, both men got compliments along with a boisterous shout of "Go Yankees" from visiting and transplanted New Yorkers.

"Ah, the winning team!" beamed Laszlo.

"What will you do when you go back to Romania now that your former boss has bought the farm?" asked Sol.

"Bought the farm?" asked Laszlo.

"It means kicked the bucket."

"Oh," said Laszlo. "What does kick the…"

"Dead, deceased, dirt nap," interrupted Sol.

Laszlo nodded. "I might sell castle and live in more modest dwelling. Castle is much too big and drafty for me."

Sol thought about the situation. "Hold on, I thought Tibor owned the castle?"

"Castle has been in my family for centuries. Somehow, evil Tibor commandeered it from naive relatives. I worked for him to find out truth. Before his dirt nap, as you say, I was able to correct deed from under his nose. You see, I am lawyer by trade, and cutthroat like JR Ewing from Dallas program show."

"I guess so," said Sol. "Glad it worked out for you."

Laszlo smiled. "I knew Tibor would meet his end. "All vampires eventually do."

"If you sell the castle, what are you looking to buy, a nice quaint cottage on rolling acres of land, maybe start a farm?"

Laszlo shrugged. "Nah, I like condos."

"Is Dumbraveni now officially free and clear of vampires? I'd love to visit again, but I sure as hell am not going to go through that again!"

"Absolutely... hopefully," uttered Laszlo.

They walked to Laszlo's hotel. Sol turned to him. "You know, after everything we've been through, I don't even know your last name."

Laszlo grinned and replied slyly. "DiMaggio."

"Laszlo DiMaggio? As in New York Yankee, Joe DiMaggio? Are you busting my coconuts?"

"No coconut busting, my friend," said Laszlo. "Joe DiMaggio visited troops in Europe during World War II," he said with a glint in his eye.

"Wow, Joltin Joe, the Yankee Clipper," said Sol, still not thoroughly convinced. "So, what are your plans for this evening?"

"I have hot date with beautiful woman, Helene."

"Wonderful," replied Sol with a morsel of envy. "Are you taking her out to dinner?"

"Yes. We go to Joe's Stone Crab restaurant."

"Ooh, fancy schmancy," said Sol. Both he and Myrna had been there a few times. "Those stone crab claws are to die for." Seeing Laszlo's confused look, he explained it meant the claws are really yummy.

Sol walked home to the condo and took the forever elevator up to the eighth floor. He took out his keys when he looked up.

Waiting for him was Helene. Sol unlocked the door and ushered her inside. He walked over to the kitchen table and found a note from Myrna, who was taking in a movie with Barbara.

"To what do I owe the pleasure…" She cut him off.

"Sol, I need to know if you had anything to do with Robbie's death or the bouncer from the disco." She was practically shaking as she spoke.

"Who's Robbie?" he asked.

"My ex-boyfriend, you know. He showed up late that night in the parking lot?"

"Oh, I remember now," said Sol, his face blushing. "Yeah, the guy that sucker punched me then drove off in his swanky sports car. Why?" He offered Helene something to drink. She declined. Sol grabbed a beer.

"They found him dead by some old pier in North Miami Beach," said Helene. "Please tell me you didn't have anything to do with his death."

"I swear I had nothing to do with his death, and by the way, I'm sorry for your loss."

"Thank you," said Helene. "Um, and what about the bouncer? You remember, from the disco? I thought I saw him in the front passenger seat of your car. Was it him?"

To her stunned surprise, Sol was candid. "Actually, yes, it was him. That meathead tried to beat me up because he thought I had snuck into the disco. I told him he had let me in, but he didn't believe me. Probably suffered too many concussions from playing football."

"So, what happened?"

"I must have a face people want to punch; you know?" joked Sol. "Anyways, he followed me to the back of the parking lot. He pushed me down and then hit me. I used to be an amateur boxer, so I still know how to throw a punch.

He came at me again, and I threw a left hook, then a right cross, and down he went, like a cut-down tree. He must have knocked himself out when he hit the pavement. I didn't know what to do, so I put him in my car and dropped him off at 163rd by some clinic. That was the last I saw of him."

Helene thought about it. Can I ask you one last question?"

"Shoot."

"All that talk about vampires at the baseball game. You guys were putting me on, right?"

He asked Helene to sit in Myrna's comfortable recliner. Sol sat in his. He took a gulp of beer. "You really want the truth?"

"I can handle the truth," said Helene, not certain if she wanted to hear a crazy story about vampires. She didn't like scary.

"Well, if you must know," said Sol, "When the four of us traveled to Romania, I was bit by a vampire bat. You remember that guy with the beard, Tibor, from the baseball game, how he mysteriously vanished? Well, he was the vampire."

"Okay," replied Helene. "I'm sorry, what?"

Sol acknowledged Helene's confused expression. "Yeah, I know, it's a lot to comprehend right off the bat, no pun intended."

He then delved into the heart of the story. "When we returned home, I was feeling like crap, sleeping in late, the whole shebang. I thought I had the flu. Turns out, I was turning into a vampire. Now, not a one hundred percent, full-fledged blood-sucking vampire like Tibor. See, he explained that as a vampire bat, his fangs didn't penetrate my neck all the way. I have Donnie to thank for that." He took another swig of beer and continued.

"Sure, you don't want anything to drink? Beer?" he asked.

Helene wasn't sure what to believe. "Uh, I think I could use something stronger. Vodka?"

Sol went into the kitchen, poured her a shot, and returned. "Here you go. Cheers."

"Where was I. Oh, yeah. So, I started changing, and hated the sun. It irritated me worse than a bout of hemorrhoids. Then what else? I started to develop a taste for human blood. Now, not too much, mind you. Just enough to wet my whistle, so to speak. By this time, Myrna was really concerned, so she called her mother back in Romania, who said she knew someone that could help me."

"Laszlo?" guessed Helene.

"Correct," said Sol. Helene downed her shot with vigor, then asked for another. He went into the kitchen and poured her a refill, then brought out some snacks in an orange plastic bowl. He handed the glass to her. "Laszlo, by the way, he's a real pisser, ain't he?" Helene nodded. Sol continued.

"So, Laszlo flies over here to the States and says he can subdue my cravings, but only temporarily. He says that in order for me to return to normal, the source needs to be eradicated. And that person was…"

"Tibor?" said Helene.

"Bingo," said Sol. "You're really good at this." Helene shrugged.

Sol took another sip of beer. "Then out of the blue, Tibor shows up at the baseball game. Turns out he had the hots for my Myrna with plans of taking her back to Romania to be his bride. That, of course, would mean eliminating yours truly, which I wasn't gonna let happen. Now, Laszlo had his suspicions about Tibor, who he worked for at his castle motel. Excuse me for a sec." Sol got up and went into the bedroom and retrieved the splintered baseball bat.

"But when Reggie Jackson's baseball bat shatters in the bottom of the seventh inning, this part nails that son of a bitch right in his heart. Bam!" Helene jumped. Sol apologized. "And just like that, Tibor the Vampire dies on the spot, reducing him to mere ashes. Thankfully, I was able to turn back to my normal self. The end." He reached for the bowl of snacks. "Bugle?"

Helene declined. Sol grabbed a handful and chomped away. "Anything else you want to know?"

Helene sat there with her jaw dropped. She finished up her vodka and stood up.

"Thanks for clarifying things for me," said Helene, dumbfounded.

Sol showed her to the door. "If you're working tonight, we'll be there for dinner at seven PM, mas o menos." She nodded yes.

Before leaving, she turned to Sol. "So, vampires. Here in Miami Beach?"

Sol smiled. "It's a good a place as any."

THE END

About the author:

DiVitto is originally from Cincinnati, Ohio, spent time in New Jersey, lots of time in South Florida, before settling in the Piedmont of North Carolina. He's written multiple novels (some horror, some for tweens), screenplays, a short story collection, along with a television comedy show based on his warped experiences working in public libraries.

He has a master's degree in Library Science from the University of South Florida and was the former editor of the Seminole Tribe of Florida newspaper. A certified diver, DiVitto is also a papier mache artist/instructor, creating everything from colorful sharks to 5-foot Pop-Tarts. Visit him at www.divittowrites.com.

www.ingramcontent.com/pod-product-compliance
Lightning Source LLC
Chambersburg PA
CBHW050726180626
46814CB00002B/622